Lifeblood

Books by Penny Rudolph

Listen to the Mockingbird

The Rachel Chavez Series
Thicker Than Blood
Lifeblood

Lifeblood

Penny Rudolph

Poisoned Pen Press

Poisoned
Pen
Press

Copyright © 2007 by Penny Rudolph

First Edition 2007

10 9 8 7 6 5 4 3 2 1

Library of Congress Catalog Card Number: 2006934076

ISBN: 978-1-59058-346-3   Hardcover

Poisoned Pen Press
6962 E. First Ave., Ste. 103
Scottsdale, AZ 85251
www.poisonedpenpress.com
info@poisonedpenpress.com

Printed in the United States of America

To Warren Murphy, for his solid advice, staunch support, and, especially, his responses to SOS messages no matter where, or how busy, he is

Acknowledgments

The author owes much gratitude to:

Michael Siverling, investigator with the Sacramento, California Public Defender, friend, advisor on the ways of California law enforcement, and a super novelist in his own right

Sorche Fairbank. If there's a more helpful, generous agent out there, I haven't heard of one

Barbara Peters. Not for nothing is she known as one of the best mystery editors in the western world

Dave Bryant, Police Detective in Tampa, Florida, one of the funniest men alive, and a great instructor on how ordinary people can defeat bigger, stronger opponents

Marilyn Hutton, for her indispensable plot and character suggestions, even when we were tossed out of restaurants for overstaying the lunch hour

Ralph Rudolph, for his unwavering encouragement and astute suggestions, to say nothing of his tolerating the foibles of a writer-spouse

Dr. Elena Gonzalez for her many useful comments and recommendations

Rob Kresge, for his wonderfully analytical critiques and essential advice

Goldialu Stone, for her thoughtful, practical, and wise counsel

Michael White, for his excellent, incisive critiques

Lois Hirt, for her humor and assistance

Jane Sampson, for her aid, ideas, and advice

Sharon Winters, a booster and a pillar of support

Kim Jackson, International Parking Institute, for her willingness to answer even witless questions

Gayle (Roz) Russell, for her open-handed, enthusiastic critiques

Laine Conway, for her friendship and her discerning assistance with plot planning

Chapter One

It came in the darkness, in the middle of the night, a faint metal-on-metal tapping, knocking, drumming, riding an echo through the empty building.

Even faint as it was, it waked Rachel. She thought it was just one of the street people, gone a bit nuts—such things happen around downtown Los Angeles—someone rapping with a spoon or something on one of the doors to the parking garage below her apartment. She didn't want to hike all the way down to the street level in her nightshirt to find the cause. Nor did she want to call the cops about some, probably harmless, poor soul and make an already unlucky life worse. So she turned over and went back to sleep.

◇◇◇

The following morning arrived fresh, sunny and clear. In a few days it would be October. The heat was gone, the smog fading. Rachel had quite forgot the night's disturbance.

Having overslept, she was still licking the crumbs of a breakfast of bagel and cream cheese from her lips when she strode down the ramps to her glass cubicle on the parking garage's street level. Walking through the parking levels gave her the chance to check on things like burned-out lights, litter, wall damage, and what vehicles had been left overnight—which was okay as long as they belonged to regular clients and weren't left there too long.

She was surprised to see a dirty white van parked behind one of the big cement pillars in the area generally reserved for fleet cars belonging to InterUrban Water Agency. But the agency's cars were all black sedans. Had the van been there a while and she just hadn't noticed? She wasn't sure.

The garage didn't cater to public parking, the signs outside the building said so. Rachel's spaces were leased by nearby businesses, but every now and then some interloper got in. The occasional freeloader was the price of avoiding the expense of installing machines and gate arms and issuing cards.

She had been operating the garage for several years. Inheriting it from her grandfather had more or less saved her life by pointing it in a fresh direction.

Did the van belong to someone at one of the businesses that leased space? Hard to know. The places cars parked had more to do with when they arrived than where their drivers worked. Still, most people noted the *Reserved* signs in the areas held for fleet cars and didn't intrude.

Running a few minutes behind, Rachel hurried to get the garage open for the early arrivals. She'd have to check on the van after the morning rush. With any luck, someone would pick it up by then and she could forget about it.

She unlocked the huge doors, and watched as they rose, crunching and creaking, above the driving lanes. Next were the doors to the sidewalk, the people doors. Remembering now the sounds in the night, she examined them for marks. She had painted those doors a few months ago. Dark red. She admired the way they looked in the white brick wall. No chipped paint, no sign of damage, no indication that anyone had banged on them with a metal instrument of some sort.

Opening rituals done, she took up her post in the cubicle as the early cars began to swarm in like bees hunting for the best flower. Rachel liked to be on hand in case someone had a dead cell phone, a flat tire, a defunct battery, whatever. Happy clients would keep her garage, and herself, financially afloat. No small trick these days.

Catching sight of her reflection in the glass of the cubicle, she turned her head from side to side. Hank had persuaded her to let her hair grow longer. She hadn't wanted to at first, but examining her image now, she found she liked the change—straight hair, almost to the shoulder and parted in the middle. Her eyebrows were still too level, chin too strong—her mother had called it stubborn. Continual plucking might force her brows into an arch, but Rachel knew she wouldn't have the patience to keep it up.

Her father thought the new hairstyle made her look too Chicana.

"But you're half Mexican," she told him. "That makes me part Mexican. I shouldn't look it?"

For the first time she wondered if her father was anti-Mexican. That would be tough. How could you be anti-part-of-yourself? If that was the case, it might be because her mother's parents were sort of anti-Mexican.

Marty Chavez would have done absolutely anything to keep Rachel's mother happy; even stop being Mexican. But Madeleine had slipped away from both Marty and Rachel after being thrown from a horse.

No. The horse accident was only part of it. Madeleine might have recovered from that. She died after Rachel had taken time off from caring for her invalid mom, and left their farm in the Sacramento-San Joaquin Delta for a shopping trip to San Francisco. She had long ago forgot why she wanted to go shopping or what she had bought. What she couldn't forget was that she had brought back a very nasty virus.

It seemed a lifetime ago but Rachel still could hardly bear to think of it. Neither she nor Marty were ever the same again. The nightmare of it all had sent them skidding down a slippery slope with nothing to break their fall. Madeleine had been the one who gave their little family stability.

◇◇◇

The time was heading toward eleven when Rachel remembered the van.

She found its dusty sides wedged between two black Cadillac fleet cars that had parked a bit over their lines. The rear plate on the van was Arizona. That might not mean anything. Newly transplanted California residents often waited as long as possible before paying the taxes and doing whatever it took to pass the emissions test and register and tag their cars. This particular van looked more like a panel truck than a passenger vehicle.

Was it abandoned? Stolen? Damn. That would be a pain in the butt. It happened a couple times a year, and Rachel was less than fond of dealing with cops.

There was that record of her DWI and possession arrest up north after her mom died. And there was the incident that had put her on a collision course with the power players in California's water politics. The CEO of InterUrban Water District had been killed by someone driving a company car, and Rachel had found the guilty car in her garage. Bad headed for worse and she'd had to report her own part in the grisly mess, undergo interrogation and the interminable waiting, wondering if she would be charged with murder.

In the end, she wasn't charged. And the ordeal did have a silver lining. It had brought her Hank, a water resources engineer at InterUrban.

She tried the rear door of the van. Locked. Not surprising. The inside of the rear windows had been sloppily painted white. Turning sideways, she slid between the van and its neighbor. The window in the driver's door was heavily tinted.

When that door proved locked, she moved to the front window. Now she could see brown plush front seats, worn and empty except for a couple of squashed beer cans and some crumpled balls of paper on the passenger side. An abandoned vehicle? Maybe stolen and dumped after serving some shady purpose.

Rachel was sliding back along the front fender when her eye caught on something behind the front seats. A metal grill of some sort.

Cupping her hands above her eyes, she peered through the windshield. Was that a cage? With something inside? She pounded the window with her fist. If someone had left a dog locked up here, she would personally hunt them down and turn them over to the authorities.

She strained to make out the image in the shadows behind the seat.

It wasn't a dog.

She was looking at a small, thin hand.

Chapter Two

"Hey!" Rachel rammed the side of her fist against the window. "Hey, in there!"

The hand didn't move. She rocked the van. Still nothing.

Back at the driver's door, she hammered the tint-darkened window, but that only hurt her knuckles and she couldn't see the hand from there. Leaving the van, she hurried back to her cubicle to find the jimmy she used to help the amazing number of clients who managed to lock themselves out of their cars.

The driver's window was tightly shut and she had trouble slipping the jimmy inside. Slamming her fist against the door in frustration, it occurred to her that the van probably didn't belong to a client or to anyone she knew. Its presence here was illegal, its use possibly criminal.

Rachel ran back to the cubicle, wrestled a toolbox from under a cabinet, and took out a hammer. A few seconds later she was raising the hammer and swinging it at the white-painted window in the left rear door.

The glass cracked and buckled but didn't give way. A wisp of foul smell seeped out.

Inside, no sound. Nothing seemed to move.

The third swing made a hole in the window large enough to put her hand through. Her arm raked against the jagged glass. Blood dribbled across her wrist as she tried to find the latch release. Maybe there wasn't any. Panel trucks were generally used for hauling stuff, not people.

Her sense of urgency building, she slid back along the side of the van, raised the hammer and brought it down on the driver's window until again there was a hole she could reach through. This time her fingers reached the switch. Door open, she climbed inside, peered over the seat back.

On the floor of what looked like a makeshift animal cage, two boys sprawled, eyes closed. But no way could they have slept through the racket she had made. Rachel searched the panel of buttons on the armrest, then under the seat before finding the right lever to release the rear door.

At the back of the van, she grabbed an outside handle and pulled the door open. Only a metal stub remained where the hand release for the back door should have been. A rush of stale, musty air enveloped her.

The door to the cage inside, held closed and inoperable by the back door of the van, swung open. One boy lay prone, his face turned away, the other was curled in a fetal position, a hand held out toward her, a small metal bolt clutched between his fingers.

The odor of dirty diapers was strong. But these children weren't infants, they looked maybe nine, perhaps a small ten. Whoever had left them here hadn't provided a potty.

Both boys were dark-haired, taffy-skinned. They looked Mexican or Guatemalan, Salvadoran—from somewhere south of the border.

Rachel grabbed the shoulder of the boy closest to her and shook him. His head flopped back and forth but his eyes didn't open. She grabbed the arm of the second boy. No response. She jammed a middle finger under his jaw trying to find a pulse. Was there a faint tremor? No time to wonder. Or to bring help.

Leaving the van's doors ajar, she ran down to the level where she kept her own car, backed the new-to-her but aging Honda Civic out of its space, drove it up the ramp and edged it as close to the van as she could. She jumped out, opened the hatchback and lowered the back of the rear seat.

Neither boy weighed much, but she was afraid of hurting them. "It's okay. It'll be okay," she whispered, knowing they couldn't hear her, but saying it anyway.

"Please, please, please…," she murmured over and over, hoping there really was a God who could fix this. It took a few moments to deposit each boy gently into the hatch.

Back in the Civic's front seat, Rachel rested an elbow on the steering wheel, held her hand to her temple, and tried to slow the panic in her head. The hospital wasn't far. But what was the fastest way to get there?

She revved the motor, popped the clutch and broke her own speed rules exiting the garage.

Wheels complaining each time she zigged or zagged around a corner, she caught the stale end of a yellow light, drove through the red, hung a hard left and entered the hospital parking lot neither noticing nor caring that she was in the exit lane. The lot was huge and packed with cars.

Skidding to a stop at the emergency entrance, she leaned on the horn. The brick wall of the hospital stretched on a block or two. Jefferson Hospital was old and rambling, built onto many times, but its reputation was top notch.

The glass emergency doors reflected the clear sky. Where the hell was everyone?

Rachel leapt out of the car, opened the hatchback and hurried toward the glass doors, which slid open automatically as she approached. "Help!" she yelled. "Please help me. I have two kids out here. If they're not already dead, they don't have long."

That galvanized two men and a woman in loose, pale green shirts and pants who appeared in the hall across from the door, and trotted forward. The gurney they steered bumped past her and down the ramp outside the emergency door. She followed them to her car.

By the time they had lifted the first boy onto it, a second team had appeared. Clasping the other boy, one of the medics raised his eyes to Rachel's, then transferred the small frame to the second gurney.

The glass doors whipped open again. A woman stepped out and motioned to Rachel. "Park your car and come in," she called. "There's paperwork."

"I don't know these kids," Rachel said. "I just…sorta…found them."

"That's fine. But please come in." The woman jerked her chin over a broad, sharp shoulder. "We still need a signature." She moved aside as, one behind the other, the gurneys bounced up the ramp on their rubber wheels, rolled through the doorway, and disappeared.

The woman wagged her head at Rachel and motioned again. She was square-jawed and looked like a third-grade teacher— definitely a match for any unruly class. "Come."

Sighing, Rachel nodded. She closed the hatch, got back behind the Honda's wheel, and hunted for a parking space. It took a while. She had to circle the lot four times.

The woman met her at the entrance door.

"I don't know those kids," Rachel told her. "Not even their names. I found them locked in a panel truck parked in my garage. I never saw them before. I have no idea who they are or where they're from, or why or when they were left in that van."

As if she hadn't heard a word, the woman led the way to a small office, offered Rachel a chair and sat down behind a small metal desk that was about the same color as the scrubs worn by the emergency room staff. "Mrs. McCarthy," the woman pro-nounced, looking at Rachel over granny glasses perched near the end of her nose. "They call me Mrs. Mac. You want someone to look at that arm?"

Rachel glanced at the cut from the window glass. The blood had congealed. Her medical insurance had a big deductible. "No thanks. I'm fine."

Without further ado, Mrs. Mac began asking questions.

For the third time, Rachel was saying no, she couldn't pay for the boys' medical care and didn't know who might do so, when a short man wearing what looked like a large shower cap stuck his head in the door. "You the lady who brought in those two kids?"

"Yes, but I don't...." Rachel stopped when she saw the look in his eyes.

He plucked off his eyeglasses, wiped the back of his hand across his forehead, and removed his cap revealing dark, curly hair. "I'm afraid I have sad news."

For a fraction of a second Rachel's eyes closed almost involuntarily. "I got them here as fast as I could."

"It wouldn't have mattered much. The one kid's been dead a while."

The back of Rachel's index finger rose and covered her mouth as if to stop a sound.

"The good news," the man was saying, "is the other is alive. Badly dehydrated, but alive. We'll be admitting that one."

Chapter Three

Dr. Emma Johnson strode down the hospital corridor faster than most people could keep up with. Her Hush Puppy walking shoes squeaked a bit on the vinyl tile.

A child for God's sake. Ten or eleven. And the other one DOA. What the hell…? She passed four rooms and turned left into the fifth.

The new arrival was in the third bed, nearest the window. Emma scanned the chart. Blond hair just beginning to gray swung forward as she studied it, and lines deepened in a face saved from plainness by wide-set blue eyes and a smile that dazzled even the most frightened children. But she wasn't smiling now.

The child she was examining was not conscious. Contusions at the left shoulder and both wrists, abrasions along the right leg. Dehydration. Malnutrition. *But alive.*

She examined her new young patient from head to foot. Was this one of the two she had seen briefly earlier? Maybe. Maybe not. Mexican, though. Or if the child lived in the area, maybe Central American. Spanish/Native at any rate. The damn Spaniards had gotten around.

Emma brushed the child's short hair back looking for more bruises. There was another abrasion at the right temple. Most injuries had been duly noted by the ER people, but they had missed the abrasions at the ends of the thumb and first two fingers of the right hand. What was that all about? She tapped the plastic bag that hung from the stand at the head of the bed and eyed the tube that led to the needle taped against the lax arm.

Laying her hand for a moment against the thin cheek she wondered how this happened. This degree of dehydration. Probably a wetback. Probably couldn't keep up. Abandoned. No parent or guardian listed. How could a parent leave a child like this behind? Surely this one was too young to have crossed the border alone. Had the agribusiness barons stooped to luring children this age to pick strawberries or whatever? Did anything need to be picked in October?

Was this a candidate for a stay in the charity ward? Emma examined the child's face, the narrow shoulders and thin arms. That might be better than whatever lay ahead for this one. No, he was just too young. She took a ballpoint pen, tapped it across her lips.

The child's head rolled from one side to the other. Life was returning.

◇◇◇

Gabriel Lucero squinted at the prescription he was filling. The toothpick he was chewing broke. He removed it, picked the bit of wood from his tongue and bit down again on the remainder. He'd quit smoking ten years before, but he'd be damned if he would give up toothpicks.

A little too much sun had added a year or two to his appearance. His eyes once had a flash of humor behind them. Now they were just a somewhat stale brown. The tie below his chin was badly knotted and light-years beyond its prime. Above the toothpick, the broad nose was a little crooked, adding to a slightly scruffy look. Brown hair had just enough curl to outwit his efforts to tame it. Not that he cared. Not these days anyway. Gel was out. Not that it was vain or sissy. It made his hair feel like it was made of plastic.

Gabe had left Albuquerque, after Ronnie, his wife of eleven years, had discarded him like a coat gone out of style. Someone else went better with her new wardrobe. Monty something. Monty owned a winery. Gabe hadn't even been suspicious when she kept talking about vitriculture and oenology, which he later decided sounded like a pathogen discovered by a doctor wearing rubber gloves.

Ronnie was a CPA and Gabe thought the bottles of Merlot she brought home were just "professional courtesy" gifts from a client. Right.

He didn't miss Ronnie so much anymore, but he did miss Wendy. His Little Miss. Nine years old and already it was obvious she was going to be drop-dead gorgeous. Maybe he should have stayed in Albuquerque. But it was too damn painful when he ran across Ronnie and Wendy with Monty-the-oenologist.

So Gabe had taken the first job he found that let him work four ten-hour days a week. The work schedule at Jefferson Medical Center's pharmacy allowed him to fly out often to see Wendy. At first he'd gone back every weekend, but there wasn't a lot you could do with a kid in a hotel. The Albuquerque zoo was world class, but how long could you gaze at gorillas?

Now, a few months after his arrival, Gabe didn't much like LA. Way too much traffic, for starters. Everybody rushing out to sit on the freeways and suck in that car exhaust. No wonder the smog was so bad. Amazing that anyone lived past the age of sixteen without coming down with black-lung.

The so-called Metro system was a joke unless you worked and lived in exactly the right places. And if CalTrans had a game plan for improving traffic it seemed aimed at making commutes so miserable that people would move to Alaska or Ohio or anywhere else. And then there was the added insult of the brush and forest fires. His eyes burned even with the doors and windows of his South Pasadena condo closed.

Maybe he should move to Santa Monica. Less smog, but a quantum leap in commute time. Why did so many people want to live in this God-forsaken place?

Gabe stared again at the prescription, closed one eye, then the other. MDs weren't exactly known for decent handwriting, but usually he could make it out. He was barely forty. Did he need bifocals already?

"Hey-hey my friend."

Gabe swung around.

"It's a glorious day out there." Gordon Cox grinned at him like a Dodgers pitcher after a no-hitter. Gordon had one of those forever-little-boy faces: soap-scoured apple cheeks, ears that despite their small size managed to stick out a little. At eighty Gordon would look like a choir boy with gray hair. Or if he dyed his hair, he'd look like Dick Clark, except nobody would remember Dick Clark by then.

Gordon was maybe five-ten, with narrow shoulders and a small-boned body, impeccably neat, with just a slight paunch beginning to appear at his belt. He was always, unalterably pleased with life. Gordon was the Zyrco Pharmaceuticals rep.

Gabe smiled in spite of his foul mood. "You mean you can actually see the mountains?"

"Well, not quite that glorious," Gordon said. "You wait till winter, though. That's when you can see the mountains. I never figured that out."

"You mean there are maybe four days a year you don't need a gas mask?"

"Something like that. But what a small price to pay to live at the center of the universe. This is where it happens, my friend."

Gabe removed the remains of the toothpick from his mouth and tossed it into a waste basket beneath the counter. "New York might quibble with that. And some of us see this particular center of the universe as a black hole."

"Maybe." Gordon set two black cases on the floor.

Gabe watched him brush off the sleeves of his suit jacket. "How do you do it, Gordo?"

"Do what?"

"How do you stay so neat? You could pass for a Mormon any day of the week. Or if your neck was just an inch or two thicker, you'd look like standard issue FBI. Dark suit and tie, white shirt, shoes with a mirror shine…."

"I keep telling you, Gabe, this is LA. If you want people to notice you, go for the neat, bland look. Makes you stick out like a topless dancer in church."

Gabe grunted. "More likely, it's the salesman mystique. Neat. Orderly. Interchangeable smiles."

"I'm not really a salesman."

"Funny. You look like a duck, quack—"

"Come on. You know full well there's a lot more to my job than that. I'm the pharmacist's best friend, to say nothing of the docs'." Gordon unsnapped one of the cases and tossed a fat brown envelope toward Gabe, who grabbed it before it hit the floor.

"The ten most prescribed medications in the U-S-of-A are in there," Gordon said. "Free samples. When you get someone you know is having trouble paying for their pills, slip 'em some freebies."

Gabe knew that Gordon, like any pharmaceutical rep, was into sales big-time. None of them would have a job if they didn't sell a lot. But Gordon didn't hound the docs like some of the reps. He didn't hand out Dodgers or Lakers season tickets or other personal freebies. Gordon did his business by just being a great guy. Friendly, funny, helpful.

You might even call him a philanthropist. Gordon could be counted on to be there if you needed him.

Chapter Four

Rachel was having dinner with Hank Sullivan at Luigi's, a little Italian restaurant that had opened on Wilshire. After the ugly mess of her day, the kids, the hospital and all, she had called him to postpone their date, but he had sounded like he was really looking forward to it, so she made up another reason for calling.

He had wanted to take her to Azalea at the New Otani downtown. "But you know me," she had said. "It's been so long since I have dressed like an adult, I've forgotten how."

Now she swished a slab of still-warm bread around in the plate of olive oil, garlic, Parmesan cheese and herbs, and finished recounting her awful discovery in the back of the white van.

"Pretty awful, all right," Hank said. "On the other hand, it was lucky for the one boy. You probably saved his life."

Rachel frowned thinking about it. "Why would anyone do something like that to children? Why were they locked in that van and left to starve?"

His sandy eyebrows tilted up as they often did when he looked at Rachel. "God only knows, sweetheart." He flicked a shock of straight hair away from his eyes. He needed a haircut. He often did.

Rachel gave a small smile in spite of herself. That stubborn hair the color of winter wheat was one of the reasons she loved him. "They were kids who should have been in grade school, middle school at most," she said, smile disappearing. "They were just left there to die, Hank."

"What about the van?" he asked. "Maybe the cops could trace it."

"It was gone when I got back from the emergency room. The murderer had great timing."

"Murderer?"

Rachel's eyebrows tightened into a straight line. "What else would you call it? Those boys were left there to die. And one of them did."

Hank peered into her face and shook his head. "Damn, sweetheart. I'm sorry this happened."

The lines in his face where dimples might have been, deepened. "Mind if I have a glass of wine?"

Mouth full of salad, Rachel just shook her head. Which was a lie. Tonight she did mind. The morning's events had shaken her. She was depressed and uptight. And okay, irritable. And she, too, wanted a glass of wine. But alcoholism was a tricky, beguiling fiend. Even one sip could put her on the path back to the hole she had crawled out of a few years ago.

The waiter brought a glass of Shiraz and Rachel tried not to watch as Hank raised it to his lips. She dropped her eyes, picked up her glass of ice water, then set it down harder than she meant to. The lemon slice inside swirled in its choppy sea of ice.

Rachel made her way through a plate of fettuccini Alfredo.

Hank kept eyeing her as if she was a river and he needed to find a safe place to cross.

When the table had been cleared and they were sipping cappuccino, he reached over and touched her hand—the left one where the diamond sparkled. "The papers have come," he said. "The divorce is done. Let's set a date."

Rachel gaped at him.

"A date," he said again. "As in getting married. You want to go to Vegas?"

"Now?" Rachel reached again for her water glass and hid the flush she could feel rising into her face by taking a swallow.

Why this reaction? He had been there—*really* been there for her—more than once. She loved him. Didn't she?

"Why Las Vegas?"

"I hear there's less red tape there."

"I, uh…I'm not sure this is a good time." She was used to being engaged. Engaged was wonderful. Marriage, well, that would be different. She needed a little time to contemplate it.

Hank frowned. "You want to wait?"

"Maybe. A little while."

"Like till when?"

"I don't know. It just seems so sudden. I wasn't thinking along those lines. I need a little time." *Don't be a fool. You'll lose him. What did you think engagement meant?*

"We're not exactly kids, Rachel."

"What did you have in mind? Just up and run off some weekend?"

Hank put his hand back on his side of the table. "You don't seem like the type to want a big do."

"Well, I do have a father, and I wouldn't want him to get within a hundred miles of Vegas. He gets into enough trouble right here in Gardena." Marty, Rachel's dad, was a serious gambler—sometimes so serious he forgot to eat and sleep, to say nothing of running out of money.

Hank's shoulders and eyebrows rose in sync. "Okay. Then what—"

Rachel cut him off. "You don't seem to understand. I can't talk about it right now. I heard this tapping in the middle of the night. One of those kids had worked a bolt out of someplace in that van and was dinging it against the door trying to tell someone he was dying. I heard it and I was too damn lazy to get up. If I had, just…." Rising, as tears distressed her further by threatening to spill, she brushed at her face with her napkin and headed for the door of the restaurant.

Hank hurriedly dropped enough money on the table to cover the bill and went after her. Two blocks down the street, he caught up with her and led her back to his green Mustang.

"I'm sorry," she said, her face collapsing again.

"It's okay. I know it was awful. Especially after everything else." He put his arms around her but it was awkward. Maybe it was the bucket seats.

Neither said anything more as he drove her back to the garage.

"Shall I come up?" he asked.

Key already in her hand, she shook her head, got out, unlocked the red side door of the garage and closed it behind her.

Chapter Five

"Okay, it's terrible," Goldie said. "So you want to go to MacArthur Park and look for worms to eat? Or maybe I should hold your arm nice and steady while you aim a gun up your nose?"

Under the streetlight, teeth flashed brilliant bluish white in the black woman's face. She and Rachel were sitting on the bench in front of the garage where they had met and become close friends. Goldie supervised a crew that worked nights cleaning nearby offices.

Downtown traffic was practically nil after ten p.m. A lone car passed, weaving across two lanes. "That one has a snootful." Goldie folded her arms across her chest, watching Rachel from the corner of her eye.

The night was chilly. Rachel pulled her shapeless old cardigan sweater closer about her. "You saying I'm over-reacting?"

"You? Over-react? I'd never say that about you, honey. I just think you sometimes get your hair on fire and can't figure how to put it out."

"So how do I put it out?"

"Stick it in a nice bucket of ice water."

"Goldie! This isn't funny."

"Well, it isn't easy getting a fix on where you are, you know. Like trying to tape Jell-O to a board. And you wouldn't be down here this time of night if you didn't want some such answer from me."

"I've gone and had a fight with Hank, too."

Goldie tossed her head. "Aaaah…That was real smart. That guy would throw himself in front of a semi for you."

Rachel leaned back on the bench, brought a foot up under her, and propped an elbow on her knee. "He wants to get married. Like soon."

"That's bad news?"

"I don't know."

"You don't know? When did that happen, you don't know? What's the matter with you, girl? What's that rock on your finger? A paperweight?"

Rachel was examining the home-made gauze bandage that covered the place where the broken glass in the van's window had ripped her arm.

Goldie pressed on. "You gonna give that ring back?"

Rachel blew a stream of air from pursed lips. "I just want to wait a while."

"So tell him that. He'll understand."

"I tried. He didn't understand."

"Did you stick your head in that bucket first, before you said it?"

"I guess not." Rachel was silent a moment. "Goldie, those kids were…." Her voice caught and it was a moment before she continued. "They shouldn't have been left there."

Goldie put a hand on her friend's shoulder. "I know, honey. But they were. There's nothing on God's green earth you can do to change that."

Rachel was staring into the middle distance. "You think it had something to do with their being Mexican?"

"Well, I don't like people who are always playin' the race card, but with those two boys, I imagine it did have something to do with their being Mexican."

"Is it that bad? Are Mexicans just non-people here?"

"Sometimes. In some ways."

"You sound like an oracle or something," Rachel said impatiently. "I'm part Mexican. No one ever treated me bad because of it. Not that I know of anyway."

Goldie drew in a long breath and peered over her glasses at Rachel. "You are just a quarter. What do they call that?"

"Quadrexican?" Rachel said, and they both laughed.

"Anyway, that hardly counts. It's just a pinch," Goldie said. "Besides, you're different. Even the quarter you are isn't cultural."

"What does that mean?"

"Like your family didn't follow the culture, did they? You're not even Catholic. And you probably don't even know what a piñata is."

"I do so know about piñatas."

"And your family was well off."

Rachel made a face. "*Was* is right." After her mother died, her father had bet their very real farm in a poker game—and lost it.

"That still don't make much never-mind compared to a lot of folks. Especially to lots of Mexicans."

"Maybe that's why I can't shake this awful feeling," Rachel said, not sure exactly what she meant. "You know what else is odd?"

"Now what?"

"I brought two kids to the emergency room. One dead, one almost. Whatever had happened to them, it was criminal negligence. Not that I like talking to cops or anything, but don't you think it's odd that the police haven't been around asking about those boys?"

"Yeah," Goldie said. "But nothing surprises me about Rampart." Rampart was the nearest LAPD station. "They might be too busy bustin' the old folks for playing chess in MacArthur Park."

"But wouldn't you think some kind of report would have to be filed? Some routine investigation?"

"I guess."

"Well, the only questions I've been asked are about almighty money, like who's going to pay the hospital bill. Not a single soul has asked if I have any information about how one of those kids got sick and the other got dead. Don't they care about that?"

"You got me." Goldie glanced at Rachel. "Come to think of it, there is one thing you can do about this. And maybe it'll make you feel better."

"Like what?"

"Get your butt down to that hospital tomorrow and visit the kid who's still alive."

◇◇◇

The next morning was hectic. Two clients locked their keys in their cars. One had flipped the door lock and wandered off, leaving the motor running. He must have really heavy stuff on his mind, Rachel thought. She didn't know his name, but she recognized his car. She used the jimmy to unlock the car and turn it off. Then she left a note in the driver's seat for the owner.

It was ten-thirty or so when she spotted Irene, sitting on a pink blanket on the sidewalk in front of the garage, playing solitaire. Irene's persona changed from time to time, like that of an actress, depending on the clothes she put on. Today, in a pink apron over a long blue skirt dotted with pink flowers, she looked as though she had flounced off the pages of a Jane Austen novel.

Rachel left the glass booth and walked over to her. "Who's winning?"

"I am, dear girl. Wouldn't have it any other way, would I?" A gray felt hat with floppy pink and white flowers all but hid her face. "Would you like a Twinkie?" She pointed to the somewhat battered supermarket cart pushed up against the fire hydrant on the corner near the bench. "I found some in the Dumpster down at Farmers Market. Unopened, of course." Irene nodded her head up and down until it threatened the hat's ability to remain seated.

"No thanks, really," Rachel said. "I had a bagel earlier."

"Good girl. Your age, you got to watch that figure." Irene patted the long skirt that covered her round stomach. "Luckily, that age passes."

"You want to make ten bucks?" Rachel asked.

Irene removed her hat, exposing hair shorn drastically short. "Of course, luv." Peering into the hat, she drew out two chiffon ties. "You want I should mind the shop?"

"Just for an hour or so. I need to visit someone in the hospital." Rachel had once had someone to help with the long hours the garage required, but with Lonnie's long detour into drug use, she'd found herself both paying him and running the place alone. After he died, she had decided to get a bit ahead on the bills and maybe even put a little money into savings rather than hire someone.

Irene replaced the hat, tied the chiffon in a bow under her chin and cocked her head at Rachel. "Not your dear dad in the hospital, I hope."

"No, no. He's fine."

"A friend, then."

"One of the kids I told you about yesterday. I just want to see if he's okay."

Irene tilted her head. "How thoughtful you are, dear girl."

A rendition of the William Tell Overture began softly somewhere nearby and grew louder. Rachel glanced up and down the street looking for the source.

"Ah, me, I forgot. You haven't seen my latest accouterment." Irene pulled a phone from the ruffled pocket of her pink apron.

Rachel blinked and nodded. There was no use wondering how someone who apparently lived on the street managed to have a cell phone or why Irene wanted or needed one. Acutely aware of her own need for privacy and reluctance to make her own life an open book, Rachel had never asked Irene much about her lifestyle, believing the woman might rightly call her impertinent.

"Hello," Irene was saying into the phone. "Hold on." She peered back at Rachel.

"You'll sit in the booth and answer the phone and all till I get back?" Rachel asked quickly.

Irene scooped up the cards with her empty hand. "Of course, luv. Didn't I say I would?"

◇◇◇

Rachel parked in the main lot this time and entered the hospital through the front door. Two women and a man sat at counters, behind Plexiglas panels with little speak holes, fielding questions from people who stood in line to ask them.

When Rachel reached the front of the line, a woman in a bright blue blouse, with frizzy black hair and pallid skin, just stared at her when she asked about the boy who was admitted from the emergency room about noon yesterday.

"A Mexican boy, I think," Rachel added. "One of the medics in the emergency room said he was very dehydrated."

"Name?"

"Mine or his?"

The woman frowned. "His, of course."

"I don't know his name."

The woman stared at Rachel, two red splotches appearing on her cheeks. "You want to see someone, but you don't know the name," she said flatly.

"I…uh…yes."

"Yes, you do know his name?"

"No." Rachel tried to throttle her frustration. "Look, I own the parking garage down the street. Yesterday I found two unconscious boys in a vehicle parked there. I brought them to the emergency room here. The doctor or nurse or whatever he was said it was too late for one of them, but the other was alive. I was just hoping to check on him. He was very young, maybe only nine or so, and I don't even know if he has any parents."

The woman in the blue blouse tapped on the keyboard in front of her computer monitor, then looked back at Rachel. "Sorry, I can't help you."

"What do you mean? I just want to see him, or at least find out how he's doing."

The woman drew together thin red lips outlined in a darker color. "No one of that description was admitted here yesterday," she said slowly, her tone underlining each word, as if speaking to someone who had little command of English. "Not after nine a.m. anyway."

"That's impossible. I brought two boys here about eleven-thirty. One was admitted to the hospital."

The woman tapped some more keys and shook her head. "Sorry," she said, then looked past Rachel to the person behind her. "Next."

Chapter Six

"Just a moment." Rachel's voice rose. "Please. He has to be here."

"No boy of that age or diagnosis was admitted from the ER yesterday. Period." The woman looked a bit wild-eyed, as if Rachel had sprouted a horn in the middle of her forehead. Then she picked up a phone, punched three buttons, and murmured something into the mouthpiece.

Almost immediately a tall man in navy pants, white shirt and a string tie, appeared. He raised his eyebrows at the woman behind the desk. She dipped her head at Rachel.

The man put a firm hand at Rachel's elbow. "Come with me, please, ma'am."

Glancing at the people in the lobby who were now looking in her direction, Rachel let him steer her to the door.

"Sorry ma'am," he said. "Is there anything I can help you with?"

Rachel explained it all again. "The second boy was being admitted. Now she says he wasn't, that they've never heard of him. How can that be?"

The man gave her a calm stare, as if he dealt with unhinged people every day of the week. "I don't know. But if they say he isn't here, he isn't here. I'm sorry, but if there's nothing else we can help you with, you'll have to leave."

◇◇◇

Irene rolled her eyes when Rachel got back to the garage and told her the hospital had no record of the child. "Doesn't surprise me dear girl. No, doesn't surprise me one whit."

"Why not?"

"First off, that is one big hospital. You know how many patients?"

Rachel shook her head.

"I hear they have room for seven hundred patients. I reckon they might misplace one here and there."

"It still doesn't seem possible."

"Stranger things have happened," Irene said sagely.

Rachel handed her a ten-dollar bill. Sometimes Irene was a total realist. Other times, just a tad, well, eccentric.

When the woman had gone back to her card game on the sidewalk, Rachel sat down in the booth, thought for a moment, then picked up the phone and touched a few numbers.

"I just want to apologize for last night," she said when Hank answered. "I don't know what got into me. I guess I'm a little stressed out."

She could almost see him lift one shoulder, as he often did when perplexed.

"Happens to all of us," he said. "I guess I picked a bad time. Whatever."

"You know that kid I took to the hospital? The one they admitted?"

"Yeah."

"I went over there today to see him and he wasn't there."

"At the hospital?"

"No record, no nothing. He's just gone, missing, lost, kaput."

"Maybe they transferred him somewhere else."

"Wouldn't they have a record of it?"

"If my experience with medical billing is any indication of medical record-keeping…."

Rachel made a bitter sound meant to be a chuckle. "Well, that's a point. Maybe they didn't check him in the right way, so he sort of disappeared." She stopped, but Hank didn't fill the gap.

"Well, I'm sorry. Really."

"Apology accepted…." This time it was Hank who paused. "Have you given any more thought to it?"

"To what?"

"Setting a date to get married."

"Yes," she said, "I'm thinking on it—oops, gotta go. I've got another call."

The incoming call was not good news.

"Ms. Chavez, please."

"Speaking."

"Gerald Mason, Patrick Hutton Advertising." Hutton leased almost three-quarters of the third level of her garage.

"Yes. Thanks for calling back. As you probably know, your parking lease expires next week. I guess we need to talk about a renewal." Normally she would have seen to this a month ago but she had mismarked her calendar. Hutton had been with her from the start, always paid on time, and always expressed appreciation when she went out of her way to help their staff, so she wasn't worried, but the lease did need to be renewed.

"You mean no one contacted you?"

"Contacted me? About what?"

"We won't be renewing," Mason said. "I'm afraid notifying you must have slipped between the cracks. I'm sorry. We're moving to the Valley. We're in the process right now. We'll be out before the lease is up. I'm really sorry no one told you."

Rachel put her hand over her mouth as if to stop it from shouting *Omigod!* Then, "I see. Well, it's been a pleasure serving you." The reduction in cash flow would be serious.

Well, it's not the end of the world. Then again, she wasn't so sure.

◇◇◇

The overhead lights in One-Eyed Jack's poker club shone brightly as the dealer laid out two hole cards face down on the green baize tabletop in front of Marty Chavez.

A drop of adrenaline charged through him as he lifted the corner of the top card just enough to see what it was. Marty always peeked at one card at a time. Looking at the cards that way had become something of a fixation for him. He wasn't sure it brought him good luck, but maybe it warded off bad luck. If there ever was a time for good luck, this was it.

He could almost feel his short salt-and-pepper hair rise on his scalp like that of a dog that sees a choice morsel.

The first card was the king of diamonds.

His eyes slid from face to face around the oval table, watching for signs the other players were pleased or unhappy with their hole cards. A "tell." The faces didn't betray much, but Marty had played often with each and knew them well. Sometimes all it took was a twitch, a lick of the lips, a scratch of the nose to give him an idea about the cards a player held.

Not that his instinct was always right. Rachel would never forgive him for losing the farm that way. Not that he missed the place—he was never cut out to be a farmer. But Marty would never forgive himself for doing Rachel out of her rightful home. He'd been trying to make it up to her ever since.

His second hole card was a diamond ten. When the bet came to him, he pushed forward a stack of black checkered chips. Hundred-dollar jobbies.

With a sweeping motion, the dealer laid out the first board card. A seven of spades. Not great. But Marty met the raise from Louis, who sat across the table.

The next board card...a jack of diamonds. *Yes!* A line appeared between Marty's eyebrows as if a ghost had pressed a finger there.

He pursed his lips to confine a sound that wanted to leak out.

Today just might be the day.

Chapter Seven

It was after midnight, but Rachel wasn't sleepy. She was compiling a list of businesses within walking distance of the garage. Clancy was sprawled over the top of her computer monitor supervising her work. Clancy was a large orange tomcat with a torn ear doubtless gained during a feline equivalent of a barroom brawl. He was clearly a street fighter before they met at the animal shelter. It was love at first sight.

Rachel's work was slow going, using first the Yellow Pages, then her computer to transfer nearby addresses into Google maps to see if they were within the distance people would be willing to walk to and from work. It might take weeks to find all the possible firms, but in the morning, she would start calling the places she identified tonight.

She couldn't last long without replacing the revenue from Hutton. She made a note to add to her standard lease boilerplate a clause about sixty days' notice to vacate.

Through an open window, she heard someone calling her from the street. "Rachel? I know you're still up. I can see the light. Let me in."

She ran down the ramp and opened the people door. "Pop? What are you doing here at this hour?" She caught a whiff of whiskey, but he didn't seem drunk. Marty's problem wasn't booze.

"Came to celebrate." He produced a bottle of champagne. Nearing sixty, he was still a good-looking man, not tall or heavy, but solid, with a complexion that always looked like he had just left the beach. The crevices in his face only seemed to enhance it. His deep baritone voice could have landed him a job at any radio station.

She locked the door behind them and started up the ramp. "Celebrate what?" she asked, afraid she knew the answer. This was typical when Marty did well at the poker tables. A week or so of over-confidence would soon cost him more than he'd gained.

"Biggest win ever," he exclaimed, turning to beam at her as they reached her apartment door.

His excitement was contagious. Rachel threw her arms around him. She had decided some years ago that there was no point in depriving him of this moment. The outcome would be the same, regardless, so he might as well have his short season in the sun.

"I mean *really* big, this time." Marty's grin nearly split his face.

"That's wonderful." Rachel tried to sound enthusiastic as she set out two stemmed glasses on the countertop of the kitchen bar that separated her living room from the eating area. She gestured for him to open the champagne and took a bottle of club soda from the refrigerator for herself.

"Damn, Rachel, my mind must be going, I don't know how I forgot," Marty said as he wrested the cork from the bottle, which gave out a loud *pop*. "I was just so excited."

Rachel had to smile. "I haven't seen you like this in a long time." Even if it wouldn't last long, it was nice to see him happy.

"But I shouldn't have forgotten your…thing."

"No problem," Rachel said. "Other than wasting some of that champagne. You can't take an open bottle with you in the car, and you can't leave it here. So we'll have to pour it out."

"Maybe you know somebody you could give it to."

"Nope. I won't have it in the house. Period. Except for right now with you here."

"I never really believed you were an alcoholic."

"Well, believe it, Pop. And it isn't *were*. Or was. I *am*. Once an alcoholic, always an alcoholic."

"I know that's what they say. You still going to AA?"

"Yes and no. I haven't been in a while. I'll go as soon as I have time." She settled onto the arm of the sofa. "So tell me about your good luck."

Marty launched into a card-by-card description of his game. Rachel was always amazed at how he could remember every play. Clancy climbed into her lap and she petted him, pretending to listen until Marty finished.

"How long were you there?" she asked when he reached the finale.

"Ten hours or so."

"Did you eat?"

Marty thought for a moment. "I don't think so."

"You can't drink on an empty stomach."

Rachel moved Clancy from her lap and got up. "So A, you're going to spend the night here, and B, you're going to eat something right now."

"Aw, Rachel…."

But she was already putting a frying pan on the stove. Taking a carton of eggs from the refrigerator, she stopped and leveled a look at him. "Okay. I should tell you I'm really glad you won, Pop, because it will be a while before I can help you out again. I lost a client today. A fairly big one."

"But that's just it," Marty said, watching her grate some cheese, "now I can help you."

"No you can't. I won't let you. You save that money. How much is it?"

"Almost fifty-six thousand."

Rachel almost dropped one of the eggs she was breaking into the frying pan. "You're kidding!" She tilted her head and watched his face to see if he was fibbing. "You have fifty-six thousand dollars?"

"Well, I owe Charlie eleven something."

"Eleven what something?" Rachel asked, stirring the eggs. She stared across the stovetop at him, hoping she was wrong.

"Thousand. Eleven thousand."

Rachel's eyes flashed. "And who is Charlie?" She already knew the answer. No bank would loan Marty that much money, even if he had something to put up for security, which he didn't.

"Just a guy who loans money."

"Jesus, Pop! A loan shark! Are you out of your mind?" Rachel banged the wooden fork she was using on the counter, splattering raw egg. "You borrowed eleven thousand dollars from a goddam loan shark?" She grabbed a paper towel and mopped up the globs of egg.

Marty was wearing his best poker face. "I guess."

"Dammit, Pop! You're gonna wake up some day with busted kneecaps."

They both were silent as she finished scrambling the eggs, topped them with cheese and a spoonful of green chile, and put them in front of him. "Just the way you like them, *que no?*"

Marty nodded and began to eat. "Really good. Thanks."

"You save that money, Pop. You put it somewhere that you can't get your hands on it real easy. Open an account in a bank in New York or Timbuktu or somewhere you can't put your hands on it too easily."

Marty swallowed a forkful of eggs. "Umm-hmm."

"You want some coffee?"

He shook his head. "No thanks. Must be getting old. It's started keeping me awake."

Rachel was cleaning up the kitchen. She frowned. "Did you hear what I said when I handed you the eggs?"

Marty shrugged.

"I said, *que no.* You taught me that when I was little. That and a couple other words, but that's all. Not even sentences. Why didn't you teach me any more Spanish?"

"Your mother wouldn't have liked it."

"She would have loved it. You know she would."

"It would have made her uncomfortable."

"Because of Nana and Gramps?"

Marty raised an eyebrow and gave a little shrug, but said nothing.

"Well, they've been dead for years and years. So teach me some Spanish now."

"Can't."

"Why?"

"I don't remember any."

"Okay, let's both learn some Spanish. I'll bet one of the community colleges offers a short course in conversational Spanish. You can use some of that big win of yours to take us to Mexico, to where you were born."

"No."

"Why not?"

"I just don't want to. Where did all this interest in Spanish and Mexico suddenly come from?"

The lines between Rachel's eyes deepened. "Can't I just want to know where you came from?"

"Seems sort of silly at this stage of the game."

Well, dammit, you owe me a little something about my own history."

"I don't think I do."

"Bullshit! I knew everything about Mom, her family, where she was from. All I know about you is you're half Mexican, half Irish and I guess there were problems with her parents over the Mexican part. Which was incredibly stupid, but it doesn't matter any more."

Marty gave her a hurt look. "I came over here to offer to help you out." He caught her look. "Okay, pay you back for some of the times you bailed me out of money trouble. And you just want to yell at me about being Mexican."

"I am a quarter Mexican! I have a right to know about that part of me."

"You are not a quarter Mexican."

"I am so." She stopped, staring. "Omigod! Are you telling me you're not my father?"

Chapter Eight

Marty's eyes were avoiding Rachel's. "Don't be silly. I'm saying you are half Mexican."

"What?…Like from where?"

"From me."

"You're half Irish."

"Far as I know, my blood is one hundred percent bonafide Mexican."

Rachel didn't say anything for a moment, then, softly, "You were lying all this time?"

"I guess so."

"But you have blue eyes."

Marty moved those eyes to hers. "Yep. That was a puzzlement. A bee in the old ointment. It caused some problems for my mother. My father's family gave her a real hard time about it. When I was about six, even the padre told them it could happen and pointed out that already I looked more like my father than my brother and sisters did. A recessive gene maybe, from some Spaniard who escaped the Moors, or some guy who got over the fence long, long ago."

"Your father didn't trust your mother?"

"Nope. And he wouldn't let up. When I was fourteen, we started fighting a lot. Physical stuff. One night he broke my arm. A couple months later I was in San Francisco. My mother arranged for me to go to her sister there."

"You have papers?"

"Of course."

"How did you get them?"

"We weren't poor. My mother paid a lot. They were good papers. The best. I think she knew the whole thing eventually would be necessary. She was probably getting ready for it."

"What happened to her?"

"I wrote her many times." Marty looked down, avoiding whatever he saw in Rachel's eyes. "I never saw her again."

Rachel walked over to her father and drew him close. "Jesus," she said, voice almost a whisper. "You're an illegal alien?"

◇◇◇

The next morning, Rachel was still trying to digest her father's news. He had obediently spent the night on the sofa and was complaining over an early cup of coffee that Clancy had insisted on sitting on his chest and staring at him. "As if I was a mouse. A very large mouse."

"More like a rat."

"You still mad?"

She shook her head. "Of course not. It just takes some getting used to."

"Good. I was afraid you might turn me in to the Border Patrol."

They laughed, shyly at first, then the kind of laughter that brings tears to the eyes.

Marty left early, wanting to get his car off the street before the rush hour.

Rachel opened the garage and as soon as the flow of cars slowed, she climbed into the glass booth and began dialing the businesses she had listed as within walking distance. She left messages at the first three, hating the whole thing, the calling, the spiel, the phone tag, but it had to be done. Before she could punch in the next numbers, her own line rang.

"Archie Van Buren," the voice said when she had identified herself, "with Jefferson Hospital business office."

Had they found the boy she had been inquiring about? But why the business office? Were they were going to try to twist her arm again about paying the bill?

"That's Van Buren, capital V, capital B. We have a few problems you may be able to help us with."

"Yes?" Rachel drummed her fingers, waiting for him bring up the boy's bill.

"You have some available space in your garage?"

"Yes. Yes, I do." She would have to rethink her disbelief in magic and genies and fairy godmothers. "As it happens I've just gotten word that one of my clients is moving to the Valley. I have at least a hundred spaces. I could give you a firmer number in a couple hours."

"Good."

Then it occurred to her this might not be quite the pure stroke of luck it seemed. "You realize I'm not open all night. I close the doors at ten. And I'm not in a position to collect individual fees."

"Of course. No problem. For the most part, we only want to be able to park a few of our medical staff there on weekdays. Nights and weekends there's room in our own lot."

"A few…?" Rachel asked. "I thought you wanted more like a hundred."

"At least a hundred," he said. "To me, that's a few. We have something like nineteen hundred on the staff."

"Good heavens, that's a lot."

"Of course they're not all here at the same time. But when they are, we have to be able to park them. And right now we're at least a hundred spaces short."

"Do you want to write up the lease yourself or use one of my forms?"

"We'll do the lease. But there's one other thing. You have a helipad there, do you not?"

"Yes." She had visions of medics and gurneys and ambulances racing through the garage. "Several clients use it during business hours, but there isn't proper lighting for use after dark, and I don't think it could accommodate patients even during the day."

"No, of course not. We don't accept helicopter transfer patients. We're not a trauma center. Our emergencies arrive from the street. But your helipad might be handy for medical supplies from time to time, and for some particularly perishable items."

"That would work," she said. "If it's only occasional, I could even do delivery and pickup."

"I'm sure we can work something out."

When they had hung up, Rachel leaped from her stool in excitement. What a windfall! A bonanza, a break. Financial disaster would stop looming. And she wouldn't have to make any more calls to beg for business.

Her delight would not last long.

Chapter Nine

Archie Van Buren didn't waste much time. That same afternoon he called again. When she confirmed the number of spaces, he asked if she would be available the next morning to go over the lease.

She would. Absolutely.

Dressed in her only suit, navy chino, and a prim white blouse, Rachel got to the medical center ten minutes early, was escorted through what seemed like miles of corridors to the administrative wing and hence into a huge, elegant conference room. The mahogany table was so highly polished she could have used it to put on eye shadow.

Rachel wasn't sure whether to put her purse on the table or on the floor next to her chair. It was a very special handbag, with an intricate design on the flap—an impulse purchase from a leather worker at an arts fair back when she could afford such things. The purse really was a work of art. She decided to place it flat on the table.

She was soon joined by Van Buren and two other men. One was introduced as a vice president of something or other, the other apparently was the attorney who drew up the paperwork.

She wondered briefly if she should have her own attorney look it over, but the lease, neatly printed on legal-size paper, was not fundamentally different from those of her other clients. So a couple strokes of a pen and a few pleasantries later, Van Buren was escorting her back through the lobby, and she left the hospital with a check for the first three months' rent in her handbag.

In mid-afternoon, Rachel looked up from her eternal book work to see a black man in navy jacket and pants, white shirt and solid red tie, standing quietly in the door to her cubicle. Below round cheeks, soft eyes like melting chocolate, and a gentle chin, his middle strained a bit at the confines of his belt.

"Dan Morris," he said, with a somewhat shy smile. "I'm in charge of security at Jefferson Medical Center. When you have time, I just need to take a look at your license and whatnot."

"Of course." Rachel gestured to where the license and certificates hung in diploma frames just below the glass windows.

Morris studied them and nodded. "Mind if I take a look around? I doubt we'll be stationing anyone here since it's just the day staff that will be parking here, but I'd like to know the layout and all that."

"Sure. Go ahead. Anywhere you like." There was something about his eyes that spoke of sadness—maybe something he'd seen he couldn't forget—a little like some of the war vets she knew from AA. She watched him wander up the ramp with the rolling gait of a man whose few extra pounds had done little to hinder an innate grace.

He must have been thorough because it was a good half hour or more before he returned.

"About the helipad," he said.

Rachel frowned. "Something wrong? If so, I'll get it fixed right away."

"Nope. No problems I can see. When can we start using it?"

"Well, your lease is dated the first of next week, but if you need to send or receive something sooner, that's okay. I bill once a month based on the number of times a helicopter touches down for you."

"Good. We'll be needing to send something off. In about an hour. That okay?"

"I don't see why not."

"What's the procedure with you?"

"Well, I'd like to meet whoever will be going up there. I don't like strangers wandering around the place. But generally, I keep the door to the pad unlocked and once I've met whoever it is, if I'm here, that person might just stop and give me a nod so I know what's going on and I can record the use. If for some reason I'm not here, which won't be often, please just leave me a note—stick it under the door of the booth."

"Mostly, I'll be that person."

"Okay. How often do you think you'll be using it? The pad, I mean."

"Could be every day weekdays. Outgoing that is. There may be other stuff coming in. I can't predict that right now."

"Good heavens. I'll have to check my insurance about that much use. If the premiums go up, I'll have to raise the fee to cover."

Morris hitched up his pants and smiled. "I'm sure that'll be fine so long as you justify it."

Half an hour later, he was knocking at the window of her kiosk hoisting a package of tightly taped Styrofoam measuring about eighteen inches high by a foot wide and deep. A blue plastic handle was attached to the thick black rubbery-looking elastic bands that bound the parcel.

"Looks like you're going on a picnic," she said.

He smiled. "Don't I wish."

She nodded. Watching him check his watch, waiting for the elevator, she decided his muscles might be a little soft, but all the same, she wouldn't relish tangling with him.

Less than ten minutes later she heard the loud thrum-thrum-thrum of the helicopter.

And a few minutes after that, he tapped on her window, made an O with his thumb and forefinger, then ambled toward the street door.

"Hey, wait a minute," Rachel called after him.

He turned and ambled back with an inquisitive look.

"You're with the hospital. Maybe you could help me out on something."

"I'll sure try."

"I found a couple of young boys locked in a van here and took them to the emergency room. I was told one of the kids was dead but the other was okay, just dehydrated."

He nodded, raised eyebrows, waiting.

"I got to wondering about the kid who was alive, sort of felt responsible for him in a way, I guess."

"Sure," he agreed.

"So I went back over there to see if I could visit him." She stopped, remembering that it was probably someone on this man's staff who had ultimately escorted her to the door to get rid of her.

"Was he okay?" Morris asked.

"I wish I knew. That's the problem. They said he didn't exist. They said there was no record of any kid like him being admitted to the hospital that day."

Morris turned his head slightly, narrowed his eyes, and hitched up his pants.

Rachel fiddled with a pencil. "I guess I should add that I made a little bit of a scene because I figured that wasn't possible. One of your guys came and showed me the way to the door."

Morris' dark eyes examined hers. "If he wasn't courteous, you tell me what time it was and what he looked like and I'll have a talk with him."

"Oh, no," Rachel said quickly. "He was perfectly nice. My question to you, since you must know hospital procedures, is can you think of any reason I would be told by the emergency room people this boy was okay, that he was just dehydrated, and that he was being admitted to the hospital. But instead he disappeared?"

Morris stared at his feet, as if examining the condition of his shoes. "Well, I think dehydration can be pretty serious. Maybe they were wrong about this kid's condition. Maybe he died before he was admitted."

Chapter Ten

Weekend chores and errands gave Rachel little time to think, but by Sunday night she was again dwelling on what Morris had said.

If both boys were dead, all her efforts had been wasted. The worst of it was that the second boy's death would be on her conscience. She knew only too well that one of them had been knocking that bolt against the side of the van, desperately trying to alert someone to the plight of the two locked inside. And she hadn't responded.

The next morning, she was standing at the garage entrance watching Irene laying out tarot cards for a passerby the old lady had cornered, when someone tapped her on the shoulder.

She turned to find a harried-looking woman holding up a cell phone. "Can I help you?"

The woman raised both hands in the air in a helpless gesture. "My car won't start, my cell is down…."

Rachel led the way to the glass booth. "I've got several chargers. Let me see your phone."

The second connection she tried fit. "Good. Now let's see about the car."

"It's in C-3," the woman said. C was the area newly leased to Jefferson.

Rachel followed her client to a pale blue BMW. "Mind if I give it a try?"

The woman handed over the keys. She didn't look like the helpless type, but she obviously didn't know much about cars.

The engine ground over with plenty of strength but didn't catch. Rachel popped the hood, opened it, and looked around for something obvious like a stray distributor wire.

The woman was pacing back and forth behind the bumper.

"Okay, my guess is it's the fuel pump. There's no smell of gas, but I'm no expert," Rachel told her. "Couple things we can do. If you have Triple A we can give them a call but no telling when they'll get here and all they'll do is tow it—you pick the place. Or, I know a guy who will come out, take a look, and if it isn't too serious, he'll fix it right here. He's not as expensive as some repair places because he knows where to get most parts at the best prices. But I don't know how busy he is or exactly when he could take a look at it. Take your pick. Triple A or Johnny Mack. For that matter, if Johnny takes a look and decides it has to be towed, Triple A can do it then."

The woman looked relieved. "You can vouch for this guy?"

"As much as I'd vouch for anyone. And if you wind up having to rent a car, I could probably give you a lift to some car rental place."

The woman's face lost its harried look and gained one of the nicest smiles Rachel had ever seen. "I didn't know that kind of service existed any more. I will certainly let the business office at Jefferson know what a good deal they have with you. Let's give this Johnny Mack a try."

Rachel punched three numbers into her phone, explained the situation, and listened, nodding, then turned to the woman. "He can come by between two and four, If you leave me a key, you don't have to be here. But if it is the fuel pump, you may have to rent a car for a day or two. Up to you."

The woman handed over the keys. "Let's do it." When Rachel finished the arrangements, she added, "Will you at least let me buy you lunch?" She held out her hand. "I'm sorry. How rude of me. I'm Emma Johnson."

"Rachel Chavez." She took the hand, which was long-fingered and surprisingly strong.

"Chavez." The woman pronounced it the right way, with the accent on the first syllable. "Have you ever been to Pedro's Cantina, over on one of those streets off Olvera?"

"No."

"Well, one of the reasons I was especially upset about the car going out right now is that Pedro only has *cabrito* once a month and this is the day. I try never to miss it."

"*Cabrito?*"

Emma Johnson looked at her quizzically. "You're not familiar with Mexican food?"

"Sort of. But I don't know the language. Or at least not any more than the couple words you learn here and there on the streets."

"*Cabrito* is goat."

"Goat?"

"If you don't feel up to trying that, there are lots of other things on the menu. Real, genuine Mexican. Not this phony Cal-Mex or Tex-Mex nonsense. Even *menudo*, although I doubt you'd want to try that."

Rachel was nodding, liking the idea. "Okay. You're on."

Emma started up the ramp, then turned back. "Damn. How stupid of me. We'll have to get a cab."

"Not to worry, I can drive. Wait here."

Rachel went to the garage entrance and called to Irene, who was dealing tarot cards for a newcomer. Today's hat bore butterflies. When Irene raised her head, Rachel jerked her thumb back toward the cubicle. "I'll be back in an hour—two at most."

Irene waved. "I hope it is fun, dear girl, not work."

Rachel got her Civic, picked up Emma at the exit, and the woman expertly directed her to the restaurant without a single wrong turn.

Pedro's Cantina was exactly what its name implied—a Mexican diner with a small bar that served Dos Equis and Corona beer in bottles, another brand on tap, and a dozen kinds of tequila.

The place was swarming with people, but as Rachel and Emma entered, an affable swarthy man caught sight of them and moved quickly through the throng wiping his hands on his apron. Pedro himself. He took Emma's hand in both of his own. "Ah, *Señora médica. Muy bien.* Is good to see you again."

"*Y tu, Pedro,*" Emma said.

"You are late. I worry."

"I had car trouble. You know I wouldn't miss the *cabrito.*"

"That is why I worry." In spite of the crowd, there was an empty table, the only one set with white tablecloth, red napkin and a single setting of shining silverware. Pedro led them to it.

"I see today you have the *amiga,*" he said, grabbing an empty chair from a neighboring table and holding it out for Rachel.

"You must come here often," Rachel said when Pedro had gone in search of another place setting.

"We're old friends. I worked for a time in Mexico. I knew some of his family."

"Where in Mexico?"

"Chiapas. You've heard of it?"

"I've heard of it, but not much more that. It's way south, isn't it? Down near Guatemala?"

Emma nodded, an inscrutable look crossing her face.

"What's it like?" Rachel asked.

"One of the poorest states in Mexico, or anywhere for that matter. If you haven't seen it, you cannot imagine what that means—the insects are healthier than the people. The stench of human waste, the swollen bellies, and arms of children like this." Emma held up a hand, thumb and forefinger forming a small ring. "It is one thing to see adults starving. It's quite another to see children."

Rachel's straight brows drew together and her eyes darkened as she contemplated a poverty that hellish. Had the boys she had tried to save come from somewhere like that?

Pedro returned with tableware for Rachel and two tall glasses of ice water. The glasses were thick and heavy and rimmed with wide cobalt blue rings. "You wish the usual?" he said to Emma, who gave him a nod and a broad smile that showed the early lines of age. Her fair complexion looked recently scrubbed with soap and bereft of any sign of makeup.

"And the señorita?" He made a small bow toward Rachel.

"What do you recommend?" Rachel asked Emma.

"You're not a vegetarian or a fussy eater?"

"Not at all. Well, maybe I'd draw the line at stewed eels or fried grasshoppers."

"I agree about the eels, but you should try the grasshoppers sometime," Emma said. "You trust me to order for you?"

Rachel nodded and Emma spoke rapid Spanish to Pedro, who then disappeared without writing anything down.

"I just told him to bring two of everything I usually have, mainly lots of lettuce, tomato, and *cabrito*."

Rachel opened her napkin and laid it over her lap. "You were talking about Chiapas. What were you doing there?"

"Working at a clinic."

"Doing what?" Rachel knew Emma worked at the hospital, but that could be many jobs.

"Treating some very ugly diseases, among other things."

"You're a doctor, then."

"Of course," Emma said, then added thoughtfully, "I should talk about Mexico more often. It would help me keep stupid little things like cars and cell phones in perspective."

When Pedro brought their lunch, Rachel approached the *cabrito* suspiciously, then smiled when she tasted it. "I thought goat would be tough."

"After cooking slowly for two or three days, nothing is tough. Mexican cooks are magicians with food that shouldn't be edible at all. But only on very rare occasions did we have *cabrito* or any kind of meat in Chiapas."

"But you worked there anyway. Treating diseases," Rachel said.

"Oh, I did a little surgery, mostly when someone got injured. And I delivered lots of babies. I preferred surgery."

"Why?"

"You feel like you're actually curing someone, accomplishing something. Somehow surgery seems more *active* than other medical specialties. Have you ever seen surgery done?"

Rachel made a face. "Only with a veterinarian."

"Really? How so?"

"I used to live on a farm. Mostly we grew vegetables, but my mother kept horses."

Emma studied her companion for a moment. "Would you like to watch sometime?"

"A real operation? Good heavens. I've never imagined such a thing. You mean like in a sort of theater, behind glass, like on the TV shows?"

"Oh no," Emma said. "We're not really a teaching hospital, although sometimes students come to watch. For us, it's much more intimate. The rooms are small, and you'd have to stay quiet and out of the way. But it's not unusual for non-medical people to be observers in operating rooms. Reporters, photographers, our own public relations people."

"You mean scrub and everything?"

"Seriously clean and careful, yes."

Rachel shook her head. "I don't think so, no. The surgery I saw was kind of gruesome. And the horse died."

Emma laughed. "Well the Jefferson O-R is a little different. There's hardly any blood. Especially with laparoscopic surgery. That's what I specialize in."

"I've heard of it," Rachel said, "but I don't know exactly what it is."

"I make only a few incisions, one for my fingers, one for a special scope—a sort of camera. There's much less risk to the patients, they recover more quickly, and scarring is minimal."

"What kind of surgery? It can't be abdominal."

Emma nodded. "But it is. That's what I do. Mostly kidneys."

"And you decided to become a surgeon because it was more active?"

Emma seemed to think about that. "I guess I formed a lot of my opinions while I was in Mexico."

"How did you happen to work there?"

"When I got my MD, I joined Doctors Without Borders. I wanted to work somewhere I could practice my Spanish. Delivering babies, patching people up, and treating nasty diseases in a place where there wasn't much food and less money."

Rachel leaned forward, fascinated by this woman.

"I wasn't crazy about obstetrics," Emma went on. "Not that I don't like babies. But in Chiapas, hardly any of them lived very long. For that matter, no one did. I couldn't help wondering how bad it would be for the poor little tykes and how wrong it seemed to bring them into such a world."

"Maybe it's different there now."

Emma laughed. "You don't know Chiapas. It will be much the same for a very long time. Everyone is young. Half the population is under twenty, only the hardiest, maybe ten percent, reach forty-five. And many babies don't survive their first year. They're soon gone, all elbows and knees and gaunt faces, they look like helpless baby birds."

"It sounds so sad."

"It is sad. Misery, ignorance, pestilence, and early death. A few lucky ones earn a pittance working in the amber mines or for one of the companies sinking little wells to find out how much oil is under Chiapas. I hear there's quite a lot. Some of those lucky ones—mostly lucky because their family has died, so there's no one they have to support—earn enough to stay healthy until they are maybe twenty. But once the women have three or four babies, and the men begin drinking tequila, it is too late."

"Why don't people leave?" Rachel took a drink of water. The blue rim of the glass was very thick.

"They don't know anything else. Some try. But they must go on foot and Guatemala to the south and Oaxaca to the north are just about as poor as Chiapas."

"When were you there?"

"Late eighties, early nineties. When I was young enough to believe I could make a difference."

"But you must have made a difference. How could you not?"

"Not enough difference. I was there the New Year's Eve when the Zapatistas took over. Everyone had such hope about that. I left that January. I was about your age then."

"Zapatistas?"

Emma gave a quizzical smile. "How is it you know so little? Didn't you say your name is Chavez?"

"I guess my father had reasons for keeping me sanitized of anything Mexican."

Emma raised her eyebrows, but didn't comment on that. Instead, she said, "We will keep the Zapatistas for another time. Enough about me. Tell me how on earth you came to own a parking garage."

"My grandfather left it to me."

"And you wanted to operate it?"

Rachel hesitated, wondering how much to tell. She didn't know this woman very well. Emma seemed so direct and honest. But then Emma's life was probably an open book. "Oh, I wanted to do something new and different," Rachel said, and sketched the barest outline of what had brought her to Los Angeles, leaving more than a few gaps. Then she changed the subject.

"Do you like working at Jefferson?"

Emma gave her a broad smile. "Very much. I get to do what I do best."

"Surgery?"

"Mostly, yes. With some of the best people in the field and an administration that is totally supportive. I simply can't imagine working anywhere else."

Rachel eyed the woman across the table. "It's really a good hospital?"

"The best. Why do you ask? Have you had a problem there?"

"I guess you could call it a problem. A few days ago, I found a couple of boys, Mexican kids, I think, locked in a van in my garage. Unconscious."

Emma frowned and pursed her lips. "Dear God, how awful."

"Sure was," Rachel said. "I rushed them to the hospital. Turned out one was dead, but they said the other was just very dehydrated. They were admitting him when I left."

"That's sad about the one. But it was hardly the hospital's fault."

"Oh, that isn't what bothered me. It's that the next day I went back to the hospital to see how the boy who survived was doing."

"How nice of you."

"Well, the people on the desk didn't think I was very nice. In fact they had a security guy escort me out, like a barroom bouncer."

Emma drew her head back. "Good heavens. Why would they do that?"

"Because I made a bit of a ruckus."

"About what?"

"Because they claimed there was no record of the boy. So either they lied when they told me they were admitting him, or they lied when they said he wasn't there."

Emma had shifted her gaze to a little wooden carving that stood in a niche in the wall across the room. She looked back at Rachel. "Actually, there are many possible explanations. I seriously doubt they were lying."

Rachel looked down at her plate, then up at Emma. "You may be right. I've been given an assortment of explanations, from the kid maybe dying before he was admitted, to a parent picking him up. But what parent would leave a kid locked in a car to die, then pick him up before he could be admitted to the hospital?"

"I don't know." Emma cleared her throat. "It is odd. I'm sorry it happened. Hospitals do screw up. We like to think they don't, but they do. And Jefferson is awfully big. Seven hundred beds. It's hard to keep track of everything."

"You mean patients get lost?"

"No, not patients. But records, maybe." Emma picked up her purse from where she had placed it under the table. "Are you ready to go?"

As they left the cantina, Emma handed something to Pedro. It certainly covered the cost of their meal and a tip. It was a hundred-dollar bill.

Chapter Eleven

The phone was ringing when Rachel got back to the garage. She had to run to the cubicle and hunt for the receiver under a mass of papers. When she finally pushed the talk button she was frustrated and breathless. "Yes?"

"It's me, doll." Hank.

They had a date for dinner. Rachel was going to cook it herself. Her interest in cooking had been gaining ground lately and she was planning on picking up some fresh fish that afternoon. The two of them needed to get back on track as a couple.

Hank's voice sounded a little strained. She had apologized, but men can be weird about things like marriage. They always think you're just waiting for any chance to walk down that aisle and into washing diapers and baking chocolate chip cookies. Not that she had anything against babies and cookies. Did she?

"I'm at LAX," he said. "They're sending me up to Sacramento for a couple weeks."

Rachel wasn't sure what to make of his waiting until he was at the airport to tell her that. "Well, okay, thanks for letting me know."

"Sorry about the short notice. Hope you didn't go to a lot of trouble for tonight."

"Of course not."

"Some kind of problem with the levees. A tiny little earthquake and they think it's an emergency. Barely moved on the Richter…. They're calling my flight. I'll try to give you a call tonight."

Rachel slowly set the receiver down, thinking this might give her a little more time to figure out why the sudden approach of marriage had panicked her. All she seemed to be doing now was avoiding thinking about it.

On the other hand, why was he so nonchalant about their plans for the evening, not bothering to call until he was practically on the plane? Hank spent quite a bit of time in Sacramento. He knew people up there. Probably some were women. Did she care?

Yes, she did. She cared a lot. Hank was the Love of her Life. Capitalized.

Wasn't he?

◇◇◇

The helicopter hovered, then slowly, very slowly edged toward the rooftop. Inside the doorway at the top of the stairs Rachel waited for the *whupp, whupp, whupp* of the propeller to subside enough that the down-draft wouldn't sweep her away.

Clinging to the railing, she approached the cockpit. The box she handed the pilot was large but light. He exchanged it for a box that rattled and a yellow padded envelope, then silently waved his hand toward the top few floors of the hospital, which showed above the railing. Words would just be blown away by the chopper. He saluted and waited while Rachel dashed back to the doorway before easing the flying machine upward.

The address on the envelope was the Jefferson pharmacy, the box was for the lab. Dan Morris was appearing almost daily to pick up or send off packages. Rachel could wait and give these new arrivals to him if he showed up this afternoon, or she could call the hospital for a pickup. Or she could just walk the parcels over herself. It was a nice sunny day, the packages weren't heavy, and nothing much went on at the garage in the afternoon.

No harm in polishing client relationships with a little personal attention. She'd make the delivery herself.

She enjoyed the walk. There had been little time lately for jogging and it was good to stretch her legs. At the hospital, she chose a side entrance and soon regretted it. The entrances and exits on the various levels were confusing, while the maze of hallways inside seemed to lead every which way and then go on forever.

The whole place seemed a bit like an airline terminal. The guy who had called her about renting the parking spaces had said there were what? Seven hundred beds. Probably an average of two to a room. So that would be three hundred fifty rooms, and obviously a whole lot of corridors. And Jefferson was old, with many annexes probably added over the years.

But how on earth did the staff find their way around, much less the poor patients?

Finally arriving in the main foyer, Rachel approached the only open reception window, hoping the face behind it wouldn't belong to the woman who had called for a security guard to escort Rachel out of the hospital when she had inquired about the Mexican boys.

It wasn't. A man covered with freckles smiled and directed her to the left when she asked for the pharmacy.

But that hall led her to a gift shop. She stuck her head in. Helium-filled balloons bounced along the ceiling. Warm and fuzzy stuffed animals exuded joy. The aura of determined cheeriness was almost daunting. "You don't have a pharmacy in here, do you?" she called to a woman barely visible behind a pile of brightly colored plush toys.

"No, no." A face with perfect teeth and too-red cheeks smiled brightly. The woman pointed.

Indeed the pharmacy was there, behind the gift shop. Glass walls and little windows everywhere. And more stuffed animals and balloons. Two men seemed to be sorting something behind a glass wall. They both looked up as she placed on the counter the envelope delivered by the helicopter.

"Didn't think I'd ever find you. This place doesn't have the best sign system," she said to the man who met her there. He wasn't much taller than she. His nose looked like it had been broken sometime long past, and beneath it a toothpick bobbed as he chewed on it.

He put an elbow on his side of the counter, rested his chin in his hand, raised his eyebrows and said around the toothpick, "Anything else you'd like to complain about?"

Rachel's eyebrows drew into a straight line, but she said nothing.

"Your name?" he asked, looking sad now, like an abused beagle.

She couldn't think why, or why it mattered to her. And the wondering itself flustered her. "What?"

"Your name."

"Why?"

"Are you always this grumpy?"

She tried a small laugh. "Not always. But I guess you're right about now." She flushed, uneasy. Why was this man with the broad brow, short broad fingers and the nose of a wrestler somehow oddly attractive?

"Well, the grumpy act is usually my job," he said. "So what's your name?"

"Rachel Chavez. But I don't see—"

"I can't very well find your prescription if I don't know your name, now can I?" He had turned away and was riffling through a tray of white envelopes. "C-h-a-v-e-z?"

"I'm not here to pick up a prescription," she said, brusquely businesslike, and tapped the package on the counter. "I'm here because, best I can tell, this is addressed to you."

He picked up the envelope, glanced at the address label, then gave her a quizzical look. "How did you get it?"

"I own the parking garage around the corner and down a few blocks. The hospital leases some parking space for staff and the daytime use of the helipad on the roof."

He stared at her. "You own a parking garage." There was no question mark at the end of the sentence.

"Right."

"Gabe Lucero." He stuck out his hand and a smile transfigured his face.

His grip was strong and she felt her own smile broaden.

"Hey-hey." Another man materialized behind Gabe. "Where's my introduction?" Bright, dark eyes that missed nothing separated a pair of ears that almost qualified for "loving-cup." He looked like a freshly bathed and brushed schoolboy.

"Meet our local drug pusher," Gabe said, tilting his head toward him.

Rachel wasn't sure how to react.

"Pay no attention to Gabe. He loses his manners every morning on the freeway on-ramp." The hand the man extended had a few strands of dark hair on the backs of surprisingly long, narrow fingers. "Gordon Cox. Zyrco Pharmaceuticals."

Gordon was taller than she, but so neatly groomed, right down to his manicured fingernails, that Rachel felt gawky beside him. "Nice to meet you."

"Usually this place is filled with pharm staff," Gabe said. "But this is like siesta time for the patients, and maybe the docs, too, for all I know. Not many prescriptions this time of day so I'm the only one on duty at the moment. Gordon here sometimes stops by to hassle me."

"I see you deliver parcels," Gordon said to Rachel. He cleared his throat and his even features grinned boyishly. "Messenger service? Competing with FedEx?"

"Occasionally." Rachel wondered if she should set him straight and decided not to bother.

"She owns the parking garage down the street," Gabe said. "I guess we rent use of the helipad on the roof."

Gordon frowned. "I thought there was a helipad on the roof of the garage here."

"Apparently it needs some repairs," Rachel said.

Gordon cut in with a change of subject. "What time do you get off?"

"Excuse me?" Never mind that he looked like everyone's next door neighbor, was he hitting on her?

"Work. What time do you get off work?"

"I don't, actually, ever get off," Rachel said stiffly. "I live there."

"Let me put it another way." Gordon glanced at his watch. "I've got two more stops before I can call it a day. How about you join us for a drink at the Pig 'n Whistle? Gabe here gets off at six-thirty, so how about seven?"

Gabe was watching Rachel's face.

She glanced at him. "Oh…no. Sorry, I can't."

"Why not?" This time the question was Gabe's.

"I have to deliver this." Rachel held up the remaining package. She felt the blood rushing to her cheeks and drew back a step or two, hoping they wouldn't notice.

"That takes four hours?" Gabe asked.

"Hardly." Rachel backed a few more steps. "But I have to see to the garage. A lot of things happen during rush hours. Besides, I don't drink."

"So don't drink. Have a soda." Gabe glanced at Gordon. His look seemed to be telling the other man to keep his mouth shut. "Tell you what. Gordon and I will be at the Pig—you know where it is?"

She nodded.

"We'll be there at seven. If you change your mind, you're welcome to join us. Otherwise…." He shrugged.

A beat went by before she said, "Okay, thanks. Nice meeting you." She turned on her heel, and gave a small sigh when the door of the pharmacy closed behind her.

Chapter Twelve

Rachel moved down the hall hoping the laboratory wouldn't be as hard to find as the pharmacy. She stopped again at the gift shop.

Either the clerk was delighted to be of service, or a too-tight facelift gave her a perennial smile. "Second floor," she sang out. "Take the elevator in the east wing. You'll find the hall to that on the far side of the lobby."

Another long air-terminal-like hall. Good exercise, though. And a good cure for nervous energy. A thin stream of people passed Rachel going the other way. If she did this often there would be no need to go jogging. Finally reaching the elevators, she went on past and opened the door under the exit sign. The stairwell was a utilitarian beige and white high-gloss enamel. She took the steps to the next floor. The door there gave way to an empty hall that dead-ended at a window just beyond the elevators.

Nothing resembling a laboratory was in sight, just a potted plant that looked out of place and sad. For that matter, the whole area looked neglected.

Arriving at a T where the elevator hall intersected another, Rachel swung the box against her leg, annoyed. The least they could do was post some signs. Two big doors blocked each end of this short hall. The lab had to be one way or the other. She turned right.

The doors were dark wood, somewhat chipped despite wide brass plates. The plates up the sides bore fingerprints, the ones across the bottom, scuff marks. Rachel pushed against the right-hand door. It resisted, but when she put her shoulder against it, it gave way, letting her into a cheerless corridor with mud-colored wainscoting and mustard-yellow walls in need of paint.

The lab couldn't be there. It must be at the other end of the hall.

A foot-square piece of plastic lay face down on the floor beneath the door. She picked it up. Big red letters outlined in black spelled AREA CLOSED FOR REPAIRS.

She was turning to retrace her steps when from behind her came the sound of shattering glass, punctuated by a sharp yell followed by words she couldn't understand. Spanish? Then there were several voices talking over each other.

Puzzled, Rachel followed the sound and found herself in a long corridor with six or seven doorways on each side. Directly across from her a door stood open to a large room, and she could see the ends of three beds.

Halfway down the hall, a man and a woman, both in white, perhaps nurses or techs, emerged from one room and crossed the corridor to another. They didn't look toward where she stood in the shadows.

Guessing she had stumbled on some sort of overflow ward, Rachel made her way back to the double doors and pushed her way through. If this wing of the hospital was in use, why did the sign say it was closed?

But her main need was to find the elusive laboratory, deliver the brown envelope, and get back to the garage. She strode to the other end of the hall, swung open the doors, and found herself next to a nurses' station. Here the linoleum reflected the bright fluorescent lights.

One of the nurses looked up as she approached.

"Excuse me."

"Oh, dear," the nurse murmured. She was a big-boned woman with frizzy red hair. "How did you get here?"

"Sorry," Rachel said. "I'm looking for the clinical laboratory."

The nurse shook her head. "It's downstairs. The floor below the lobby."

"Below the lobby? I was told it was on the second floor."

"That is the second floor. The lobby is the third floor." Catching Rachel's look, she added, "I know it's confusing."

"Thanks." Rachel turned back toward the elevators.

"No, no. Not that way," the nurse called behind her.

"But that's the way I came."

"That's a restricted area. There's an elevator down there." She pointed to the opposite hall, where glossy white woodwork and floor tile ran between bright blue walls.

Rachel shrugged and moved obediently down the hall of the pointing finger. Were all hospitals this hard to navigate? Still preferring to walk, she found another staircase next to another bank of elevators. If this was one floor above the lobby, the one she wanted should be two floors below. She started down.

The banister was metal painted GI khaki and cold. Even Rachel's light footsteps echoed. Must be some sort of psychological test, she was thinking, to see if patients can get around the building without losing themselves or their tempers. As for her, she was failing on both counts.

Above her, the door she had come through opened and footsteps came down the steps toward her. She looked up, but could see only the underside of the stairs, not whoever was on them.

"The lab is another two flights down?" she called.

No answer. The footsteps had stopped too.

Chapter Thirteen

An unexpected chill rippled down Rachel's spine. *Don't be silly. Probably just someone who forgot something and stopped to think.* Just the same, she ran down the steps, not pausing until she reached the door that should lead to what they called the second floor.

Inside were dazzling blue walls and a sign that read CLINICAL LABORATORY. Clever place for the first sign, she thought.

A white-jacketed tech behind the counter relieved her of the box. "How do I get out of here?" she asked.

He tilted his head toward yet another hall. "Easiest way is through the emergency waiting room."

It was getting late. This time she took the elevator and ran all the way back to the garage, plagued by two equally unwanted thoughts.

Why are there people, presumably patients, in a wing of the hospital marked closed? Nothing to do with you and none of your business.

What on earth is so attractive about that pharmacist? Compared to Hank, he's a one-eyed dwarf with warts.

So when Rachel found herself in front of the Pig 'n Whistle at ten after seven, it was because she had persuaded herself that the first question about the odd hospital wing might be answered by the pharmacist. Or at least that's what she told herself.

The bar was dimly lit and filled as always at that time of night with the shadows and chatter of people who for whatever reason would rather be there than at home.

She pushed through the crowd looking for Gordon Cox, who she thought would be hard to miss. A perfectly groomed, dapper fellow should stick out among these loosened collars and awry ties. Besides, she didn't really want to look for the pharmacist. What was his name? Gabe.

A hand tapped her shoulder. She spun around to look into the beaming face of Gordon Cox. "Over here. We have a booth," he said, and a surprisingly firm hand grasped her elbow and led her past the people perched on bar stools.

"Thanks." She scooted onto a padded black plastic bench.

"No, that's my place." Gordon motioned her to the place beside Gabe, who was furiously chomping a toothpick. He removed it only to take a swallow of the beer from the mug in front of him.

"What do you want?" Gordon asked Rachel. "I'll get it from the bar. We're not likely to see a waitress."

"Club soda," Rachel said, "with lots of ice, some lemon and a straw."

"I told you," Gabe said to Gordon. "This is a woman who knows exactly what she wants."

If only. Rachel watched Gordon disappear into the mass of shoulders. She thought the only thing missing from the neat figure was that he should be wearing a derby. The guy sure was a sweetheart.

Gabe moved the toothpick to the other side of his mouth. "Glad you changed your mind. I'm new around here. Don't know many people. Gordon says I should get out more."

"Is he your keeper?" Rachel asked, and in spite of the fact that his leg was too close, she didn't move hers.

Gabe gave her an amused look. "He's a good guy. Better than most."

Gordon reappeared holding a glass of clear liquid with tiny bubbles breaking against the floating lemon slice.

Gabe removed the toothpick and wrapped it in his napkin.

Gordon set the glass in front of Rachel, slid onto the bench across the table, then reached up and fingered the knot of his tie before picking up his own drink, which looked like scotch on the rocks. "I won the bet." He gestured at Gabe. "This gentleman thought you wouldn't show."

"He was close," Rachel said. "I didn't think I would, either. But I have a question, and it occurred to me one of you might be able to answer it."

Gordon tilted his head toward her. Gabe was wiping up a wet spot on the table with his napkin. They both said the same thing. "Shoot."

The bubbles buzzed up her nose as Rachel took a sip of soda. She set the glass down and pressed her napkin to her lips. "It's about the hospital. The east wing on the," she stopped to count, "I think it's the fourth floor. The one with the sign that says *Area Closed for Repairs* or something like that."

Gabe shook his head. "No clue. I've only been here a couple months and I hardly ever get out of the pharmacy. When I do, I go outside, not upstairs."

Gordon was examining his swizzle stick as carefully as if it were the entrails of a sacrificed animal. He glanced at Gabe. "Maybe she means the celebrity wing."

Gabe frowned. "What celebrity wing?"

Gordon rubbed a finger along the end of his thumbnail. "You mean you don't know?"

"So what's there to know?" Gabe asked.

"Where are we?" Gordon asked. "Could this possibly be Los Angeles? More celebrities than anywhere in the world? Okay, maybe New York has more per square foot, but a load of famous people right here, no?"

Rachel's eyes moved from Gabe to Gordon. She took another sip of soda.

"So where do you think they go when they get sick?" Gordon asked. "Or maybe even when they just get a facelift?"

Gabe broke into a smile. "Son of a gun, is that right? You mean we might have Paris Hilton up there?"

"Of course they're quiet about it. No one wants to be mowed down by a mob of star-struck fans," Gordon said. "Or worse, a platoon of paparazzi scaling up the outside of the building. I've heard that some of the big-time pols, even a president or two, have been here at least once. They know Jefferson will protect their privacy."

Rachel put her glass down. "Okay, that probably explains it. Thanks."

Gordon glanced at her. "How did you find out about it?"

"I stumbled across it earlier today when I was lost, and couldn't help but wonder."

It wasn't until she had left the bar and was driving home that it occurred to her that the mud-colored wainscoting and mustard-colored walls didn't exactly connote celebrity. Incognito or not.

Chapter Fourteen

Later that night on the bench in front of the garage Rachel mentioned to Goldie the Jefferson ward that Gordon thought was reserved for celebrities.

"Makes sense," Goldie said. "If you're Julia Roberts and you're getting tucks here and there, you don't exactly want your fans running through the halls, barging into your room, askin' for autographs and seeing you without your face on. Ditto photographers."

"If it's a secret place for celebrities, why the ugly color scheme, the dingy look?"

Goldie shook her head, crossed her arms, peered over her eyeglasses and gave what Rachel called her school teacher look. "You ever think that may just be the point? The Army has a name for it. Dis-information or something."

"Okay. Maybe," Rachel agreed. "But come to think of it, the room I saw had three beds. Three celebrities in a room?"

"So maybe they have people who stay with them. Secretaries, beauticians, people like that."

A truck lumbered by, its tires clicking on the pavement, its exhaust fouling the night air.

"That's two weird things about my newest client. Jefferson Medical Center loses track of kids brought to the hospital, and has a mysterious ward that's in use, but has a sign—of the few signs in the whole damn place, by the way—that says it's closed."

Goldie thought about that. "Okay, there was a sign. But it wasn't hanging on the door. You said you found it on the floor. Maybe it was meant for somewhere else, fell off a cart or something."

Rachel scratched the end of her nose. "Maybe. But AREA CLOSED means area closed. And the area where the sign was looked like it should have been closed, only it wasn't."

"Maybe it's closed some of the time," Goldie said. "Maybe it's an overflow area."

"You're probably right. That's what I thought when I first saw it."

"I've heard of women having babies in the halls of some hospitals. Or maybe it's some sort of charity ward that they open when they need it."

Rachel thought about that. "I guess that's possible, too." She leaned forward. "What do you think happened to that boy I took to the emergency room?"

Goldie pursed her lips and blew out a stream of air that sounded like a punctured tire. "You got me, sweet pea. Maybe he did pass on before they got him admitted to the hospital, like that security guy said."

"If that was the case, they'd have to file some kind of report, wouldn't they? He wouldn't just disappear. After all, the kid was a victim of criminal neglect, at the very least. Surely the cops would be called in."

"Seems like. But that's probably the very sort of thing that falls between the cracks."

"I'd sure like to get a better look at that ward."

"You got some fool notion they stashed that kid there?" Goldie drew back. "Don't you be giving me that look. Nosiree! I am not going to help you nose around that hospital."

"Okay. I didn't ask, did I?"

"I already did that once for you, over there." Goldie nodded toward the building across the street. "My heart will never beat normal again."

She had sneaked Rachel into InterUrban Water Agency's headquarters with the cleaning crew so they could search the office of the CEO who had been killed—murdered, as Rachel had suspected. They were caught red-handed by the chairman of the board and Rachel had lied their way out of it.

"I said okay. I'll figure out...."

"I didn't say I wouldn't help." Goldie paused and flashed a grin. "It *was* kind of awesome."

"And I was right."

"Yeah, you were right. You sure were." Goldie grinned. "Hoooooooo-*ee*! That was exciting."

Rachel pulled a wry face. "Maybe you miss that stuff. I sure don't."

"I think that may be a wee bit of a fib."

"No way," Rachel said. "I hated every minute."

Goldie was silent for a moment. "You know what? If there are celebrities in that wing, or even if there aren't, you can be damn sure they aren't cleaning those rooms themselves."

"And?"

"I might see if I can find out who is cleaning over there and ask what's up."

"Would you?"

"Uh-huh. I just might do that very thing."

One by one, the cleaning crew was leaving the office building across the street and streaming toward them. They were all young. Six of the nine had chubby round faces and rounder cheeks. Rachel had trouble telling the boys from the girls because all had hair about the same length and their nearly identical overalls hid any physical dissimilarities. Most were Down's Syndrome people. All were earning a living. Most lived at a sort of halfway house named, for some peculiar reason, Downers Grove. Maybe the naming was deliberate. My kids, as Goldie had explained, don't have much use for political correctness and prettified terms.

"Get in the van," Goldie called to them. "I'll be right there."

"Right-o, Golda," a voice shouted, and several giggled as they all turned and headed for the big van parked in a short half-circle driveway in front of the office building.

"I love those kids," Rachel said. "Don't they ever get tired?"

"Never tired, never crabby," Goldie said. "Well, hardly ever."

"We should all be so lucky."

Goldie got up to follow the cleaning crew. "Why don't you give Rampart a call? See if they know anything about those Mexican kids you're so curious about."

"You know why."

"Well, Rampart has been butt deep in its own scandal. They play high-and-mighty with you, I believe I would gently remind them that you've been clean a lot longer than they have."

"I'll do that. I'm sure they'd enjoy hearing it. Especially from me."

"'Bout time you get over that, girl." Goldie called over her shoulder as she crossed to where the kids stood in a cluster under the street light.

It wasn't that Rachel had a grudge against cops. She just figured they would discount most of anything she had to say. But that was her own fault. Six or so years ago, up north around San Francisco, she had been high on booze and a snootful of meth to boot. She'd run a car off the freeway. It was pure luck the father and son in the car weren't hurt.

She got out of doing jail time thanks to a clever attorney. And she'd never taken another swig, snort, or drag of anything. But she was sure any cops she talked to would somehow be able to look up her record and then would chalk up anything she had to say as chatter from a junky.

◇◇◇

Four days later, Rachel was still trying to rid her head of the image of the kids on the squalid floor of that van. No matter how many times she told herself it had nothing to do with her, it somehow did. What kind of a world was it if everyone just looked the other way? Just ignored what happened to others? Especially kids that young.

As soon as the morning rush hour was over, she worked up her nerve, picked up the phone and called the infamous Rampart police station. A woman answered, put her on hold, then cut her off. Rachel called back. On hold again she pictured some of the cops she'd seen. They looked like Marines on steroids with necks as thick as thighs and so much muscle they were bowlegged. On the other hand, there was a police captain who occasionally showed up at her AA group, and he looked, acted and sounded like a university professor. Go figure.

After being transferred for the third time, she was muttering to herself about the possibility that if you called a police station and said it wasn't an emergency, they transferred you to some job that had been outsourced to India and your call was handled like corporate customer service. She drummed her fingers trying not to give way to annoyance.

Finally, a raspy voice asked if its owner could help.

For the third time, Rachel described finding two young boys and taking them to the emergency room at Jefferson Hospital. "It was too late for one of them," she said, amazed at the dispassionate sound of her voice. Maybe if you say something often enough you don't care anymore.

"And the other?"

"That's what I'm trying to find out. They said he was being admitted, but he's not at the hospital. I don't know what happened to him. Would they have to file some kind of report if a kid was brought in suffering from what was obviously criminal negligence if not worse?"

"Yes and no."

"What does that mean?"

"The one who was dead, that would be the coroner's office. You'll have to call there."

"And the one who was alive?"

"Well, maybe he died, or maybe his parents came and got him before the hospital admitted him."

"Would there be any kind of report made, in either case?"

"I can look. The date?"

She told him.

"Hold please."

A few minutes later, he was back on the line. "Sorry. Nothing like that on that date." And without another word, she was listening to a dial tone.

Chapter Fifteen

Rachel reached for the phone book and thumbed through the pages. How would the coroner's office be listed? Under City of Los Angeles? County? Looking up, she saw Irene peering into the garage, one hand on her supermarket cart, which seemed to have gained a bright blue and yellow striped blanket. Beneath the blanket, something protruded that might be the tail of an animal.

"Hallo, dear girl."

"I like your new blanket," Rachel said as the woman pushed the cart into the garage. She never asked where Irene acquired things.

"Getting on toward winter. Got to be prepared. Wait till you see this." Irene reached into the cart and drew a fur coat from under the blanket. Pulling it over her plump shoulders, she twirled. The coat reached nearly to the ground.

"That is spectacular," Rachel said.

"There's a small tear in the back." Irene slowly spun about holding the right side of the coat out like a model. "Otherwise it's perfect. My old mother had one of these. I think it's raccoon. Found it out behind the Rainbow Theater on Beverly. They are closing, you know. Tossed out a lot of costumes. I had me a very good day, I did."

"That's wonderful."

"You haven't had use for me lately."

Rachel closed the phone book. "I'm sorry. It wasn't that I didn't want your help. I had a client move out of town and I was worried about money. About keeping this place afloat."

"Ah, that I understand. I do indeed. But your credit is good with me, luv. Anytime. Remember that."

"Well, thank you. But I think I'm okay for now. I got another client pretty quickly."

"Good to hear it. Yes indeed. That's very good." Irene took off the coat, folded it and put it back under the blanket in the basket. "Did you ever find that poor boy you were looking for?"

"No. He seems to have disappeared."

"Doesn't surprise me. Doesn't surprise me at all."

"You said that before. I don't understand what you mean."

"Oh, I hear things, I do."

"Like what?"

"Things a girl like you would rather not know," Irene said.

Rachel raised her eyebrows. "Try me."

"Life on the street is not always good, you know," Irene said. "Every now and then someone disappears, never to be heard from again."

"Well, that's not at a hospital."

"Not always, dear girl."

"People sometimes disappear at hospitals?"

"They might," Irene answered cryptically.

"You ever hear anything about that particular hospital? Jefferson?"

"Well, I could say yes, or I could say no. Like what?"

"Like do they have a lot of celebrity patients?"

"I expect they do, dear girl. Celebrities get sick just like you and me, you know. Yes, I've heard of limousines pulling up there. Saw one or two myself. Neil Diamond, it was once. And another time Sean Penn. They always dress like plumbers, movie stars do."

"Plumbers?"

"Yes, indeed. All in gray. Gray shirt, gray pants, gray jacket. Black shoes, though."

The phone rang. Rachel punched the talk button and said, "Chavez Garage" into the mouth piece.

Irene turned to push her cart back to the sidewalk. "You let me know if you need me, you hear? I gave you my cell number, didn't I?"

Rachel shook her head.

Irene reached into a pocket, drew out a business card and handed it to Rachel.

Irene. Fortunes And More.

Rachel wondered what the "more" was and decided it might be wiser not to know.

"Your credit is plenty good with me," Irene said. "You remember that."

"I will." Rachel waved as the woman went back to her supermarket basket, then said into the phone, "Sorry. Can I help you?"

"Rachel, honey?" It was Marty.

"Hi, Pop. How's it going?" Had he already lost all his winnings and needed some money? It wouldn't be the first time.

"Okay. Real well, in fact. I want to bring you something. When's a good time?"

"Bring me what?"

"A surprise."

"Pop, I don't like surprises." Rachel peered through the glass of the cubicle at what looked like the shadow of someone leaning against the garage wall a few yards away.

"Well, you'll like this one. When's a good time?"

She sighed. She knew the routine. When her dad won big, he liked to shower friends and family with gifts and cash. Eventually he would lose big and want back whatever cash was left, along with any pawnable gifts. She sometimes wondered if he deliberately gave the kinds of gifts that pawnshops liked.

"I suppose it'll have to be something like noon," she said. The previous day's poker games tended to wind up by noon and there was a lull in the afternoon, at least at the club where Marty played.

"Noon is good. Tomorrow? We can go for lunch."

Rachel was idly watching the shadow on the wall. It probably was not a person at all. "If it doesn't matter to you," she said into the phone, "I'd rather stick around here. A lot of people take their cars at noon and you never know when somebody will need something."

"Sure. Okay. I'll bring lunch. How about Chinese?"

"Okay. But look, Pop, I'd love to see you tomorrow. I don't want to seem ungrateful, but I really don't need anything." The shadow moved, lengthened, grew shoulders. Rachel glanced at her watch. Mid afternoon. Still, the local lowlife didn't keep special hours. There were always enough around to cause problems.

She pulled the three-year-old book of yellow pages from a shelf and opened it. Inside, her old thirty-eight rested where the center pages had been carved out to hold it. Marty had given it to her years ago for her birthday.

"Come on, Rachel," Marty was saying. "I'll give my little girl a present if I want to. Noon tomorrow. Your place. Lunch."

She gave up. "Okay." Then, "I gotta go." She pressed the off button.

With the gun pointed at the floor, Rachel stepped out of the booth. Not for the first time she was glad that back on the farm, Marty had taught her how to shoot.

She stepped quickly and quietly toward the shadow.

Chapter Sixteen

"What are you doing here?" The words exploded from her in relief.

"Waiting for you to stop gabbing long enough to say hello." Hank swept her into his hug.

"Why didn't you call?" she sputtered.

He took the wrist of the hand that held the thirty-eight. "What the hell is that?"

"I saw your shadow. How was I supposed to know it was you? Why didn't you call?" she asked again.

"I'm only here for a couple hours. Keith was coming down in the Water and Power plane and at the last minute, offered me a ride…. Put that thing away. It reminds me of how we met."

At that, she had to laugh. They had met in the garage when, during a power outage, they bumped into each other in the dark and Rachel, thinking him a thief or mugger, had floored him with her knee.

"Well, do tell. It's the Water Man." Irene waddled toward them, her smile almost as broad as she was. "How have you been, sir?" She offered him her hand. Somewhere she had come into possession of a beanie, which somehow gave her a look of youthful surprise.

"Couldn't be better." He brought the woman's hand to his lips in an Antonio Banderas imitation that made Irene fairly squeal with delight. "Now, can you take care of the shop while

I whisk my dearly beloved away for a soda or snack or whatever she wants?"

"Of course dear boy. I was just a few minutes ago complaining that she doesn't make use of me enough." She turned to Rachel. "All work and no play, dear girl. You don't want to become dull."

Rachel nodded, wondering if she was part of this *tête-à-tête* or just the audience. Hank could at least have asked her instead of Irene. *Don't be so irritable. He flew all the way down here just to see you.*

How do I know it was just to see me?

"I do think I should have your spare set of keys. You know. In case you want to take off the whole night," Irene said with her most ingenuous deadpan.

◇◇◇

The Pig 'n Whistle was almost deserted. The bartender, whose name tag read *Randall,* wordlessly laid out napkins and cardboard coasters imprinted with a chubby pink pig in a Scottish kilt, and gave them a raised eyebrow.

Hank ordered a Guinness, Rachel asked for her usual club soda with lemon. She felt oddly safer these days at the Pig since Randall had come to work there. He was a member of her AA group.

"Haven't seen you lately," he said as he delivered the soda.

Rachel hung her head, knowing he meant at meetings. "I've been sorta busy."

A frosted mug and a dark brown bottle arrived in front of Hank. He tilted the bottle and poured into the glass but got mostly foam.

"What does he mean he hasn't seen you lately?" he asked Rachel.

Rachel lifted one shoulder. One does not "out" a fellow AA member. She took a sip of the fizzy soda water.

"I hear you were here a couple days ago," Hank said. He was still having trouble getting any beer into the glass without the foam overflowing.

"Obviously, you don't drink a lot of beer," Rachel said.

"Not a lot," Hank agreed. "Even less if I don't count the ones I drink from the can or the bottle. Must be a trick to using a glass."

"You have to tilt it and pour down the side."

Hank frowned at her.

"Trust me. Among all the odd jobs I've done, I was once a bartender." She took the glass, squeezed a little of the lemon from her own drink into the mug, and the foam wilted. Tilting the glass, she poured in half the bottle of beer.

"Now it'll taste like Mexican beer," Hank said.

"Maybe. So?"

"It's Irish beer."

She gave him a wide-eyed look. "Really?"

"*Were* you in here a few days ago?"

Rachel felt her face flush. About what? A silly glass of club soda with Gabe? She looked away from Hank toward the clock. "What if I was?"

"I'm just asking."

"I guess I'm asking why you're asking. Like who told you, and what's it to you if I was?"

"Oh-oh. Sounds like a storm warning."

Rachel sighed. "I'm sorry. But I am curious."

"Curtis Jacoby in Water Quality mentioned he saw you in here with a couple of guys he'd never seen before."

"I don't even know Curtis Jacoby."

"He thinks he knows you. I guess he's seen us together. He parks at the garage. Whatever. He and I don't always agree on things, so he probably could hardly wait to tell me."

"Is that why you suddenly came back? Without calling first? You trying to catch me in an assignation or something?"

"Assignation?"

"With my pants down."

"Good God, Rachel."

"You having people watch me?"

"Of course not. I told you—"

"You think I'm running around on you?"

"Of course not."

"Well, I'm not." Her voice skidded to a halt as she thought about that, then plowed on. "If I ever do I'll tell you. Me. I'll tell you. Not somebody else. Count on it."

"Rachel, I'm not trying to check up on you."

"Why does it smell like that, then?"

"I don't know. I'm sorry if it does."

They both fell silent.

Rachel rubbed her palm across her forehead, mussing her hair. "Why is this happening? I don't want it to be like this."

Hank looked like he was trying to rein in words that had gotten away. "Actually, you're right. I have no right to make these noises."

"No, you don't."

"Maybe I'm just…I don't know, scuffing up sand. So you don't look at me too closely."

"What does that mean?"

"Okay. Maybe I'm the one who should 'fess up."

"What does that mean?" she said again.

"I took a woman out for dinner in Sacramento."

"Oh?" Rachel's face went expressionless. She smoothed her mussed hair and looked at him, weighing his words.

"Just an engineer at the State Water Project. I guess I was feeling sorry for myself."

She gave a slow nod. "Maybe you should go on doing that."

"What?"

"Feeling sorry for yourself."

"Are you serious?"

"Oh, Hank."

Without tilting the mug, he poured in the remaining beer. Undeterred by the rising foam, he drank down the contents, then plunked the glass on the counter and wiped away the bubbles that coated his upper lip. "You go out with some guys here, and somehow, it's my fault."

"Not really." She was wondering how they got from square one-A to square two-hundred-Z.

"Then what?"

"I don't know. I guess I'm just having a bad-hair day. I seem to be having a whole string of them."

Hank looked at his watch. "I gotta be back at Burbank in an hour."

Rachel turned and put a hand on his sleeve. "Hank, I didn't."

"Didn't what?"

"Didn't date anyone else."

"Okay."

"But you're telling me you did?"

"Rachel, it was dinner. Just dinner."

She turned her back on him and motioned to Randall to bring her another club soda. "Okay. You'd better go. I'll walk back."

Chapter Seventeen

Rachel didn't sleep well that night. She dreamed of carrying a small package that was light as a slip of paper in the beginning. But she was on a road than seemed to grow longer with every step. The little package remained the same size, but grew heavier and heavier until she was exhausted.

She woke drenched in perspiration, with teeth so tightly clenched her jaw ached. She got up, went to the kitchen, poured a cup of milk and heated it in the microwave. After that and a chocolate chip cookie, she took a *National Geographic* magazine from the floor-to-ceiling bookcase that lined one wall of the living room and went back to bed. Clancy climbed in next to her and purred so loudly she couldn't concentrate on an article about ancient Peru.

Finally she finally fell asleep, but woke feeling as though she'd spent the night running, whether away from something or trying to catch something, she wasn't sure.

Coffee helped, but not enough. Wishing she could go back to bed, she instead went down to open the garage. There were days when having an ordinary job would be nice. Then one could call in sick.

When the morning rush had filled the garage, and slamming car doors and rapid footsteps had given way to silence, Rachel sat, still tired and rooted to the stool in the cubicle, looking out at the street but not noticing what was there. The phone toodled. She pressed talk. "Chavez Garage. Can I help you?"

"Probably not. But you can bet your sweet biffy you're going to find this interesting." Goldie.

Rachel sat up straighter. "What did you find out?"

"I kept asking around until I got the name of Jarvis Barry. He heads up the sanitary engineers—which is to say the mop-and-flop people—at that medical center. Turns out Mr. Barry is the brother-in-law of one of my kids. Anyway, I find out his hours and go talk to him about his maybe taking on one of my crew who's about ready to graduate to bigger and better things than we can offer."

"You're so good to those kids."

"Damn straight about that," Goldie agreed. "So while I'm talking to him, I say I've heard about a closed-off ward on some floor in the east wing and that maybe the hospital plans to open it, so I thought he might be needing some extra help."

Rachel grinned. "What a clever liar you are."

"I've had some good teachers. Present company included."

"So what did he say?"

"He looks at me like I've lost my mind and says, 'Where'd you get that idea? There's no empty ward of any wing on any floor of this hospital. The whole place is just about full up all the time.' And I say, 'I don't remember, but I thought someone mentioned a wing that they sometimes used for celebrities, or overflow, or some such thing.'

"He says, 'We do get celebrities sometimes, but they get suites on the top floor of the main building.' He said *suites,* can you believe it? In a hospital. Must be nice. Anyway, I say, 'Well, I guess I got the wrong information. I heard something about the fourth floor. East wing, I think it was.'

"'Oh that,' he says. 'Twelve rooms, mostly triples, and it's full all the time. Sometimes they even bring in extra beds, have a couple in the hall. But it sure isn't movie stars or anything close. Those people are packed tight.' That's what he said, 'packed tight.'"

Rachel rubbed her chin and stared thoughtfully at her reflection in the cubicle glass. "Why would it have a closed sign then?"

"We've already been over that. If I had an answer I'd spit it out. But I couldn't really ask this Jarvis a lot more without letting on I knew more than I was saying."

"I guess."

"Anyway, I killed two birds. He is looking for more cleaning crew. That staff of his is huge. He said he's always looking. Maybe I'll be able to place more of my kids there as they come along. Anyway, he gave me an application form for Clarence to fill out."

"That ward is full but not with celebrities. That's what he said?"

"Umm-hmm. I see you were listening for once. This guy should know if that area is in use."

"I'd sure like to get a firsthand look at that ward."

"Well, don't look at me."

"I'm not even looking at the phone."

"You know what else that guy told me? The food at that hospital is good. You ever hear of good hospital food?"

"Sounds like a contradiction in terms."

"He said there were a couple of black guys there—brothers, mind you!—who make the best greens in the whole United States. And a couple of Mexican women who make better red enchiladas than you can get anywhere in LA. We got to go have lunch in that cafeteria sometime."

"Go out for lunch to eat hospital food?" Rachel's voice rolled out without expression.

"My mama makes real good greens, but she don't do it very often."

"Greens."

"Lord, woman. You have eaten greens haven't you?"

"I guess."

"You sound funny. You okay?"

"I had another fight with Hank."

"I thought he was up north."

"He was. He caught a ride down for the afternoon yesterday in somebody's company plane."

"So why did you fight?"

"He accused me of messing around. Some guy he knows saw me at the Pig with the pharmacist from the hospital and that drug company rep."

"Well, guys are funny that way about their women. That shouldn't be hard to patch over."

"It got harder when he told me he'd been seeing some woman up there."

"Yiiii!" Goldie drew out the exclamation, then paused. "I'll check the bench after I get the crew started tonight. If you're there, we could talk if you want."

"I didn't sleep much last night. I don't know if I can stay awake."

"If you aren't there, we won't talk." Rachel could almost see her friend's plain no-nonsense face as she rang off.

She twisted the engagement ring on her finger.

Chapter Eighteen

It was a little after noon when a shiny silver Toyota 4Runner drove up the ramp to the booth. Not sure she'd seen the vehicle before, Rachel leaned out the cubicle doorway and waited until the SUV window began sliding down. "Sorry," she called. "This isn't public parking."

"I know that." The face that appeared in the open window was Marty's. He held out a plastic bag with a semi-circle of red letters that spelled *Chow's Chinese Kitchen*. "Where's an empty space?"

She took the bag. "Where'd you get that car?"

"Never mind that right now, Rache. Find me a slot."

"Third one on your left, down there." She pointed. Now what?

The sweet-and-sour aroma from the bag made her suddenly hungry. Sweeping aside the papers on her desk, she dug out a package of paper plates from a file drawer.

"How's my girl?" Marty set down the box he was carrying and spun her about for a hug.

"Have you become a car thief?" She laughed into his collar, feeling better for some reason she didn't quite understand.

"The apartment or the bench?" Marty asked.

"I haven't had my full dose of smog yet today." Rachel picked up the bag of take-out cartons.

Carrying the box, he followed her out onto the sidewalk. "Gorgeous day," he said as they settled on the bench in front of the garage. "Not much smog at all."

Hoping it wasn't the present he'd mentioned, but knowing it probably was, Rachel nodded at the package that Marty set down on the sidewalk in front of him. "Better move that under the bench, or someone will steal it."

"In broad daylight?" But he did as she suggested.

Rachel balanced a plate on her lap. "I saw a rollerblader make off with a woman's purse while she was sitting on this same bench. The jerk was out of sight before it even registered on her what had happened."

Marty watched her dish out fried rice and General Tso's chicken. "Your hair," he said.

"What about it?"

"I still think it makes you look too...."

"Chicano?" She handed him a plate.

"Chicana," he corrected her.

"Well, it's not my fault you didn't teach me proper Spanish. I only know a couple words I've picked up on the streets." She moved her eyes to his. "Why shouldn't I look Chicana?"

Marty concentrated on his food. "You don't think it makes people...I don't know...look at you differently? Treat you differently?"

"My last name is Chavez. I have dark hair and brown eyes. Maybe they should think I'm Swedish?" She raised her face to the sky. The day was warm and bright. "I don't get enough sun." She held out and arm and pulled up a sleeve. "Look at this bar-room pallor."

The lines over Marty's eyes deepened. "Bar room?"

"Oh, Pop. It's an expression. I'm not drinking. I'm not using. I'm so pure I'm boring." She changed the subject. "The new 4Runner," she said, not wanting to know but asking anyway. "Nice. It's yours?"

"First off, it's not new. It's three years old, low mileage, thirty-five thousand."

"Still, those babies aren't cheap."

"I told you what I won."

"That wasn't your last poker game, Pop." She didn't say that pawnbrokers don't do cars and a quick sale to a used lot would bring only about half what he probably paid.

Marty grinned, ignoring her implication. "I bought it for you."

"You what?"

"That old Civic of yours has seen better days. You need a good car. I thought I'd trade you. I don't drive all that much. You take the new one, I'll take the old."

"Pop, I can't do that."

"Why not?"

"The last time you drove a car of mine you were run off the freeway by someone who was probably trying to kill me."

"No one is trying to kill you now." Marty paused, examined her face. "Is there?"

"Nope. Nothing is going on in my life except this garage." Rachel finished the last of the rice, folded her plate and put it in the bag with the empty cartons.

"Any luck landing a new company to replace the one you lost?"

"Didn't I tell you? Turned out, I was hardly out a week's rent. Jefferson Medical Center."

"That's wonderful, Rache."

"So one of these days, I can buy another car myself."

Marty put his plate in the bag. "Is that the hospital where those two kids disappeared?"

"One was dead. It's possible the other boy died in the emergency room—before he could be admitted to the hospital. But I guess you could say they both disappeared because I can't find out what happened to either one, dead or alive." She turned to look at her father. "I think it has something to do with the fact they were Mexican."

"Why?"

"Don't you think that might be part of the reason they came to be locked in that van in my garage?"

Marty glanced at her, then away. "I don't know. Maybe."

"I had lunch with one of the doctors at Jefferson who's now parking with me. She worked for a while in Mexico. Chiapas. She says things were pretty awful there."

"Chiapas is just about the poorest place in the country. Maybe in the world. Always has been."

"Was all your family wealthy?"

"You'd probably call them filthy rich. We had servants."

"You never go back. You never see your relatives?"

Marty shrugged. "Tia Inez was good family. The best."

"Your mother's sister? Where is she now?"

"She died. Breast cancer. She lived just long enough to see me through college."

"Did Mom ever meet her? Did she know…?"

"No. Inez was gone by then." His eyes flicked back to Rachel's face. "You're all the family I need."

She took his hand and squeezed it, thinking how hard it must have been on a young boy to be thrust into a strange country, a strange culture. He would have been about the age of the kids she had found in the van. Maybe the family was wealthy, but her grandfather must have been an asshole.

"Why didn't your mother leave him? Take you and your brother and sisters and come live with Tia Inez?"

Marty shook his head. "That sort of thing wasn't done in my family. It simply wasn't done."

Rachel gazed into the middle distance and tried to imagine being rich and having to tolerate abuse.

Marty took the opportunity to change the subject. "So when are you getting married?"

She tilted her head and made a face he couldn't see. "I don't know. We'll set a date one of these days."

"You want a big wedding?"

"Good God, no," she sputtered. "You have any idea what a big wedding costs these days? You didn't win that much. We'll go to a chapel in Burbank or something. I can't afford a big do, let alone a dress I would only wear once."

Marty reached under the bench and brought out the package. "That's why I brought this along."

She frowned. "A wedding present? We don't even know when—"

"No-no." Marty placed the package in her lap. "Open it."

Rachel gave him a perplexed look. Not wanting to deal with this, but seeing no way out, she undid the plain brown wrapping. The large box inside was a yellowish white. She lifted the lid and her eyebrows drew together.

"It's white. Satin or something. I can't open it here on the street. Tell me you didn't buy me a wedding dress, Pop."

"I didn't."

"Then why does it look like one?"

"It was your mother's."

Chapter Nineteen

When her clients began collecting their cars for the evening rush hour Rachel was still trying to sort out her feelings about the wedding dress. She had no urge to take it out of the box to try on or even just to admire. She could see the fabric was beautiful. Even after all these years, it fairly glowed.

At first she had put the box on top of the filing cabinet. When she had trouble concentrating on the figures she was posting in the ledger, she had taken the box up to the apartment and slid it under her bed.

Why was everyone who mattered in her life determined to see her married? She glanced down at the engagement ring, wiggled it, then pulled it off. It dropped to the floor and bounced out of the cubicle. She chased it to the front wheel of a parked car and put her foot out to stop its roll.

Did she want to end the engagement? No. Maybe she was just tired.

But Hank is messing around. He even admitted it.

He said he had dinner with someone. Dinner. Period. Big Deal. Right.

She put the ring back on, then took it off again, put it in an envelope, and the envelope inside the top file drawer.

After several interruptions, Rachel was still sitting over the ledger, deep in thoughts that had nothing to do with accounting, when someone knocked on the cubicle window.

She jumped, startled.

"Whoa," came the voice on the other side of the glass. "Sorry. I didn't mean to scare you."

She peered, puzzled, at the speaker. The light in the garage was always dim. He moved a little closer, and the light from the cubicle lit his face.

"Just wanted to say hi," Gabe said. "I'm parking over here now. Most of the pharm staff is. I guess they figure we just sit around all day and need more exercise. Six blocks' walk each way is supposed to extend my life. Saw you when I came in this morning, but you were busy."

"Nice to see you," Rachel said.

He gestured at the ledger. "Are you finished? For the day, I mean."

"As much as I'm going to be, I guess."

"Could I interest you in dinner?"

Rachel looked at her watch to buy some time while her mind raced. *Well, why not?*

Too many reasons to list.

"You'd have to pick the restaurant, I don't eat out much and don't know LA very well."

Hank is probably having dinner with that woman in Sacramento right now.

"Okay," Rachel said. "Thanks. I'd like that."

A smile broadened itself across his face. "Where to?"

"Someplace casual. And close. I have to be back to lock up. Have you been to The Pantry?"

"Not yet."

"It's been here forever. Very plain and straightforward. No frills, no nonsense." She stopped. A smile played about her lips. "Like me."

"Are you?"

"Sort of. Get your car."

"You're on." He headed up the ramp.

A white Integra pulled up next to the booth. He lowered the window and clicked the door lock. "Hey lady, want a ride?"

Suddenly flustered, Rachel got in and turned her face to the passenger window so it couldn't be read, though she wasn't sure what might be seen there. "The Pantry's on Figueroa. Downtown. It's not far, but the one-way streets are a pain. And with all the construction you can't be sure a street that was open yesterday will be open today. I'll try to navigate."

After a few double-back turns, she pointed to a small parking lot that was emptying of day traffic. The night life hadn't picked up yet.

The Pantry, however, had a waiting line. "Popular place," Gabe said as he and Rachel joined the queue.

"Plain, good, cheap food, and lots of it," Rachel said. "That'll do it every time. An ex-mayor owns the place now. I hear politicians do power breakfasts here."

"I guess 1940s retro is in these days," Gabe said when they were finally seated at a scarred Formica table next to old photos of a younger Los Angeles.

"What is that waiter carrying?" Gabe asked.

"A billy club."

"A what?"

"They're open all night and I guess the clientele isn't always the tuxedo crowd. I hear the waiters don't hesitate to conk a noisy diner, but that might be apocryphal. I once saw them chase a guy who tried to leave without paying. Awesome."

"Cheap enough," Gabe said, looking at the menu. "You sure the food is edible?"

"Very. The rib eye is good. The other steaks are a little tough. The pork chops are good."

A waiter stopped at their table and fidgeted until they both ordered rib eyes.

Rachel tried to ignore the tingle that went up her back when Gabe's dark caramel eyes held on hers. *Pheromones,* she thought. *I hate them.* "So how's your friend?" she asked. "Gordon something. The drug salesman."

"He doesn't like to be called a salesman."

"Why not?"

"He sees himself as a philanthropist. And in a way, he sort of is."

"How so?"

"Oh, if some guy—somebody one of the docs knows or one of us in the pharmacy hears about—needs an expensive med and doesn't have prescription insurance, Gordon gets it for him free. If it isn't his company's line, he trades another rep for it."

"That's nice of him. But it doesn't exactly make him a philanthropist. I mean it doesn't cost him anything but time."

"These days, most people would rather give money than time."

Rachel thought about that. "You're probably right. Okay, he's a nice guy."

"One of the best." Gabe glanced around the room at the decor. "In Albuquerque, we're into the Route 66 craze, but it's more '50s. Booths with red plastic benches."

"That where you're from? Albuquerque?"

He nodded. "I've got a little girl there. And an ex-wife. I'm thinking of going back. I sort of promised to stay a year when I signed on at Jefferson and I'd hate to renege, but I'm not crazy about LA."

"Recent divorce?" Rachel had to raise her voice. The restaurant was filled with chatter.

"Almost a year."

"You probably won't like anywhere for a while."

"You've been there?"

"Not personally. Divorce, I mean. Albuquerque, either, for that matter. I've heard people talk about marriages splitting up." A lot of people she knew in AA were divorced. "Why don't you like LA?"

He made a wry smile. "Don't get me started."

"What's Albuquerque like?"

He chuckled. "Used to be a wide spot in the road. Fifteen, twenty years ago, some of the streets weren't even paved. Now it's LA without an ocean. Backed-up traffic, smog, housing developments multiplying like white mice. It's growing so fast we'll probably run out of water and be rationed to three cups per person, per day."

"So why would you go back?"

Gabe laid his knife and fork across his plate. "You don't have any kids?"

Rachel shook her head.

"It makes everything different."

"I'm sure it would." She scooped up the last bite of steak, chewed, swallowed, then looked across the table at him. "Question."

"Shoot."

"A week or so ago I found a couple of kids in a van someone left in my garage. Not a regular customer. Someone who just got in and parked." Trying not to notice Gabe's eyes riveted on hers, she took sip of water.

He tilted his head toward her. "And?"

"Mexican kids, I think. Young. Nine, ten, something like that. Unconscious. I put them in my car and raced them to the hospital. Jefferson."

Gabe frowned, took a cellophane-wrapped toothpick from his pocket and laid it on the edge of his plate.

"It was too late for one of them," Rachel went on. "That's what they told me at the emergency room. The other one, they said was just dehydrated. They said they were going to admit him."

"And?" Gabe prompted again.

"I went back to see how he was doing."

"Nice of you."

"No. As a matter of fact, it wasn't. At least the hospital didn't think so. They kind of pitched me out the door."

He gave her a hard look. "You're joking."

She shook her head. "Well, I probably got a little intense when they insisted no child like that was admitted at that time on that day."

Gabe's eyes softened. He made a small smile and ducked his head.

She wondered if that was to prevent her from seeing something in his face.

"Somehow, that isn't hard to imagine," he said when he looked up.

"So, you're an insider at the hospital. You have any idea what might have happened?"

"Dehydration can be really serious. You probably know that."

"So you're saying maybe he died."

"It's possible."

"Other people have suggested that. But wouldn't there be some kind of record?"

Gabe shrugged. "I'm not familiar with Jefferson's procedure for admissions from Emergency. On the other hand, dehydration can be very mild. Maybe a little IV drip did the trick, and he just walked away."

"Would they let a child that age just walk away alone?"

"I suppose that would depend on his story. Then again, he might have just got up and sneaked out or left AMA."

"AMA?"

"Against medical advice. Without a by-your-leave. A hospital isn't a prison."

"I don't think he was old enough to know that. But even if he did, why no record?"

"I'm not a good one to ask. No idea." Gabe peeled off the cellophane and placed the toothpick in the corner of his mouth. Then he removed it and asked, as one does about smoking, "Bother you?"

Rachel shook her head. "Of course not."

He replaced the wooden pick at the edge of his smile.

She was thinking she was surely the only human in the world who thought that was sexy.

"Great place," Gabe said, looking around again. "I don't suppose they do Cointreau or anything."

"Unlikely."

"You want to adjourn to one of the hotels?" He caught her startled look and, flustered, added, "For an after-dinner drink."

"Not tonight, but thanks."

They paid, crossed the street to Gabe's car and drove back to the garage. He pulled into an empty parking space near the entrance.

"Look, I'm not blind," he said, turning to her. "I saw the engagement ring before. Now I don't see it. I don't know what that means."

Avoiding his eyes, Rachel saw the pale place on her finger where the ring had been. "Truth is, I don't know what it means, either."

"So that's why you picked the most unromantic restaurant in California."

"It was close and quick."

"Will I be rude if I ask who's the guy?"

"Yes," Rachel said, then added, "okay, he's an engineer. He's on assignment in Sacramento right now."

"A quarrel?"

"You could call it that."

Gabe got out of the car, and she was wondering if he was just leaving her there without a goodbye when he appeared at her door and opened it. She slid out of the passenger seat. They were very near the same height.

He didn't step closer, but put both palms against her cheeks and gave her a very quick, small peck on the cheek.

Chapter Twenty

"Gabe isn't as good looking as Hank," Rachel told Goldie over a lunch of greens and macaroni and cheese in Jefferson Medical Center's main cafeteria. "I don't know what it is that attracts me to this guy. Just chemistry, maybe."

"Maybe it's something plain and simple. Like you're just mad at Hank."

"You think he took that woman out to dinner because I didn't leap at the chance to set a date to get married?"

"People have dinner all the time. Doesn't mean they go jumpin' between the sheets with whoever is sitting across the table."

Rachel took a forkful of the greens. "This stuff is fantastic. What is it?"

"Turnip greens, mustard greens, collards, whatever's in season; a little bacon or ham, a little vinegar and the rest is a secret."

"A secret? Why?"

"Because whites can't make it. They shouldn't even try. It takes a black hand to stir the pot."

"Goldie!"

"All right. Truth to tell, I don't know. I don't cook."

"You should learn."

"I will one of these days. Haven't had time yet."

The noise in the cafeteria was growing louder as it filled with people, most in whites, a few in street clothes, some in O-R greens. "This place is big as a gymnasium," Rachel said. "And Jefferson has another restaurant as well?"

"That's what I hear."

"Looks like this is where most of the staff eat."

"Course they do. They know where the good greens are."

Rachel devoted her attention to her meal for a moment, then looked across the table at Goldie. "My dad brought me something yesterday."

Goldie peered at her expectantly. "Yes?"

"My mother's wedding dress."

Goldie rolled her eyes. "Men have the worst timing of any animal on the planet. They must learn it in boys' gym class."

"Do all men think women can hardly wait to get married?"

"Yep," Goldie said emphatically. "I was close to getting married once. Kenneth. A little boring, but nice. He managed a Chinese restaurant over in Toluca Lake."

"Was he Chinese?"

"Course not. There you go doing stereotypes." Goldie gazed out the window next to their table. "Everyone I knew, my family, friends, guys and girlfriends alike, were in such an all-fired hurry to get me to the altar they just about greased me down and slid me there."

"So what happened?"

"I did what you're doin'. I got my back up. If everybody wants me to do something, it's for sure I don't want to do it."

Rachel stopped the forkful of macaroni halfway to her mouth and looked at her friend. "You sorry?"

Goldie shrugged ambivalently. "I saw him the other day. At Disneyland. I took my two nephews and Peter, the kid on the crew. Kenneth obviously had found himself another woman right quick. Good lookin' one too, and two little kids—one so little he was carrying it in one of those slings around his neck."

"You wished you hadn't dumped him?"

"I don't know. I wished something." Goldie pointed her chin at Rachel's left hand. "You took off your rock. You gonna break up with Hank?"

"Maybe." Rachel paused, asking herself the same question. Not finding an answer, she changed the subject. "I asked Gabe about that Mexican kid. What might have happened. He said the same thing everybody says. Maybe they both died. Or maybe the one wasn't as sick as they thought and he just walked out of the hospital before he was admitted."

"I don't know," Goldie said. "If the kid was unconscious, how could he recover so fast?"

"I've been wondering something else lately. You think whatever happened to those two kids might have something to do with that peculiar closed-but-full-of-people ward upstairs here?"

Goldie gave her a disparaging look. "If you aren't the limit. I told you before. You're just rolling two puzzles into one lump. What could that ward have to do with the kids you're talking about?"

"I don't know, except both things are weird and both have to do with this hospital."

"You're adding two and two and getting seven." Goldie shook her head. "Weird things happen all the time. They don't have to be related."

"How many rooms did your friend say are in that ward?" Rachel asked.

"Twelve, wasn't it?"

"Each with three beds?"

"Most. That's what the guy said."

"More than thirty patients in an area that's supposed to be closed."

"You got…me," Goldie said. A man rose from the table behind them and, carrying a tray of dirty dishes, passed their table. Her eyes followed him. "Now that is one good-looking dude."

"Dan Morris," Rachel said. "Security guy. Seems very nice. I don't know if he's married, but no ring. You want me to see if I can find out?"

Goldie cocked her head until it gave her an attitude. "You might just do that, girl."

"I sure would like to get a look at that ward."

Goldie made a face. "I don't want to meet him that bad."

"I didn't mean you. I meant I'd like to see it."

"You going to try getting lost again?"

"I'm not sure that would work a second time."

They finished eating. "There's something else weird," Rachel said as they stacked their dishes on the trays. "I never told you or anyone because I figured you'd think I was some kind of paranoid nut case."

"I suspect you have now overcome that fear."

"That day I got lost and saw that fourth floor wing. I was pretty sure someone followed me when I left."

"Followed you? You are paranoid. That sounds real unlikely. Why would anyone follow you?"

"No idea. But I could swear I heard footsteps behind me." Rachel could almost feel the slight chill she had felt that day. "The steps stopped when I stopped. I turned around twice, but there was no one there."

Goldie drew back. "Holy Jeez! And you wanted *me* to take a look around there?"

"Well, I sort of convinced myself it was my imagination. But now I'm not so sure."

"If it wasn't your imagination, it could've been my butt!"

"Okay. I'm not asking you, am I? I'm trying to figure a way to get in there myself. Doesn't that Jarvis whatever-his-name-is oversee the cleaning of the O-R along with all the other places? Doesn't the whole operating room complex have to be cleaned like anywhere else?"

"No."

"Of course it does. For that matter, it has to be cleaner than anywhere else."

"No, no, and no. I am not getting me or anyone else mixed up in this obsession of yours."

"All I want is some scrubs."

"Let me see if I got this straight. You want me to get someone to steal something?"

"If I could look like a nurse or a tech, I'll bet I could get into any part of any hospital without anyone batting an eye. I'd only use the scrub suit once. Then I'd wash it and give it back."

"No way, no how. No, no, no."

"Okay. Forget I asked. But it isn't stealing. It's borrowing. "

"Can't you just buy some? From a hospital supply place?"

"Probably. But I don't have time to hunt one up."

They carried their trays to the front of the big room where a man in a long white apron and a small white hat that failed to hide his hairnet was stacking dirty dishes. Rachel was adding hers to the pile when a sudden commotion at a table near the cash register caught everyone's attention.

A young woman with dark Slavic features and a handsome, mysterious look had climbed up on a chair and was now stepping onto the table. Her blouse was dark pink with white flowers. With the moves of a dancer, she pulled the blouse open, pulled up a pink halter underneath and two round breasts popped out. She lifted the right one and shook it at the stunned and gaping crowd.

She pulled her blouse closed, jumped down from the table and was out the cafeteria door before the watchers had closed their mouths.

"My cash drawer!" the cashier yelled. "The money's gone."

Several men ran to the door where the woman had disappeared. No one noticed the other two men leaving by the opposite door.

It was then that Rachel realized that her purse straps were still over her shoulder, but the purse was gone.

Chapter Twenty-one

"I'll never find another purse like that one," Rachel groaned to Irene when she had told her the tale of its loss.

"Ah, dear girl. Not many things one of a kind, are there? Must be another somewhere."

"I don't think so. I got it from the person who made it."

"You know his name?"

"Her name. Corazon Lopez. I remember because it was tooled in neat little letters inside. But even if I could find her, I couldn't afford to buy another one now. It was pretty expensive."

Rachel spent the afternoon calling credit card companies and her bank, then standing in line at the Department of Motor Vehicles while Irene kept an eye on the garage.

"What a pain. And I still have to get keys made," she told Irene when she got back. "I hope that doesn't mean new locks."

"No, you don't." Irene smiled angelically and held up a ring of keys. "While I was getting some made for myself, I had a whole new set made up as a spare."

Rachel didn't know whether to thank her or strangle her. She decided on the thanks.

"Gypsies, dear girl, that's what they were," Irene said, wagging her head as the feather earrings she wore swung back and forth. "An old gypsy trick, that is. They have been to that hospital before. This time I hear it's the king come down from San Francisco for heart surgery. Jefferson is very good at heart surgery. Or was it ear surgery? I hear about a hundred came with the king. They sleep in chairs and on the floor—makes no never mind to a gypsy—in the lobby and the waiting rooms."

"The hospital puts up with that?" Rachel asked.

"That and more. Those gypsies even steal the plumbing out of the bathrooms—I mean to tell you, luv, the faucets, the drains, the toilet flushers, everything."

"And the hospital doesn't throw them out?"

"Those that run hospitals love gypsies. Gypsies pay cash, dear girl. Cash on the barrel head. In advance."

◇◇◇

It wasn't until after work the following night that Rachel sat down in front of her computer, brought up Google and typed in *scrub suit*, thought a moment and added +*hospital*. Dozens of hospital supply companies turned up. The scrubs weren't expensive, but she had no idea there were many different kinds. It wouldn't work if she didn't match those at the hospital.

What kind of scrubs did Jefferson use? The emergency room techs were wearing scrubs the day she brought the two boys in. But what kind? Green. That's all she could remember for sure. But they were so nondescript she had no recollection of the style. How could there be so many styles? Pullover tops, button tops, trimmed tops. And different shades of green. Did they have to match? She wasn't sure.

Maybe she should buy the plainest, palest green ones she could find. She could ask Gabe about the style and color. Or maybe Gordon would know. He was parking in the garage now, too. Rachel didn't think he was supposed to because he wasn't really Jefferson staff, but she had an extra space, so she let him have it. He was grateful, too, kept asking if there was anything she needed, anything he could help her with.

Maybe the whole idea of trying to get into that fourth floor wing was stupid. Goldie was probably right. She was obsessing about those boys. Maybe it was just a way to not have to think about Hank.

She needed the income from Jefferson's lease. If she got caught, would that be trespassing? They might cancel the lease. And she wouldn't exactly be in a position to enforce the terms.

Just a worst case scenario. Nothing to really worry about.

◇◇◇

Watching a man leaving the garage the next afternoon, Rachel was trying to place him when he turned around, caught her eye and waved. Gordon Cox. Could he possibly be as young as he looked?

She waved back, and when he beamed with such apparent pleasure at seeing her, she left the booth and joined him at the door that led to the sidewalk.

"Hey, Rachel. When are you gonna let a couple of the nicest guys in town take you out for another drink?"

"It's hard for me to get away, Gordon. Especially now. I've been gone too much this week already. My purse was stolen, and I spent forever dealing with it, the driver's license, credit cards, the whole mess."

Gordon's baby face puckered into a frown. "That's too bad. How did it happen?"

"I was having lunch at the hospital of all places."

Gordon had already begun nodding. "Ah. The gypsies. I heard they got cash from the register and about a dozen wallets and handbags."

"They sure got at least one handbag," Rachel said. "So how about you? How's business?"

"You wouldn't believe how good. I hardly have to work any more. I just drive around and schmooze with friends."

Rachel remembered something. "Can I ask a dumb question?"

"Okay."

From the tone of his voice, she wondered if he thought she was going to hit him up for narcotics. On the other hand, maybe he was hoping she *would* ask for drugs. *Jesus. Was Gordon a pusher?* No. His company would have dozens of safeguards.

To dispel that, she asked quickly, "You happen to know where Jefferson buys its scrubs?"

A black Chrysler swooped past them.

"Scrubs? Why?"

"Well, it occurred to me that scrubs would be terrific cover-ups. Like in a garage, I'm always doing things that pretty much wreck my clothes. Scrubs would be light in the summertime. And they have a little more style than overalls."

"You're not only cute, you're clever," he said. "I've never thought about where they buy scrubs. You want me to ask around?"

"No. Don't bother. I can probably find some."

By the next afternoon, Rachel had already ordered the plainest pale green scrubs she could find on the Internet.

She would wait until maybe seven p.m., walk into the lobby as if she were a visitor, then go to the visitors' john and change before sneaking over to the east wing and up to the fourth floor. She was sure the Jefferson emergency room crew had been wearing light green—whitish green, not yellowish—scrubs. But the uniform wouldn't arrive for at least a week. And now that she had made up her mind what to do, she was impatient.

Looking up from a *Newsweek* someone had left behind, she saw Emma heading up the ramp to her car, and waved.

On her way out, Emma stopped her BMW next to the booth.

Before the driver's window had slid down more than a few inches, Rachel knew exactly what she would do. "Nice to see you again," she said.

"And you," Emma said. "I really enjoyed our lunch. We should do it again."

"Yes," Rachel said. "And next time it's on me. But meantime, I've changed my mind, I'd like to take you up on your offer to let me watch you do surgery some time."

Chapter Twenty-two

The pharmacy was behind on filling prescriptions and Gabe was trying to catch up. He counted out 30 Fondril XT and wondered why the MD didn't prescribe the less expensive generic. Doctors were so busy these days there was no way they could keep up on pharmaceuticals, but why didn't they ask? All it would take was a phone call. He guessed a lot of them didn't want to admit there was anything they didn't know.

Gabe didn't see Gordon until his friend was standing at the counter, checking the prescriptions kept on small clipboards, and preparing to help fill them. Technically, that was stretching the rules a bit, but the pharmacy had techs doing more than they probably should as well. Gabe would check each bottle before he stapled it into the little white bags with the patient's name.

He shook his head. "Why the hell do they prescribe Tynex?"

"Why not?" Gordon asked.

"The price is outrageous. Way more than a buck apiece. And people can get virtually the same thing off the shelf at Wal-Mart for about a dime a tablet."

"Well, not quite the same thing," Gordon said with a disarming grin.

"The generic is as good or better than this stuff," Gabe shot back. "You know damn well the manufacturer just did a minuscule alteration to re-brand it when the generic was released."

"Well, don't look at me. It wasn't Zyrco. It isn't mine."

"I know this patient. She's on Medicare/Medi-Cal. She can't afford to pay 10 times what this is worth. Are the docs dumb, or do they own stock, or only prescribe it to patients they hate, or what?"

"Ah, the docs are so damn busy these days, they don't have time to keep up with things like meds," Gordon said. "With the insurance companies lining their stockholders' pockets by squeezing payments to physicians, the MDs and DOs have to see a patient every twelve minutes to make as much as you and I make."

"You, maybe. Not me." Gabe was still frowning at the bag he had just stapled. He tore it open again. "I think I'll put a note in there and tell her to buy the generic off the shelf."

"The owner of this place will not be happy." Gordon was lining up the bottles in threes.

"Watch what you're doing," Gabe cautioned. "We don't need to kill some poor slob with the wrong medication."

"That's why you have insurance."

"It doesn't bring the patient back."

"But it can make the family very rich."

"Speaking of that." Gabe looked over the bottles of stock medications. "I need a favor."

"Sure."

Gabe named one of the most expensive drugs Zyrco made. Gordon whistled. "Okay."

"It's for a guy who works here," Gabe said. "Well, not him, his daughter. He just happened to mention it to me a couple days ago."

"I think I know who you mean. I've got him covered."

Gabe's eyebrows climbed toward his hair. "Dan?"

Gordon nodded. "Morris. The daughter's an adult, no insurance of any kind."

"Paying for that drug would put Dan in the poorhouse," Gabe said. "You're quite a guy." Despite the fact that he looked like a government-issue CPA—the kind they stack on back shelves and wind up at tax time. Gabe sometimes entertained himself with new analogies for Gordon's neatness. Of course that had nothing to do with Gabe's own sometimes sloppy dressing.

They filled the remaining bottles and Gabe began opening each bottle, checking the contents and replacing the cap.

"You are obsessive," Gordon said.

"That's why they pay me the big bucks."

"Not according to you."

"Well, that's why they pay me so I can pay my ex the big bucks."

Gordon sat down, leaned back, and watched Gabe work. "When are you going to find yourself another honey?"

"The first one cost me too much, and I don't just mean the money."

"How about that fair lass down the street?"

"Who?"

"The one with the cute butt."

"Rachel?"

"I may have to try her on myself."

Gabe swung around to face him. "Don't you fucking dare," he said conversationally.

"Aha!"

"Okay, so she's interesting. A little...mmm...weird, a little hard to deal with, but maybe worth it. She's interesting."

"Weird?"

"The on again, off again with the engagement ring." Gabe laid the packages out on the counter to alphabetize them by patient names.

Gordon pointed at the alphabetization process. "Why do you have to do that?"

"One of the afternoon techs is out sick, the other is at the dentist, a third hasn't shown up yet. The fourth is on annual leave. I'm not doing anything else except jawing with you. So why not?"

"So what's interesting? Other than her butt, I mean."

"Well a woman owning a parking garage is kind of intriguing."

"I guess if you want a place to park near downtown LA, it could be."

Gabe shrugged and gathered up four bags for patients whose last names began with T. "She's different. Seems to have some unusual interests."

"Like what?"

"Like she's met some MD here. A surgeon. And Rachel's going to observe surgery sometime."

"Yech," Gordon said. "When?"

"I think she said it's on for day after tomorrow. Early. I find someone who wants to do that interesting."

"More like weird. Why would anyone want to watch somebody cut up somebody else?"

"Curiosity. At least that's what she said." Gabe was finishing the last of the alphabet. "A chance to do something ninety-nine percent of the world has never done, was the way she put it."

"And wouldn't want to," Gordon said. "You wouldn't catch me doing it. All that blood. Way down my list of fun things to do."

Chapter Twenty-three

Wearing a denim jacket against the early morning chill, Rachel walked the six blocks from the garage. It was 6:05. Emma said most surgeons found their senses were sharpest early in the morning, so that's when they preferred to work. Rachel had opened the garage early and asked Irene to keep an eye on things.

She smiled and nodded at the two security guys who were copping a smoke on the sidewalk in front of Jefferson's main entrance.

This time she had to find the west wing. That's where Emma had said the O-R was. It seemed like a 5-k hike before she found a door to the stairs around the corner from a bank of elevators. Rachel went down two flights as Emma had directed.

Voices and bright light came from behind a pair of huge double doors. Rachel pushed through them. A dozen or so sinks lined the wall and at least as many people, some in green scrubs, some in street clothes, were moving about. They all looked purposeful and efficient.

She expected someone to stop her, question her right to be there, but no one did. Apparently not a lot of people wanted to crash an operating room at six-something in the morning. A bench of wood more orange than brown, with edges rounded by countless coats of shellac, held stacks of green garments arranged according to size.

Collecting shirt, pants, a mask and three stretchy bag-like things, one large, two small, Rachel studied the women moving through the room and decided that the large bag was to be worn like a shower cap, the two smaller ones must fit over shoes.

She found an empty dressing room and changed clothes. Eying herself in the mirror, she decided the scrubs were so shapeless, so nondescript, that everyone wearing them would look about the same, especially with the addition of the mask, except for height and weight. In some cases, even gender might be hard to guess.

A long row of beige lockers stood just outside the dressing rooms. A few had combination or key locks, but many did not. Most staff probably left valuables in their offices. Rachel had her purse, a replacement for the one just stolen, but she never carried much cash and she hadn't yet received the replacement credit cards. She placed her belongings in one of the open lockers. Edgy as she was about theft since her recent experience in the cafeteria, it still was hard to imagine someone stealing from a locker in an O-R. And it was a bit late now to do much about getting a lock.

People were still milling back and forth like doggedly earnest green ants.

"Excuse me," she said to a woman moving toward her. "Where can I find Dr. Johnson?"

"Emma Johnson or Ronald Johnson?"

"Emma. She invited me to watch surgery."

"Down that hall. Number four. But wash up first. Tuck your hair up a little better—all inside, every strand. Then get that mask on and don't touch anything, as in zero, zip, nothing at all. You can back through the doors."

The sink was automatic. Rachel washed, blew her hands dry beneath a blast of hot air, and holding them up in front of her, she moved to the hall where the woman had pointed. None of the people in green looked up when she entered room number four.

The patient was positioned a little to the left side, the body almost completely covered except for a space of eight inches or so just above the hip. This area was spotlighted and the green-clad people hovered around it. A woman stood at the patient's head which was hidden from the others by a short green curtain. She was the only one who could see the face and she was apparently scrutinizing it intently. Attached to a pole, a tray of gleaming instruments hung nearby.

In the corner was a small grey plastic stool. Emma had said it would be there in case Rachel wanted something to stand on to see better. She did.

Handles of what must be instruments protruded from small incisions. It all looked pretty bizarre. But there was practically no blood at all. The person across the table turned her head and Rachel recognized Emma's eyes. The eyes went back to what looked a little like a computer monitor. Emma had explained that one of the instruments was a camera and the surgery was done by watching the monitor.

The eye-hand coordination must be awesome, Rachel thought. Like maneuvering a razor inside an abdomen with a computer mouse.

A few minutes later a shiny object was brought out by an instrument just above the pelvis followed by a collective sigh from those hovering over the patient. Whatever it was, was deposited in a white box and one of the masked crew left the room with it.

Emma's work must have finished because she now came over to Rachel, blue eyes fairly glowing. The two remaining people were preparing to suture the incisions. Emma tilted her head toward the door and Rachel followed her out of the room.

Emma was still holding her hands, encased in plastic gloves, aloft, so Rachel followed suit.

"That was really impressive," she said.

When they reached the bank of sinks, the doctor shucked her gloves into a receptacle, and pulled her mask below her chin. "Isn't it marvelous what we can do these days? I have another in about 20 minutes. Would you like to watch that as well?"

"No," Rachel breathed. "Thanks, but this made me dizzy enough."

Emma peered at her. "You feel ill?"

"No. Not at all. It's just a lot to comprehend."

"It is, isn't it?" Emma set about scrubbing her hands, which could hardly need it since they had been covered by the gloves. "That patient will be good as new—well, almost—in a few weeks. And his brother will have a new lease on life."

"He was donating a kidney to his brother?"

Emma nodded. "An excellent match. They both will be fine. Thank God for live donors. It's rare for anyone to actually need two kidneys. One has to wonder why our Maker bothered to give us a pair. But I'm glad He—or She—did. Some fifty thousand people on the kidney waiting list and fewer than ten thousand suitable cadaver donors available each year."

The doctor made a sad frown. "And the waiting list gets longer every year. But laparoscopy with less risk and almost invisible scars makes it easier for a living donor to part with a kidney. And a kidney from a well-matched living donor is by far the best candidate for a successful graft."

"Why is that?" Rachel asked. The area was bustling with even more activity than earlier. No one ran, but no one moved slowly either. Few bothered to glance at the two women in front of the sinks.

"No big rush, for one thing," Emma said. "Time to do the tests and be certain we get everything right. Then, too, a living donor is generally younger, healthier." She was still holding her fingers at shoulder height—fluttering white doves without a place to land.

"And no one needs two kidneys?"

"That's not a hundred percent, obviously, but percentage-wise it's not often. We manage with one heart, one liver, one pancreas, one spleen…and you have no idea how much it means to the recipient." Emma glanced down the hall they had emerged from. "The next one should be about ready. I'd better go."

"Thanks for the chance to do this," Rachel said and watched until Emma disappeared into an operating room at the end of the hall.

Matching her motions to those of the people crisscrossing the area, Rachel followed a tall slender man with brown hairy arms through the main door and into the hallway. He made the turn toward the elevators. She found the stairway exit.

Glimpsing her reflection in the door's window, she realized she still had the cap on. The man she had followed was bareheaded. She snatched off the cap, then bent over and removed the shoe coverings, rolled up all three and shoved them into her pocket. They made a large a lump. She rolled them up again but once back in the pocket, they unrolled.

She was almost breathless by the time she had trotted all the way upstairs, past the lobby and to the east wing. This time the long corridor was almost eerily empty, like an airport before the flights begin.

Not sure what she would do if she got lost again, she climbed more stairs to what she thought was the fourth floor, opened the door and stepped into the hall. The T-shaped hall looked like the place where she'd lost her way a few days before.

A nurse with very short hair and fleshy bulges above and below the waist of her uniform turned the corner but barely glanced at her before pressing the down button for the elevator. The scrubs did seem to make one all but invisible.

Imitating the purposeful stride of the O-R people, Rachel turned the same corner and, ignoring the *Closed* sign now in place on the left door, pushed open the right one.

Chapter Twenty-four

The area seemed even smaller than it had the first time, dwarfed by the rest of the corridors Rachel had now seen. Obviously this was a much older part of the hospital.

Light was spilling from as many as a dozen doors that opened onto the hall, which hummed with a flurry of activity. The place smelled of sausage and maple syrup, and a trolley laden with trays stood next to the wall. Celebrities or no, these patients apparently ate well.

A buzz of conversations emanated from the rooms, but Rachel couldn't quite make out the words.

She walked down the hall, trying to look as if she knew exactly where she was going. People wearing scrubs would be seen as normal here, wouldn't they?

What little she could see of the rooms she glanced into seemed somewhat Spartan. Most doorways revealed the metal foot-boards of three beds.

At the foot of each bed was a holder for what must be each patient's medical records.

Two people in head-to-foot white passed with hardly a glance in her direction. Rachel's shoes were black Reebok high-tops. Would that give her away?

She passed a women's restroom, backtracked and turned in. A toilet flushed. Rachel stepped quickly into a booth and slid the latch on the door. Sitting on the toilet, she took the elastic covers from her pocket and placed them back on her shoes. Would that be less noticeable than black?

Through a crack between the booth door and wall she could see a woman in white at the sink. Had there only been one door closed in the row of booths?

The woman finished washing her hands and left.

Rachel left the booth and looked quickly right and left. All doors stood open. She went to the sink and washed her hands for the third or fourth time that morning. She was drying her palms under the hot-air machine when the hall door opened to admit an attractive woman with dark skin, high cheekbones and caramel-colored braids. Rachel returned her businesslike nod and left the john.

A pair of women in white pants and jackets exited one room, crossed the hall and entered another.

Rachel walked briskly down the corridor. All the rooms seemed alike. Stark, brightly lit, three beds, all with medical records in holders at the foot.

So why the closed sign on the entry door? Gathering what further boldness she possessed, she made a random left turn into a room.

The talk there ceased. Two pairs of eyes looked into hers from faces the color of maple syrup. The eyes belonged to patients in beds that were rolled to sitting position.

A third bed was surrounded by a grey, rubberized curtain. Rachel could see a pair of white lace-up shoes beneath the curtain. She backed out of the room and hurried down the hall. Wearing scrubs, she might look like one of the staff, but best not to have to talk to anyone.

The last room in the corridor was empty of patients but it was clearly in use. Two beds had rumpled sheets and various items on the steel cabinets next to them. The third bed, the closest to the door, was made up with fresh white linens. At the foot of each been hung papers on a clipboard.

She stepped inside, away from the door, where she couldn't be seen from the hall.

Her eyes fell on the papers at the foot of the nearest bed. Someone had scrawled *Deceased* across the top. Lifting the clipboard from its place, Rachel scanned the pages. Reading them word-for-word would take more time than she had. Knowing it was the last thing in the world she should do, she removed the papers and put the clipboard back.

The patient was dead. How much could it matter? And weren't medical records typed up every day? Whatever, she could always come back to the hospital and drop these notes in a hall where someone would find them.

Folding the papers, she left the room just as a woman in white was exiting the room across the hall. The woman stopped.

"Wrong room," Rachel muttered, spun on her heel and walked quickly down the corridor.

The woman was following, calling, "Excuse me…," softly at first, then louder.

Rachel tried not to run. Glancing over her shoulder, she stuck the folded papers in the waistband of the scrub pants. The woman had disappeared. Rachel darted into another room. It was much the same as the last, except this time all three patients were in their beds. All three still had breakfast remains on trays on metal-arm tables.

The eyes of the patient in the middle bed went so wide that white showed all the way around the dark pupil. He shook his head sharply. "*No. No hoy.*"

Rachel held out both hands, palms out. She couldn't understand the words, but she could read the panic in his eyes. "Sorry. I'm sorry. You're right."

What was he afraid of? Everyone she had seen so far seemed comfortable and healthy. Come to think of it, if that was the case, why were they in the hospital?

She stepped back into the corridor. The same woman was there again, moving toward her, a cell phone held to her ear.

Trying to smile, Rachel said, "I'm afraid I'm lost." She turned and moved quickly down the corridor toward the exit, the covers on her shoes rustling over the linoleum.

"Wait!"

Was the woman breaking into a run? Now there were more footsteps. Were more people coming after her?

Rachel didn't turn. Almost in a run herself, she reached the ward's exit doors, pushed through, raced out and around the corner. The middle elevator stood empty, doors open.

As she rushed toward them, the doors started to close. She grabbed at the narrowing space between them. Too late.

Slamming a thumb against the down button, she realized she shouldn't have run. She might explain her presence, but how explain running away? She shouldn't have panicked.

The elevator door began sliding open again.

A sound reached her, other doors, heavy doors, opening nearby.

Hurrying into the elevator, Rachel jabbed a finger on the *close* button. The equipment seemed to hesitate.

She shouldn't have gotten into the elevator. Anyone following her would expect that. She should have taken the stairs.

The elevator jerked, came to a decision, and whisked its doors closed.

But they began to open again. Someone must have pushed a call button.

She slammed her hand against the *close* button in the car and held it there.

Someone rapped on the door.

The open crack between the doors disappeared, the car shuddered. Rachel had a sudden image of the car plunging at breakneck speed, but it began its descent slowly. She let out breath she hadn't realized she was holding, and touched the button for the lobby floor.

Okay, so she didn't totally get away with it, but no one recognized her. She patted the papers through the fabric of her pocket. Maybe this was something that would shed some light on what was going on in that ward.

She left the elevator at the lobby floor, and followed the long corridor, grateful that it was now filling with people, to the west wing. In the stairwell there, she stopped a moment to clear her head enough to stop her hands trembling, then went on down the steps to the O-R, grabbed her clothes from the locker, stepped into a dressing room, closed the door, flipped the lock and sank down on the orange wood bench built into the wall across from the mirror.

Her eyes looked like dark hollows. What if the staff up there put out some sort of alert?

But she hadn't done anything.

Well, they won't look for me here.

This is exactly where they'll look for you. You are wearing scrubs, in case you hadn't noticed.

Okay, let's just calm down and get the hell out of here.

Rachel removed the scrubs, put the folded papers flat against her body, pulled on her jeans, chambray shirt, and denim jacket.

No one was pounding on the door looking for her. She opened the dressing room door. No one was paying any attention to her at all.

Tossing the green shirt and pants into a laundry bag that was stretched open across a framework of metal bars, she saw shoe covers and caps piled in a big white plastic bag and added hers. Stopping at the mirror over the sinks, she ran fingers through her hair, and backed through the doors to the hall.

By the time she had climbed the two flights and found her way to the lobby, she felt much better.

She was thinking it was stupid and silly to have let herself get so spooked when someone tapped her on the shoulder.

Dan Morris. She smiled and opened her mouth to just ask him straight out if he was married. If he wasn't, she'd ask him if he'd like to meet Goldie.

Morris' big dark eyes looked like they were going to melt and run down his cheeks. He grasped her elbow. "Sorry, ma'am. Would you please come with me?"

Chapter Twenty-five

Rachel froze, instantly certain that Morris' request was related to her escapade on the fourth floor.

"Why?" she asked, trying to keep her voice normal while her anxiety rose at mach speed. "What's going on?"

He was wearing a navy blue chino jacket with gold buttons. He tipped his head toward her, looking genuinely concerned. "Do you want to talk here, or somewhere a little more private?"

"Talk about what?" Her voice grew tight, almost broke. Was he going to accuse her of trespassing? How bad could that be? Surely not the end of the world. Please don't let them cancel the lease. Why the hell did she have to be so nosey?

Morris drew out a cell phone, pushed a button, took a few steps, turned his head away and spoke into it. Rachel couldn't hear the words. He folded the phone and slipped it back into his jacket pocket.

Gently, he nudged her forward in front of him. She felt like a rubber doll, with no control of her own as they moved through the vast expanse of lobby, past sofas where twenty or so people sprawled. Her captor steered her to the right and down a long, carpeted hall with a dozen or more doors open to offices.

At the end of the hall he guided her into an office that looked much like the ones they had passed. Rachel stopped in front of a gray metal desk. There was a large pad of paper and a phone, but no other sign that anyone actually worked there. Morris didn't enter the office, remaining instead half in, half out the doorway.

Rachel finally found what she had been desperately searching for. Her nerve. How bad could it be? Okay, she might lose a client, but they had signed a contract, so maybe not even that. She drew herself up. "Just what is this all about, Mr. Morris?"

"We will need to have you searched."

She was sure she hadn't heard right. "Excuse me?"

Morris turned his head to glance down the hall. "Please, Miss Chavez, I'm sure you don't want to make a scene."

An aghast look spread from Rachel's eyes across her face. "What do you think I've done?"

"We need a search. I can call the police and have them send a woman, or you can agree to have a woman here look through your…uh…things."

"You're going to strip search me?"

Morris was watching her, his look more apologetic than arrogant. He said nothing.

"This is totally ridiculous," Rachel sputtered. "What do you think I have? My purse was just snatched right here in this very hospital a couple days ago. So I don't have much in this one."

"I'm sorry," he said.

A rustling sound came from the hall. Morris stepped aside. A small woman strode in. She wore white. A lot of white. White shoes, white nylons, white uniform. No doubt her underwear, too, had not one thread of color. She moved past Rachel and stopped with her back to the window, making room for a second woman, this one in a dark blue dress with a scarf of lighter blue covering her hair, rimless glasses, and no makeup.

There was barely room for all of them in the small office.

The woman in blue looked at Rachel the way one looks at stray dogs at the pound, eyes emanating a sadness about life and death and the inability to escape either. The woman in white was eyeing Rachel as if she were an IRS examiner and Rachel was a highly suspect tax return.

Morris gestured to the woman in white. "This is Molly Kirkpatrick. One of our nursing supervisors." The woman nodded brusquely. "And Sister Mary Frances."

"You're a nun?"

The woman in blue dipped her chin. "Pastoral services."

"Sister agreed to give us a hand here," Morris said. "It's best to have two…witnesses."

"I see." Rachel looked at him. "It's either this or the cops?"

Morris' mournful eyes held hers for a moment before he nodded.

Rachel threw up her hands. "Okay, fine. What the hell. Excuse me, Sister. What in the name of heaven do you think I have?"

For a few seconds, the two women looked at Morris, who looked at the floor. No one spoke.

"Let's just get it over with," Rachel said. "What do you want me to do?"

"I'll leave you ladies alone," Morris said. "I'll be right out here in the hall." He closed the door behind him.

Clearly used to being in charge, Molly, the woman in white, went behind the desk, pulled the chair out but stood in front of it rather than sit. She tapped the barren top of the desk. "Why don't you just set your handbag down here?"

"What are you looking for? Cocaine? An assassin's rifle? What?"

"I'm afraid it's necessary, dear," the nun said. "Just do as she asks. It won't take long."

Rachel sighed and set down her purse where the woman had pointed.

Molly Kirkpatrick opened it and tipped it so that lipstick, comb, nail file, wallet, and coin purse tumbled out onto the desk. With the thoroughness of someone preparing a patient for surgery, she examined everything, but found nothing that interested her. She shook the purse, peered inside, ran her hand over the lining. Then, moving it and what had been its contents to the side of the desk, she said, "Now your jacket, if you please."

Rachel slipped the faded denim jacket from her shoulders and tried to shrug her arms out of it.

The nun reached over to help, then folded the jacket more neatly than Rachel had ever folded anything and handed it to Kirkpatrick, who laid it flat on the desk, reached into the right pocket, and withdrew three pieces of tissue, a key and a black marble.

The woman turned the jacket to the other side and put her hand into the left pocket. "Ah!" The sound seemed to escape without intent. She looked up. Pale blue eyes looked straight into Rachel's. She drew her hand out of the pocket, fingers clasping a squat, white plastic bottle.

Rachel gaped at it, stunned.

The woman shook the bottle. It rattled. She turned it over and read the label.

"OxyContin. I assume you have a prescription for this? Who is the prescribing doctor?"

Chapter Twenty-six

No! Rachel's head wouldn't stop shaking. *This can't be happening.* It was too much to take in all at once. Not now. Not when she had finally made a life for herself, had got her head above water and was able to pay her bills and have a little left over.

Morris had telephoned the police. The two women had sat stiffly with her in that dreadful office with the naked desk between them and Morris at the door, everyone utterly silent.

"I don't know where it came from." Voice gone dull, Rachel was saying the seven words for the third time since the two cops had arrived. "I didn't take it. I know it's a drug, but I don't even know what it's for."

The cops said nothing. They barely looked at her. She wondered if they thought she was such a low life form it would be a waste of time to notice her. A drug thief. Stealing from a hospital.

From somewhere on another planet, she helplessly watched the scene play out. Thank God for Miranda. In her frenzied state, she might have tried to answer their questions without an attorney.

Sister Mary Frances touched her arm and said quietly, "Would you like me to find someone for you?"

"Someone?" Rachel pronounced the word dumbly.

"A lawyer, dear?"

"Yes," Rachel gulped. She wasn't sure she could marshal enough rational thought on her own to do that. "Please." Her thoughts were jumping about like drops of water on a hot griddle. She couldn't focus on what all this meant.

After a short, miserable ride to the police station, locked behind a grill in the back seat of a squad car, she was led into a room. A scarred metal file cabinet stood in the corner, and a cheap table, three folding chairs, and a pad of yellow paper were just about dead center of the remaining space, which seemed large enough to echo.

A bright overhead light showed the room's countless dingy smudges. One wall had a hairline crack from the ceiling down, and bits of fallen plaster were still on the floor—the effect of the last earthquake, maybe, or, judging from the look of the rest of the room, the last six earthquakes.

Left there alone, Rachel gazed at the wall trying to collect the mass of fragments that had been her mind.

Finally she began to wonder why. Why had someone planted the bottle of OxyContin on her? And who?

Sitting in that appalling room with its ugly table, she was feeling kicked in the gut all over again. Like she had once before—was it four years ago now, or five? Only that time she was guilty.

A short, stocky cop with a big brush of a mustache appeared. His blue shirt was starched and ironed, with creases that looked sharp enough to be used as weapons. His shoes were like black mirrors.

Rachel looked up at him. "May I use the phone?" Someone, she wasn't sure who, had taken her handbag and her cell phone.

He nodded toward an ancient avocado-colored phone on top of the army green file cabinet in the corner. Perhaps back in the sixties the cops had thought the color combination stylish.

"How long are you going to keep me here?"

The man just grunted and stationed himself against the wall, arms folded, staring straight ahead, apparently waiting to monitor her phone call.

Not sure she could walk without falling over, Rachel moved slowly to the phone, dialed the garage, and told Irene she had been delayed, might in fact not be back for the rest of the day.

"Not to worry, luv," Irene said blithely. "Everything is in hand here. Not to worry at all."

Right.

When Rachel hung up, the cop, without glancing at her, left the room.

The clock on the dirty yellow wall was missing the minute hand. The hour hand was stealthily creeping up on noon. Could it possibly be six hours since she left the garage that morning?

Maybe the cops were waiting for an attorney to show up. Would the nun be able to find someone good? *Does a successful attorney actually come down to a police station when someone they've never even met is arrested?* Most likely it would be someone just out of law school, looking to cut his or her teeth in criminal law.

Or were they waiting for Rachel to get so stressed out and exhausted that she couldn't think at all? They probably would prefer to question her while her defenses were numbed out. In that case, it wouldn't be long.

◇◇◇

Edgar Harrison was wearing golf shoes, a bright green golf shirt, and about the eyes, a bland, neutral look that must have had a lot of practice.

He introduced himself as her attorney. Rachel was relieved the sister had sent her someone who was at least forty and could afford to play golf. He seemed competent and assured, and for the first time, she began to feel she might have a chance.

"You need to know two things," she told him. "First, I didn't steal that drug. I've never taken OxyContin in my life. I've heard of it, but that's about all."

"All right," Harrison said stoically. "And second?"

"I have a prior drug arrest."

"Where? When?"

"Up north. Alameda County. That time I was guilty. This time I'm not."

Judge Annette Garcia obviously didn't believe that. She set bail at a hundred and twenty-five thousand and lectured Rachel about finding a rehab program for herself and that she was despicable beyond words if she was selling drugs to others. At least that's how it sounded.

Harrison pulled a cell phone from his briefcase and called a bail bondsman.

When he was through, Rachel borrowed the phone and called Marty. "I need your help, Pop."

"What's wrong?" Marty sounded cautious.

"Are you in a game?"

"I'm at the club," he said noncommittally. He was in a game.

"I've been arrested." She listened to his sharp intake of breath and went on before he could comment, "Someone planted drugs on me. At the hospital."

"I'll be right there."

"No. Wait. I need you to bring me the deed to the garage." She knew how he hated to leave a poker game and his willingness to do so in response to her urgency made her eyes suddenly sting.

"I've still got most of that pot I won."

"No, Pop. I don't want it. Besides, it wouldn't be enough."

"But you can't risk the garage."

"I have to. I'll try to arrange a mortgage later. But right now, I need that deed. And the appraisal I had done when the deed transferred from Gramps. You remember where the papers are?"

"I remember," Marty said grimly. They both had keys to the safe deposit box.

"Thanks, Pop." She hesitated, then said again, "Thanks."

It took all the rest of the day to post bond with what was basically her entire life as collateral. Harrison gave her his card and a pep talk he probably gave all clients. Marty drove her back to the garage. As they pulled up at the curb, the moon was launching itself above the high-rise office buildings.

Chapter Twenty-seven

Rachel had forgotten the medical record papers until she was undressing that night. She barely glanced at them before slipping them under a pile of turtlenecks in the bottom drawer of her dresser. She wasn't sure why she was hiding them, except that unlike the bottle in her jacket pocket, she *had* stolen the papers. But her interest in them had waned. She now had bigger things on her mind.

It was mid-afternoon a week after her arrest and she was getting a headache. She had devoted hours every day to searching for a company that would give her a mortgage at a decent interest rate. So far, no luck.

Leaving her booth to get a breath of fresh air she saw Emma Johnson at the street door.

Rachel stopped in mid stride. There was no avoiding coming face-to-face with the doctor. Had Emma heard about the supposed OxyContin theft? She must have.

"Hello, Emma." Rachel wondered why she felt guilty when she knew better than anyone that she wasn't. Even her voice sounded guilty.

The doctor nodded, took a few evasive steps, then looked back at Rachel and shook her head sadly.

No need to wonder anymore whether she had heard.

◇◇◇

"Reasonable and finance company are contradictions in terms," she told Marty when he stopped by to see how it was going.

They were eating green enchiladas at the counter of Rachel's tiny kitchen.

"I can't find a single loan where the company doesn't want a big chunk of money just to give you the loan. Then they hit you with an interest rate so high you can't imagine ever paying it off. Then there are clauses that say I have to get permission to do anything to the mortgaged property, even to make a repair. And the loan officers treat me like I'm trying to rob them at gunpoint. I hate to think what they'd do if they knew why I need the loan. I'm afraid to tell them and scared to death they'll find out. Doesn't anyone get arrested for something they didn't do?"

Marty gave her a worried look. "Why won't you let me stake you?"

"It's not that I don't appreciate your offer, Pop. But if you really want to do me a favor, put that money in a CD."

"Okay. It's your life. But the offer stands." He pointed to the enchiladas. "You make these?"

"I've been working on the recipe. For starters, it's Mesilla Valley chile. From New Mexico. Supposed to be the best in the country."

"It comes in cans?"

"Good God no. After a little experimenting I realized there's no such thing as good chile from a can. What kind of Mexican are you?"

"We didn't eat enchiladas."

"In Mexico? You didn't eat enchiladas?"

"My father—and maybe my mother, I'm not sure—regarded enchiladas, burritos, tacos, stuff like that, as peasant food, unworthy of the upper classes. My father wouldn't have a taco in the house."

"What the heck did you eat?"

"Mostly French. My brother and I used to buy tamales on the street, but we had to hide them."

"No burritos?"

"Not until I got to San Francisco. Then, after I met your mom, well, she ate a taco now and again, but I still remember the look she gave me when she saw a plate of flat enchiladas."

Rachel remembered the looks her mother could give and they both laughed.

"She would have tried them if you had made them," Marty said. "These are very good."

"They're a job to make, but fun to see how different kinds of chile, and even how long you cook the sauce, change the flavor."

"So what are you going to do if you can't find a loan?" Marty asked when they had finished eating and Rachel was clearing the plates.

She sighed. "I don't know. The fine print, the points, the fees, the processing expenses just about drive me over the edge. It's like applying to be robbed. To say nothing of finding and gathering all the papers they insist on seeing. I'm three months shy of being formally in business the acceptable number of years, which I suspect is an arbitrary number they use as an excuse to charge me higher rates." She bit her lower lip. "There are so many hidden 'gotchas,' it scares me silly."

"I could call El Jefe." Marty had earned the man's appreciation because El Jefe's son had lost a lot of money to Marty and Marty had given it back when he learned it was the boy's college money.

"He's a criminal, Pop."

"How do you know that?"

"He reeks of gangster. You can't be that naive."

"He loves his son. He's sending him to a good college. He's repaid the debt in more ways than money, which seems pretty honorable to me," Marty said. "For that matter, I don't think he hides any gotchas. He seems very up-front, which is more than you're saying about the loan people. And I'm sure he has a lot of connections."

"Okay, what sort of business is he in?"

"I think he owns three or four companies. Maybe more."

"What kind of companies, Pop?"

Marty shrugged. "I never asked."

"He's a criminal."

"Rachel, I don't like to put it this way, but at the moment, some people think you are, too."

She groaned, and after a long moment, asked, "You don't think I did this thing, do you?"

"Not if you say you didn't. But the evidence is pretty strong. You'll have to prove someone planted it on you. And why would anyone do that?"

Rachel shook her head back and forth. "God only knows. I sure don't."

Marty's eyes searched hers and she knew there was at least ten percent of him that didn't believe her. When he looked away, he asked, "How do you feel about that attorney?"

"I don't know. This guy Edgar whatever his last name is, seems okay. But maybe I should try to get Aaron to come down." Aaron had gotten her out of jail several years ago when she had been guilty of possession.

"El Jefe might know a good attorney, too."

Twelve thousand five hundred dollars of the bail bond was forfeit regardless of her guilt or innocence. That was bad enough. But she also had to pay her attorney.

"Okay, Pop," Rachel said dully. "My back's against the wall. If you think he can get me a good mortgage on the garage, ask him."

An hour after Marty left, the banging on one of the pedestrian garage doors began.

Chapter Twenty-eight

Rachel ran down the ramps and called through the door, "What's all the ruckus?"

Goldie's voice yelled back, "I want to know what the hell is going on!"

"Okay, okay." Rachel unlocked the door and opened it. "Nothing's going on. What's got you madder than a wet hornet?"

Goldie gave her a hard stare. "Since when is getting arrested nothing?"

"How'd you find out?"

"Irene told me. I need a sit-down explanation." Goldie nodded her head toward the sidewalk behind her.

Rachel pulled the door closed and followed Goldie to their much-used bench under the streetlight in front of the garage. "How could Irene know? I never told her a thing about it."

"Well, she does fortunes, doesn't she? She hears things. And if there's anyone Irene doesn't know I can't think who it might be."

"The governor, maybe."

"I wouldn't be too sure," Goldie chuckled.

"Okay. The fact is, someone planted a drug on me. Oxy-Contin. A prescription drug," Rachel said in the tone of someone trying to believe her own statement. "Who the hell would do that?"

Goldie tilted her head back and gave a low whistle. "No clue, girlfriend. That's pretty serious shit. I hear that OxyContin stuff

is sort of like heroin. I think they even call it hillbilly heroin."
She looked at Rachel. "How about that guy you met?"

"Who?"

"The one with the pheromones."

"Gabe? Why would he plant a bottle of pills on me?"

"He works at that hospital. He's a pharmacist, isn't he? That means he's got the easiest access to just about any drug you could name. Legal drugs anyway. Controlled substances. That must be what OxyContin is, right?"

"I guess he *could* do it, but that doesn't mean he would. What reason would he have?"

"Maybe he's a pervert. Wants to see you squirm. Then when you're feeling real bad he can get in your pants."

"Goldie, that's pretty far fetched."

"Maybe, maybe not."

"I don't think it has anything to do with Gabe. If you want the truth, I think it has to do with that closed ward on the fourth floor of the hospital."

"That's what's far fetched. You have been connecting everything with that. If there's an earthquake tomorrow, you'll be thinking it has something to do with that ward. Or maybe it was because of those kids you found." Goldie nodded a couple times. "But okay, while we're at it, let's get them out of the way. Why would those kids have anything to do with someone planting drugs on you?"

"Maybe because I've been asking questions about them. Maybe someone doesn't like that, doesn't want anyone looking for them."

Goldie rolled her eyes. "Okay, then how about that hospital ward? Why would anyone connected with that ward plant drugs on you and have you arrested?"

"Okay, you're right," Rachel said slowly. "It's crazy."

At that, they sat in silence until Goldie broke it. "I can hear the gears grinding in your head."

Rachel looked over at her. "I do think I know *when* those drugs got planted."

Goldie's eyes narrowed thoughtfully. "You said they were in a pocket, right?"

Rachel nodded. "The left pocket of my jacket."

"Maybe someone behind you on a crowded elevator…?"

"I didn't take the elevator while I was wearing that jacket. I took the stairs."

"Then you got me," Goldie said.

"It had to have happened while I was in the O-R, or when I was up on that fourth floor."

"You think someone was following you or knew where you were?"

"Had to. I'm certain that damn bottle of pills wasn't in my pocket when I walked to the hospital. It's cool that early in the morning. I had my hands in my pockets."

A car sped by, a Hummer, its windows looking absurdly small in the large body.

"Come to think of it," Rachel mused, "a woman called out to me, in that ward. I think she was trying to stop me. She ran after me. And she had a cell phone."

Goldie's eyebrows climbed nearly to her hairline. "So where was your jacket at this time?"

"That's exactly the point. It was hanging in an open locker next to the dressing rooms in the O-R."

"So if she called someone, how would this person who wanted to plant drugs on you know that?"

"I'm back to square one. I don't know."

"Why would this person, whoever he, she, it, is, *want* to plant drugs on you?"

"I don't know that either." Rachel gnawed her lower lip and slowly shook her head. "To keep me from nosing around that ward? Or nosing around anywhere at that hospital?"

"Okay," Goldie said. "So what did you see in that ward that somebody didn't want seen?"

"Well, that janitor guy you talked to was right. There were lots of patients. More than thirty, I think. Other than that, I didn't see anything. I went into the john down the hall. It was an pretty ordinary john."

"So why would anybody get so uptight about your being there that they'd stick a bottle of drugs on you?"

"They didn't just stick some drugs on me, they also sicced the security guy on me. He stopped me the minute I tried to leave the hospital. And he knows me. He's the guy we saw in the cafeteria. The one you said was a looker. There's no way he would have stopped me unless someone told him to. Someone who *knew* there was a bottle of pills in my pocket."

"Maybe he's the one who planted them."

"I don't think so. He seems like a really nice guy. I was hoping to fix you up with him."

"Mmmm-mmmm," Goldie said. "That is too bad. In more ways than one."

"Why would it be a big deal for someone like me to see those patients on the fourth floor?"

"Maybe they're experimenting on people. Making Frankensteins or something."

"You've been watching too many horror movies. That hospital has a very good reputation."

"Maybe it's because they want to hang onto that reputation and if anyone found out they were making Frankensteins…. What else could it be?"

"I don't know." Rachel thought for a moment. "Let's back up a minute. What if it wasn't because of that hospital ward but had something to do with the two poor kids I found. One dead, one alive, and they both just disappeared."

"I knew you'd get back to that." Goldie leaned her head back on the bench and studied the sky. "Let's see. You went to the hospital to see how the one kid was doing."

"Right."

"And you went to the cops."

"I will choose this moment to remind you that both those things were your idea. And I called the coroner's office."

"I didn't say you shouldn't have nosed around. I just said you did. But no one had any idea what might have happened?"

"Like I told you, a couple people thought maybe the boy who was still alive died before he was admitted to the hospital. But the coroner's office didn't know anything about either boy, or said they didn't."

"Why would they lie?"

"How do I know? Maybe the receptionist is lazy and just wanted to get rid of a pesky phone call."

◇◇◇

The next morning Rachel looked up from her bookkeeping in the booth to see a large hand ready to tap on the window and behind it, the woeful face of Dan Morris. His routine had settled into a steady, almost daily schedule of sending parcels via helicopter from Rachel's rooftop helipad.

She slid open the door. "Hi, Dan. What can I do for you?"

"I just want you to know I'm really, really sorry." He sounded genuinely upset. "I've been told the parking lease will be cancelled."

Chapter Twenty-nine

"But the lease is paid…through the end of the year, I think," Rachel said.

"That's right. I just have to tell you it won't be renewed." Morris' eyes slid away. "They said…I'm sorry to put it this way…They said they can't do business with a…a felon."

"For God's sake! Aren't people innocent until proven guilty anymore? I didn't do it, Dan. I swear it."

"I believe you. I do. But I don't make the decisions. I sure don't know where we're going to find space for all those cars, either."

"And I doubt you'll find a nearby helipad." Her anger surfaced along with a desire to make Dan, as a representative of Jefferson Hospital, even more uncomfortable.

"We won't be using this one much longer anyway. Couple weeks ago the order went down to the physical plant folks to drop everything and get our own pad back in shape. We're just waiting for the inspector now."

"I see." Rachel had never billed the medical center for the frequent use of the pad, thinking it a good will gesture to keep her new client happy. She made a mental note to bill them for that extra use now.

◇◇◇

Each of the following three days, Rachel visited loan brokers and picked up applications. She tried to fill out the papers while she was on duty in the booth, but she couldn't concentrate. After most of her clients had picked up their cars, she pushed the talk button on her phone and dialed the number of Hank's cell phone. The voice mail picked up.

She imagined him taking out the phone, seeing her name and number on the readout, and turning off the ringer.

Had he heard about her arrest? Had word spread to the water agency? Did everyone know? How long before her other clients would decide they didn't want to do business with a thief?

She went up to the apartment. When she finally finished filling out the loan applications, it was time to close the garage.

But she didn't do that.

Instead, she got into her own car, took Beverly north a mile or so, and pulled into a strip mall. The neon light in the bright window was blinking *Budweiser*.

She didn't want beer.

She wanted vodka. The good stuff. The Russian stuff you could put in the freezer and it would go down like liquid silver, with a cold burn all the way. Something with a name that ended in O-V and cost a small fortune.

The store was brightly lit, the spirits arranged in alphabetical order. Vodka wasn't hard to find. With an almost trance-like intensity, Rachel examined each bottle carefully and chose Danilov. She wasn't sure whether she picked it because it was the most expensive, or because it had the ugliest label—a somewhat emaciated, weak-chinned gentleman with a pince nez perched upon his nose, and the word vodka spelled with barely recognizable letters, "BODKA."

She paid, watched the clerk place the bottle first in a brown paper bag, then into a yellow plastic one.

Putting the bottle under the frayed army blanket she kept in the back of her old Civic, Rachel told herself the blanket would keep it from rolling around. But another part of her knew quite well the real purpose of the blanket was to hide the bottle—just in case someone was there when she got back—her dad, Irene, Goldie. Or maybe Hank made another quick trip down from Sacramento to ask for his ring back.

Wouldn't want anyone to know she was drinking again.

She pulled into her usual slot. The garage was mostly empty, except for eleven vehicles whose owners were out of town. Sometimes people took a shuttle to and from an airport and arranged to leave their cars overnight.

She went through the garage-closing ritual, hearing the metal sections of the huge main doors clank into place, then locking those and the pedestrian doors.

That done, she retraced her way back to her car, opened the hatch, took out the yellow plastic bag, and walked up the ramp. The night lights shone in dusty yellow triangles along the walls. The muffled echo of her own footsteps seemed eerie, and twice she stopped to be sure she wasn't hearing other footsteps as well.

Normally Rachel prowled the garage beaming a flashlight into most dark corners to be sure some street person hadn't gone to sleep there, but the trip to the liquor store had up-ended her routine.

In the apartment, she removed the bottle from its brown paper sheath. Seeing there wasn't much room in the freezer, she threw away the remains of a pint of ice cream, moved a Healthy Choice frozen dinner into the refrigerator, and laid the bottle with its clear liquid and ugly label across the ice cube trays.

The vodka would chill perfectly in about an hour. In the meantime, she would heat the Healthy Choice in the micro while looking forward to a much less healthy choice.

She overnuked the dinner. The broad, flat noodles were dry and chewy, but she had to eat. Booze on an empty stomach was not a good idea. For that matter, booze in her stomach at all was not a good idea.

She changed into her night shirt.

Forty minutes after she had put the bottle in the freezer, she took it out, put it on the coffee table and sat down on the sofa. Why wait? Get it over with so she could stop thinking about it.

She got up again and turned off all the lights. The streetlights outside the window were enough to see by.

She didn't really want to see much, anyway. Staring at the bottle, Rachel tried to savor the look of it, the fact of it. She waited for the thrill of anticipation. It didn't come.

All her good efforts, good intentions and hard work had come to this. If she couldn't prove someone had planted that OxyContin on her—and how could she prove it?—she was looking at jail time. Where would they send her? A state prison? Chino? She didn't know anything about the jail system, but she soon might be finding out a lot more than she wanted to know.

And there sure wouldn't be any icy vodka there.

She deserved something nice for herself.

And she was going to have it.

Reaching for the bottle, Rachel felt the chill coming from it. She sat back before touching it and propped her bare feet on the edge of the coffee table.

She should drink it soon, or the chill would be gone.

She sat there for a long time.

Then she reached for the bottle.

This time, she picked it up.

Chapter Thirty

The bottle was cold. The streetlight from the window lit the big squarish letters that spelled BODKA.

After a long moment, Rachel stood up. Holding the bottle by the neck, she opened the apartment door and went out into the garage in her bare feet.

Shadows danced like gremlins across the floor.

She walked over to the wall opposite her apartment door and slammed the bottle of vodka against the concrete wall.

A couple of drops splashed on her bare ankles when it shattered. The odor of alcohol enveloped her.

Carefully, Rachel backed away, toward her apartment. She would have to get her shoes and clean up the mess. One of her clients might get a piece of glass in a tire.

A sliver stabbed her thumb while she was mopping up the last of the alcohol with a paper towel. She plucked it out with tweezers, and put on a Band-Aid. Then she changed back into her jeans and sweater and went out. Was Goldie working tonight? She couldn't remember.

She had been sitting on the bench thinking dark thoughts for nearly an hour before she saw Marvin Porter, the relief cleaning crew supervisor, and remembered it was Goldie's night off. As she got up, Peter, one of the kids on the crew, crossed the street toward her. He was carrying something.

He reached her breathless, his round face all grin.

"Hi, Peter. What is it?"

"Miss Golda not work today."

"Yes, I know. I had forgotten, but now I remember."

"You have los' your purse," he said.

"Yes," Rachel said, then corrected herself. Goldie had told her not to "mess with the kids," to tell them the truth and not talk down to them. "No. I didn't lose it. Someone stole it. Right off my shoulder. They cut the straps and took it."

"Gypsies," Peter said wisely.

"How did you know?" she asked him.

"Irene said."

"You know Irene?"

Peter nodded and held out what he was carrying—an Albertson's grocery bag with something inside. "For you." He turned to go back across the street.

"Peter, look both ways!" Rachel shouted after him.

"No cars," he called back and kept running.

It was true. There were no cars. There weren't many at this hour. But Rachel worried that one day when he didn't look, there would be.

When he got to the other side, Peter turned, waved, then disappeared into the InterUrban Water Authority headquarters, where the crew was cleaning offices.

Rachel sat down on the bench. The sight of the bag's contents made something prickle behind her eyes.

It was a purse. Not her purse and not a new purse, but a leather one. And nice. No telling where Peter might have gotten it. His older brother was once a thief and if he was out of jail, he might be back at his old tricks. But at the moment, Rachel didn't care. Both eyes welled, but only one lone tear escaped.

Down's Syndrome folks may be the lucky ones, she thought. For some reason, the tears made her feel better.

◇◇◇

The voice on the phone was unctuous. "Rachel Chavez, please."

"Speaking."

"Milton Price. I represent Jefferson Medical Center. It seems there is a problem with the billing for the use of the helicopter pad on the roof of your garage."

"What problem?"

"The leasing contract calls for the charge to be based on usage."

"I am basing it on usage. Your client has sent parcels regularly, almost daily, weekdays. And I'm only charging for two deliveries a week, although there have been at least twice that."

"You are billing through the end of the contract. Which I am told, by the way, will not be renewed."

"I have been advised that it will not be renewed," she said, her anger turning cold. "They paid for the parking spaces in advance, so I thought it would be appropriate to bill the helipad use the same way."

"Jefferson Medical Center will not be using the helipad after November fourth."

◇◇◇

That next evening, after most of the cars were gone, Rachel again left the garage, this time on foot.

She hadn't asked Irene to sit on duty. Hardly anything went on between six-thirty and ten, when she closed, just a few workaholics picking up their cars. She hated to deprive Irene of the money, but until this awful drug mess was cleared up, she wasn't sure she could afford the cost.

It was nearly dark, but she was going only a few blocks and she would ask someone to give her a ride back to the garage.

There was no way to get there without going three blocks out of her way or walking past the hospital. Rounding a blind corner of Jefferson's medical office high-rise, she nearly collided with someone who was also cutting the corner tight.

"Oops. Sorry," she said, reddening when she saw it was Gordon Cox. Did he know? And worse, if Gordon knew, Gabe knew. Of course they knew. The whole world must. Everyone at Jefferson anyway.

But Gordon didn't act like anything odd had happened since last they met. Instead of avoiding her eyes, he tapped her arm, smiling as though delighted to see her. "Rachel. Gabe and I were just saying we've been missing you. Are you out for a stroll? Do you have time for a drink?"

"N-no," she stuttered, "I…uh…I have an appointment. Maybe some other time. Thanks, though." She was grateful he wasn't shunning her. But surely he knew. He had to.

"Will you be long? Maybe we could go after. I mean Gabe hasn't left yet. We could all meet at the Pig later."

Rachel shook her head and said something that was at least half true. "I'd love to, Gordon, but I can't tonight. I'll be at least an hour or so, and then it'll be time to close the garage."

"Some other time then? Like maybe next week? I'll talk to Gabe."

"Okay," she said. "Sorry. I've got to go. I'm late."

Turning onto Wilshire, she could see the white brick storefront two blocks down. She broke into a jog and arrived a little out of breath. The front windows and the door had been painted white, but yellow light shone through the glass in the small window above the door.

She pushed the door handle and went in.

Chapter Thirty-one

The aroma of fresh coffee permeated the room. A table along one wall held two aluminum urns, one with a handwritten sign that read *Coffee*, the other marked *Hot Water*. Ten or twelve people were milling about, chatting, and sipping from Styrofoam cups. All eyes swung toward the door as it opened.

A tall coffee-colored man with short-cropped hair and modish steel-rimmed rectangular eyeglasses moved toward Rachel. He held out both hands and took hers. He wore a three-piece suit, white shirt and striped tie. He was a police captain who credited his rank to an early slide into alcoholism, which, as he put it, gave him enough time to wriggle out and still have a life. "Rachel, this is wonderful. It's been a long time."

"Hi, Brian," she said. "Too long, I'm afraid."

"Oh-oh," said the man who had come up behind Brian. "Does that mean we've been naughty?"

"No, Miles," she said. "Well, not exactly, but almost."

"A miss is good as a mile." Miles was a dental hygienist. Rachel figured he spent his salary with his employer. The teeth he flashed looked too perfect to be natural. He was short and so blond it was hard not to credit bleach, especially since his eyebrows were handsomely dark. His eyes were the deep blue of special contacts and his biceps spoke of lifted weights. Lots of weights. He wore spotless red sweats and she was sure he never sweated into them.

Someone touched Rachel's shoulder as she was opening the spigot of the coffee urn over a Styrofoam cup. "Carol!" she said when she turned and saw the heavy-set woman with very thick glasses. The bookish look was for real. Carol was a librarian.

"How nice to see you," the woman said. "It's been months, well...since Lonnie...."

"I guess it has. Nice to see you, too." Lonnie had worked for Rachel. He had died from an overdose of something he thought was a street drug.

"Well, cutie. It's about time you showed that pretty face." This man looked to be in his twenties. He was small, slight, with dark hair and a neat mustache. He was dressed to the teeth and sported a navy blue ascot.

"I just couldn't stay away from you any longer, Roger."

"Frankly my dear, I do give a damn," Roger said, taking her hand theatrically and kissing the back of it.

"Favor?" Rachel asked. "I came on foot. Can you drive me back to the garage after?"

"Sure."

There were a number of faces she didn't know, and she realized it had been a long time since she had come to a meeting.

"Okay, ladies and gentlemen, take your seats, it's time to start." Brian was standing behind a podium in front of two semi-circles of folding chairs.

People immediately began to head for second-row chairs. A few sat at the ends of the first row. Rachel looked back toward the door as a gust of air entered with a latecomer—a large man with dark hair and a belly that strained at his belt. Manny.

"Tonight we have someone with us whom we haven't seen in a while," Brian announced when the room had quieted. "Rachel? Would you like to say something?"

She got to her feet and made her way to the podium.

"My name is Rachel. This is my fourteen hundred and twenty-first day of sobriety—I think that's right." She paused, then said in a quavery voice, "I almost didn't make it past fourteen hundred and twenty." She rested her elbow on the podium and put her hand to her forehead.

The room went totally silent. Carol started to get up from her seat in the second row, but sat back down again.

"I've been accused of stealing a drug called OxyContin from a hospital."

There was a collective intake of breath in the room.

"I didn't do it. I'd barely heard of OxyContin."

The room exhaled.

"What I did do, though, was last night I bought a bottle of vodka. Danilov vodka. Real class. I put it in the freezer and I was practically drooling when I took it out."

The crowd gave an appreciative chuckle.

"Then I took it and bashed it against a concrete wall."

"You go, girl," someone said.

"Yes!" said another.

"Thanks," Rachel said. "It made an awful mess, though. And I cut myself cleaning it up. That's the closest I've come to blowing it since I got into AA.

"I started hitting the bottle really hard after my mom died. She'd been thrown from a horse on our farm up in the delta. She was in bad shape from that, but it didn't kill her. What killed her was a flu virus that I gave her. I picked it up shopping—shopping, for God's sake—in San Francisco.

"My dad's a gambler. That same summer, he sort of lost the farm in a poker game, so I couldn't go back to college for my senior year. Instead I ran a man and his two little kids off the freeway and into a ditch. A nice alternative to college, don't you think?

"Thank God it just shook them up and made some bruises," Rachel went on.

"I only had a blood alcohol content of point-one-four when the cops pulled me over. I was barely beginning to feel good. And I had five ounces of crystal on the floor of the back seat. After all, if you drink as much as I did, you need a lot of speed to wake you up. That was enough to get me free room and board at County."

The room was absolutely silent.

Rachel cleared her throat and went on. "An old family friend hired a wheeler-dealer attorney who got me off on a technicality. "Anyway," she finished, "I've been away too long. I thought I was over…it. Not over being an alcoholic, but you know, the feeling that a drink will solve anything, make anything better. But I never dreamed someone would put a bottle of drugs in my pocket and I would be arrested for something I didn't do." She looked over the room. "Thanks for being here tonight."

She left the podium and refilled her coffee cup at the urn. Three or four people patted her shoulder when she sat down.

"Next?" Brian was saying. No one got up, so he went on to tell his own tale, including his pouring the garden hose in his garage full of vodka—vodka was the hard liquor of choice for many because it leaves little telltale odor on the breath.

Rachel read the twelve steps written on a chalkboard hanging on the wall next to the podium. She wasn't sure which step she was on. Maybe that was part of the problem.

"That was a magic garage," Brian was saying. "My wife couldn't figure out how I could go in there sober and come out drunk. She searched the place from top to bottom. But she couldn't find the bottle. That's because there was no bottle. Then one day she accidentally knocked the hose off its hook…

"She has this cast iron frying pan. That's when I decided it would be better to quit the booze than to get beaten to death with a frying pan."

The people on the folding chairs nodded and laughed a little. Their stories had different words, but they all told the same sort of story.

"I've been sober for twenty-two years and four months," Brian said. "I don't know how many days that is." He smiled at Rachel, and sat down as Manny went to the podium.

When the last person had spoken, they all formed a circle, held hands, and chanted, "Keep coming back."

Roger drove her home. "You just wanted a ride in my Maserati." He wasn't kidding. The low-slung car looked and sounded like it belonged on a race track. He did makeup for some of the big studios.

"How many horses?" Rachel asked.

Roger laughed. "You can't count that high."

He pulled up to the sidewalk door of the garage and kissed her on the nose when she thanked him. Then was off in a roar of engine revs.

Feeling better, but totally exhausted, Rachel locked up the garage and decided to take the elevator for once.

She knew something was wrong the moment she reached the top level.

Chapter Thirty-two

When the elevator opened, the door to the apartment rattled a little, then swung a few inches on its hinges.

She had closed and locked it. Hadn't she? Surely she hadn't been that distraught.

"Clancy," she called, dashing into the living room, remembering another burglary when the big tomcat had gone missing. But this time he was hiding behind the sofa, all but his orange tail, which gave him away. He emerged at the sound of her voice, his grape-green eyes still big with alarm, the way they got when a car backfired in the garage.

The rooms looked normal. Almost. This burglar had been careful, even polite. Only small things like the door ajar, a few books oddly askew in the bookcase, a light on in the bathroom, testified to a visit by a stranger. There was no apparent sign of haste.

Rachel sat down on the sofa and patted her knees. Clancy landed in her lap in one eager leap, pushed his nose against her chin and began a throaty, hesitant purr.

"Who was it?" she whispered, patting his head, scratching behind his ears, calming him. "And why?" The last burglary had sort of made sense. She'd hidden something that could identify a killer. But why now? She hadn't hidden anything. She didn't have anything to hide. Then she remembered the sliced-off strap across her shoulder and her missing purse.

Rachel hadn't been carrying the keys to the garage that day when she and Goldie had lunched at the hospital cafeteria—the day the gypsies had performed in the lunchroom and absconded with wallets, handbags, and cash from the register. But the key to the apartment had been in her purse along with her driver's license giving the address of the garage. Had they now come to her apartment to see what more they could steal?

Why hadn't she had the lock changed?

She hadn't felt threatened by the theft of her purse, just severely inconvenienced. Did gypsies stoop to common burglary? Maybe they had sold her purse with everything still in it, or taken the few dollars from her wallet and tossed the rest in a Dumpster somewhere. Given the address, someone could find the garage, but how would they know about the apartment on the top floor?

Unless the finder of the key was a client.

It seemed unlikely that the business and medical people who parked at her garage would be doing Dumpster diving or burglary on the side.

She checked to be sure the apartment door was locked and bolted. A frown burning lines in her face, she began a systematic search of the three rooms she called home.

A kitchen drawer was slightly open, the stack of towels in the bathroom linen closet was at a different angle than she usually left it. But nothing seemed to be missing.

Still, there was something eerie about the whole place. Something that made the hair on her arms prickle.

When the phone rang, she leapt to her feet, heart racing. Her eyes fluttered closed when she heard the voice.

"Sorry I haven't called. You can't imagine how busy it's been up here." Hank.

"It's been busy here, too," Rachel said wanting to tell him about her arrest, how her life had slammed into a wall, and equally wanting to avoid saying anything at all about it.

"They're giving me a three-day weekend to make up for all the late nights," he said, and she could tell he was yawning.

Late nights? With whom?

"I can catch a flight late Thursday or early Friday. Can you get away from that god-awful garage for three days?" It was now Wednesday.

"It isn't god-awful. It's—"

"I know. I know. I'm sorry. That was a stupid thing to say. But you're so married to that place."

"It supports me, Hank. I am married to it."

"The question is, can you get away for a few days?"

Rachel hesitated. "I guess," she said tentatively. "Maybe."

"I'm desperate for someplace quiet," he said. "I need to just lie in a heap and listen to the ocean, or maybe the wind in the trees in the mountains."

"God, that sounds good." The words escaped her lips. She didn't mean to sound so eager.

"Are we on, then?"

"I'm not sure…I'll have to talk to Irene…."

"What else would she be doing? Shopping on Rodeo Drive?"

"That would surprise me less than you think. She does go to Santa Monica and Venice to do fortunes on the beach."

"I'll call you Friday morning."

She sensed he was hanging up. "Wait…It isn't so much whether Irene is available, the problem is I'm having some financial problems. I'm not sure I can afford to pay her and I don't like to ask her to wait for the money."

"For God's sake, Rache. With expenses paid, I've been making more than I can spend up here. Let me pay her."

"I'm not comfortable with that."

"Look," Hank said, his voice rising, "this is a dire thing for me. Don't ask me why. I don't know. I have this awful feeling that I'm losing you, I'm exhausted, my life is falling apart. Please. Just this once, let me do something for you. For me. Let me pay Irene."

She thought about that. "Okay."

◇◇◇

Rachel had made a list of things to do and was getting ready for bed when she saw the corner of the bottom drawer of her dresser was out of line. Had she checked that drawer? She was almost too tired to think.

She opened the drawer. Just her turtlenecks. Nothing missing. Who would want a worn turtleneck?

Wait. She *had* hidden something in that drawer.

She slipped her hand under the shirts. Nothing.

She had hidden something there. Something she actually had stolen. The medical record, the papers from the bed in that peculiar ward at the hospital.

Chapter Thirty-three

Despite the unease about someone rooting through her belongings, Rachel woke more refreshed than she had felt in a long time. An AA meeting could do that. She hurried into her clothes and gulped down her breakfast. Thursday was going to be a busy day. She had to get a locksmith out. That would probably set her back a bundle. But maybe this would be the day she'd land a good mortgage on the garage.

She called Alvin's Lock Shop first. Alvin told her she probably wouldn't have to get a new lock, just a re-jigger, as he called it, of the old lock and a new key.

Next, she dialed Irene, still marveling at the woman's ownership of a cell phone. Rachel was leaving a message when someone knocked on the booth's side window. Gabe.

Her blood rose until it was pounding in her cheeks.

He gave her a small tentative wave.

"Hi. What can I do for you?" Rachel's words felt a little tight coming out.

He shifted his weight from one foot to the other. "I just thought I should come by and say I don't believe a word of it."

She blinked her amazement, then managed a weak smile. "Well, thanks. I figured everyone over there was sure I was guilty."

"It's totally insane," he said. "Why would you do something like that?"

"I don't even know why anyone would bother to steal Oxy-Contin."

"It's a pain reliever."

"It's not a street drug or a party drug. Why would anyone steal a pain killer? It's a whole lot easier to go to a doctor and get a prescription."

Gabe looked at her as if he were sizing up her statement. "Are you as naive as you sound?"

Rachel lifted one shoulder. "I guess I must be."

"Ever heard of morphine?"

"Of course."

"Pain killers are among the most addictive drugs around. What makes OxyContin so street worthy is that it apparently provides a striking sense of euphoria along with pain relief."

An exiting car squeezed by Gabe, and Rachel told him to come up the step into the booth. The space was small. She stepped back and hoisted herself to the countertop, leaving the stool for him.

He didn't take it. Instead, he drew a toothpick from his shirt pocket, stripped the paper from it, lodged it between his teeth, and said around it, "People are afraid of heroin, but they think if doctors prescribe this stuff, it must be safe. They don't realize you can be addicted in as little as five days."

"Seems like pretty short-term pain relief."

"It's mostly prescribed only for severe back injury and for terminal cancer patients. OxyContin is why that nut-case assemblyman resigned and went into rehab after getting caught conning doctors into prescribing it for him. And who knows what else people do with it? Druggies are very creative, always coming up with something new. They may mix it with something else and snort it or shoot it. I hear it sells for about a dollar per milligram on the street. That bottle you had—a hundred of the eighty milligram—is the highest dosage. We get about ten bucks a pill."

"You mean I had a thousand dollars' worth in that bottle they found in my pocket?"

"You bet. And that's retail. On the street a hundred doses might fetch eight thousand."

"Jesus." Rachel examined his face as she asked, "Did it come from your pharmacy?"

"Apparently it did. It's a class two narcotic, so we keep it under lock and key. We did an inventory and a bottle of that size and type was missing."

"You keep that stuff under lock and key?"

"Of course." Gabe shifted the toothpick from one side of his mouth to the other. "People hold up drugstores to get their hands on class twos."

"But surely not your pharmacy. You're inside a hospital."

"We have a door to the street."

"You have security guards."

"We also have a lot of pretty sick, screwed-up people, and not all of them walk in off the street, or, for that matter, are patients."

"What are you talking about?"

Gabe scratched an ear. "Accepted rule of thumb is that about ten percent of physicians are impaired. My guess is that it's even higher. More often than not, impaired means substance abuse."

"You mean ten percent of the doctors over there are addicts?"

"Probably not that many. Some are alcoholics."

"Jesus. That's reassuring."

"Yeah."

"Why would that be?"

"Practicing medicine ain't for sissies. They may bury their mistakes but I don't think they ever forget them. Or stop worrying about making a career-ending screw-up. After all, they're dealing with human lives."

"What's the figure for pharmacists?"

Gabe raised his eyebrows and dipped his chin. "About the same, I guess." He gave the toothpick a few quick bites.

"Thanks for letting me know you don't believe I took that bottle. That means a lot to me."

"I don't see how you could have. Unless someone left it on the counter. I can't say that's never happened—a class two left on a counter—but it's unlikely. We're pretty careful. I've never seen that happen at Jefferson." Gabe bit down hard on the toothpick.

Rachel thought he looked sweet and didn't like thinking so.

"Who *could* have taken that bottle? Who has access?"

"All the pharmacists. Some of the techs."

"Doctors?"

"Some, yes. Maybe. But access isn't necessarily the whole point. The main question is who would want to plant something like that on you, and why?"

Rachel had opened her mouth to say she had some thoughts on the why if not the who, when Irene appeared at the garage entrance and pushed her cart up to the booth.

"Hello, dear girl. I got your message and thought I would just reply in person. No sense running up the cell bill when I've got two perfectly good feet."

"Good." Rachel turned to Gabe. "I guess I should get back to work."

He gave her an affable nod.

Rachel watched him stroll up the ramp toward his parking place. She'd have to wait to ask his take on her suspicions about whether someone would plant that bottle of pills on her because of her nosing around about those boys or that ward.

Chapter Thirty-four

Chez Chic restaurant was in a one-story, cleverly artificially aged building on a pedestrian-only street of shops in Valencia. Marty had told her to ask the hostess for E.J.

Rachel wished she had changed out of her jeans when she saw the white tablecloths and cobalt blue napkins. She'd expected something like a bistro, hadn't realized a restaurant in Valencia might be this upscale. Especially one that apparently was a front for a gangster.

The time was 1:20. Nine diners were finishing their meals at tables near the windows. The hostess wore a blue dress that matched the napkins, gold helix earrings, and a hairdo that rose in a swirl on top of her head.

Rachel asked to see E.J.

"Ah…yes," the hostess eyed Rachel up and down as if appraising her for purchase.

"You will please be seated." The accent didn't sound French, but the woman was certainly exotic. She showed Rachel to a table at the back of the room, away from the other diners, and beckoned a waiter, who brought a stemmed glass containing ice and a slice of lemon.

He poured water over the ice, causing the lemon to swim, and when Rachel didn't take her napkin, he unfurled it with a flourish, handed it to her and asked, "Madame is alone today?" He wore a single earring, and a big-sleeved shirt of soft, white fabric.

"Yes," Rachel said, feeling grubbier by the minute. "I won't be eating...dining. I'm just here to see E.J."

She assumed E.J. was in fact El Jefe. But El Jefe in a French restaurant? Mexican maybe, or Spanish. Indian. Moorish. American steak house. But French?

The waiter turned to look at the woman in blue and some signal passed between them. He turned back to Rachel. "It will be a few minutes. Would you like a glass of wine while you wait? We have a very good Cabernet."

"No, thanks. The water's fine."

The waiter dipped his pointed chin. "Good." He swept up the other three napkins on the table and disappeared into a hall opposite the door. Apparently, even if one wasn't going to dine, the table must be properly adorned.

Making a mental note never to eat there, Rachel examined the mural on the wall—a copy of Monet's painting of his garden in Giverny. She remembered it from her art history class at Stanford. In those days, she didn't exactly hunt out snobby restaurants, but when she found herself in one, she didn't feel like a peasant at a grand banquet.

Wondering if paintings were protected by something like a copyright or whether anyone could copy at whim brought her to the realization that if El Jefe owned this place, copied paintings, even if illegal, would be the least of it.

What was she doing here? Was she that desperate?

She was.

If she didn't get a loan with a decent interest rate soon.... Well, she didn't want to think about that.

The waiter reappeared. "You will come with me."

No more *Madame*. Wondering what that subtle change meant, Rachel got up and followed him past the other diners, past the entrance, into a short hall where an elevator stood open.

An elevator? The waiter entered the car with her and the door closed.

Rachel pushed down sudden panic. Where was he taking her in an elevator in a one-story building? If she went missing, how long it would it be before someone noticed?

There was only one button on the panel. He touched it. The car descended, slid to a silent stop and opened its doors without another move from the waiter. He gestured for her to leave the elevator and the doors closed behind her.

The room was long, with ceiling and brick walls painted white; the floor was chalky white stone tile. There were no windows but all the white made the space seem airy.

A hulking figure sat at a large desk at the end of the room. There were low flood lights in the corners that made it hard to see anything but a silhouette, and Rachel remembered El Jefe's penchant for that kind of lighting.

An arm motioned. A raspy voice, not exactly menacing, but clearly as much in charge as any storm trooper ever was, "Come. Sit."

It seemed like a long walk to the desk. She perched gingerly on the edge of the large padded white leather chair that faced it. The desk was bare. A computer, on a matching teak credenza behind the desk, looked pristine, little if ever used.

El Jefe leaned forward. "And how is your papa?"

Rachel cleared her throat. "He's okay. He's fine."

"He tells me that you need some money."

"A loan," Rachel said quickly. "I have collateral."

"A parking garage," El Jefe said solemnly. "How much? The borrowing. How much?"

She took a deep breath. "I guess about fifteen thousand dollars."

"For what do you need this money?"

Rachel brushed a strand of hair away from her forehead. Apparently Marty had left the explanation to her. She swallowed. "I was arrested for something I didn't do. I need the money to pay the bail bondsman and to help with the attorney's fees. I had to put up the deed to the garage and…and…."

"You are not happy with that."

"No. I don't really understand how it works and I don't trust this guy. The bondsman."

"What is his name?"

She told him.

El Jefe nodded three times, pausing to eye her steadily each time he brought his chin up. A look passed over his face. "You let me know if he does anything he should not."

The look was not unlike that of a junkyard dog. Rachel didn't know whether to be comforted or threatened. Or both.

He took a pad of paper from a drawer, wrote something on it, tore off the page, folded it into quarters and handed it to her. "You do not need an appointment. He expects you this afternoon, after three, before six."

"Thank you."

"*De nada.* Is nothing. *Poquito.* Your papa was very kind to Emilio. My son is now wanting to become an *abogado.* A lawyer. Your papa give Emilio back the money he win from him. He let Emilio have his face. In that way, he maybe even save his life."

Did he mean he might have killed his son for taking his college money and playing poker? Rachel decided she didn't want to know the answer. She rose from her chair.

"No," the big man said. "Sit."

She obeyed, like a well trained spaniel, and hoped he would not command her to fetch something or roll over.

"*Almuerzo?*"

"I'm sorry…?"

"Did you eat?"

She shook her head, hoping the failure to eat was not a punishable offense.

He punched a button on the phone and barked into it, "*Coq au vin. Dos,*" then said to Rachel, "I do not like eating alone. The *coq au vin* is very good. It is Provence." His French accent seemed better than his English one.

The waiter appeared almost immediately, as if by magic. Had he been waiting in the closed elevator?

He opened a nearly invisible door in the white wall and withdrew a handsome wooden folding table, which he set up in front of Rachel, then disappeared. This time she heard the faint whirring of the elevator.

"This is very kind of you." Her mouth was so dry her tongue stuck to the words.

El Jefe's eyes were on her face. He said nothing, but his eyes softened.

"Could I ask you a question?"

"Of course," he said, seeming to almost smile.

"Why a French restaurant?"

"Because French is the food of *importancia*. Of *importante* people. And who would expect to find such as I am here?" Now he did smile. A broad smile that flashed even white teeth.

Charmed against her will, Rachel ventured another question: "Why do you need an elevator to go only one floor?"

"Because an elevator can be stopped."

Suddenly she understood the degree to which he controlled entry and exit. Among other things, he probably didn't have to worry about hidden microphones.

When they finished eating she said, "That was the best meal I've had in years, maybe ever."

He beamed.

The waiter cleared the table and again disappeared.

She rose to go. "I have to be somewhere between three and six."

"Yes." El Jefe nodded. "You tell Abe to treat you good."

The elevator doors opened and she realized he must have a control at the desk.

Chapter Thirty-five

Rachel didn't open the paper he had given her until she got back to her car. It was white with blue lines. On it was written *Abraham Junipera*, followed by *Senior Vice President*, and the name of a large, well-known bank. The address was on Hill Street, downtown.

She got there at four. She had gone back to her apartment, changed clothes and taken a cab. Parking in that area was impossible.

A receptionist with hair blond to the point of white and wearing a dress as tight as it was short showed her to an office, then disappeared.

Abraham Junipera was a tall thin man, probably fifty-something, but already one could see how he would look at eighty. Eyes that seemed to have been gouged into his face darted from Rachel to somewhere behind her, as if he expected someone else to join them, or was afraid someone might.

He spoke her name in a deep, sonorous voice. When she agreed the name was hers, he picked up his phone and murmured something into it she couldn't hear, then suggested she close the door.

Rachel pushed the knob a little too hard and it slammed.

Junipera's eyes widened with something that almost looked like fear. He gestured to two chairs that resembled the leather seats in a Bentley or Rolls Royce.

She chose one and sat. Her eyes took in the huge window behind him. "Nice view," she said to break the silence, although she sensed he was as nervous as she. What favor could a man like this owe El Jefe?

He brushed his broad pale blue tie as if feeling for stray cookie crumbs.

Rachel decided to just wade in. "I assume you know why I'm here?"

"Of course." He sat up very straight and handed her a piece of paper. It was a check, complete with stub, made out to her, for twenty-five thousand dollars.

She stared at it, then looked up. Junipera was rising from his chair. She hastened to rise from hers. "This is more than I need."

"You can't be sure of that. It's best if you don't have to come back."

"Don't you want me to sign something?"

"That isn't necessary. You have a guarantor."

"Oh. I guess I do."

He moved toward the door as if he were leaving instead of she.

"But what are the terms? And where do I send the payments?"

He shook his head. "No payments." He handed her another, smaller piece of paper with a telephone number written on it. "If and when you have the entire balance, telephone that number and we can arrange for you to bring me a check."

"But I don't know how much interest...."

"No interest."

"But...how long...?"

His narrow shoulders swallowed most of his neck in a shrug. "Let us say three years. If you need an extension, call that number."

"Okay." Feeling a bit like Alice in Wonderland, she wondered if she might step out into the hall and disappear forever.

Junipera's smile lit the caverns in his long face. He opened the door as he might for someone who couldn't be expected to find the doorknob herself.

"Thank you." She held out her hand.

The limp way he took it made her think he would probably go down the hall to wash up before returning to his desk.

◇◇◇

"So that's all?" Goldie asked.

Rachel had closed the garage at ten, then crossed the street to InterUrban Water headquarters and waited on the front steps for Goldie. Now they sat in the Merry Maids van eating some of the Oreos that Goldie always kept there, and drinking raspberry iced tea from a thermos.

"What do you mean, all? I've got a check for twenty-five thousand dollars. It's probably hot."

"How can it be hot? It's from a bank."

"But I didn't sign anything. You ever hear of getting a loan from a bank without signing any papers?"

"Nope. Lucky you."

Rachel helped herself to another cookie. "It can't be on the up and up. Stuff like this isn't done by verbal agreement. I've been filling out loan application papers. I keep expecting them to demand a hair sample, a spit sample, and maybe an MRI scan to be sure I'll live long enough to pay everything back."

"No urine sample?"

"Very funny."

Goldie handed Rachel a paper towel to use for a napkin. "I wish somebody would just hand me a check for twenty-five grand."

"I'm going to pay it back."

"I'm sure you will."

"You think I should add interest?"

"I think I would do exactly like he told you, no more, no less."

"I could skip the country."

"They know your father. At least one of them does."

"True. Besides, twenty-five thousand doesn't go all that far these days."

"So don't look a gift horse in the eye."

"Goldie!"

"I just wanted to see if you were listening. Sometimes you do go on and on." Goldie brushed the Oreo crumbs from her shirt. "So how's my favorite hunk?"

"Hank?"

"Who else? I've never seen the other one. You are some woman pussyfootin' around two guys."

"Hank is coming down for a three-day weekend. Starting tomorrow. He wants to go to Ventura. Get a place near the beach."

"Mmm-hmm. And of course you said no."

"Wrong."

Goldie gave her a narrow-eyed look. "You tell him about the arrest thing and all?"

"Not yet."

"Mmmmm."

"I will. It's just not easy to do on the phone. I want to be able to see his face."

"Well, do it early," Goldie said. "Putting it off will just spoil the whole weekend. You gonna to put that ring back on?"

"I guess. I didn't want to wear it when I went to see El Jefe or that banker. I didn't want them to think there was anyone else I could ask."

"You wanted to appear helpless."

"No, just, you know, with my back against the wall. Which is the truth."

Goldie let out a laugh. "You gotta wonder what that El Jefe of yours did for that banker dude that he would just write out a check for twenty-five large and give it to a complete stranger."

"Maybe he knocked off somebody who was troubling Mr. Junipera."

Chapter Thirty-six

Rachel was surprised by how glad she was to see Hank.

She was still half asleep the next morning and hadn't seen his green Mustang drive up the ramp. He startled her by tapping her on the shoulder as she was bending over trying to get the keys, the jimmy, the phone numbers and everything else ready for Irene to garage-sit.

"My God! Did you come in last night and sleep in the garage?"

"What a way to greet a guy who's been gone for weeks."

Her brain locked on the realization that she had not restored her engagement ring to its proper place on her finger. Flustered, she said, "Has it been weeks?"

"You don't know?" He looked so like a puzzled little boy that Rachel couldn't help putting her arms around him. She pulled him close and kissed him on the chin. His beard was prickly. "I can't leave till about ten. That's when I asked Irene to be here."

"That'll work," Hank said. "I just drove down from Burbank. I need to go home and pack a few more clothes. I'll come back about ten."

"You came down here before you went home from the airport?" Hank lived in La Crescenta. "That's kind of the long way around from Burbank Airport."

"I wanted to see you, you silly thing."

She hung her head and shot him a smile.

But he was now frowning. "Did you lose it?"

"What?"

He nodded toward her left hand.

The lie just rolled right off her tongue. "Oh. No. I took it off to clean it. It's upstairs in the bathroom."

◇◇◇

"Dear girl, it is not as hard to run this place as you seem to believe," Irene told her. "One would think you were leaving a baby with me, not a parking garage."

"It is my baby. You can't imagine how I worry about it. If something goes bad here, there's nothing…I have nothing else."

"Don't be silly. You have your Pa, your friends, and that estimable dear boy. Yes, estimable." Irene smiled, admiring the word. "When are you two going to…you know, tie the knot?"

Rachel tensed. Was everyone in Los Angeles conspiring to get her married? "We'll set a time soon."

"I do hope so, dear girl. We're not any of us getting any younger."

Rachel was thinking she didn't need to hear that right now. She finished explaining the running of the garage for the third time.

"Yes, yes." Irene's tone politely made it clear she remembered the first two times.

"Here's the key to the apartment." Rachel handed it to her. "I do wish you would just stay there till I get back."

"I'd miss my friends in the village."

"Village?"

"On the river front, of course."

Rachel frowned. "The Los Angeles River?" The last she had known, Irene was spending her nights in MacArthur Park.

"Of course, dear girl. We move from the park now and again when the policemen don't have enough to do and pester us. I do miss the greenery. I'm scouting Elysian Park these days. I think that might be quite nice."

"By Dodger Stadium?"

"Well, not right next, you know. It's a big park."

"Is it safe where you are by the river? I've heard things are getting bad along there."

The river had long ago been paved into a concrete ditch that worked more like a storm sewer than a river, carrying water only after a heavy rainfall. Rachel often jogged along it. The so-called river's banks were sometimes dotted with clusters of cardboard boxes and supermarket carts. The clusters belonged to every type of group from transvestites to octogenarians. The boxes and carts always magically disappeared about half an hour before the cops made one of their infrequent sweeps through the area.

"Of course, it's safe, dear girl! I am with the Gray Panther settlement. One doesn't mess with the Gray Panthers, you know. Why once a thief who saw what I had in my purse took it upon himself to follow me to the village. My friends saw him coming. They knew him. One of them, Donald his name is, about eighty I do believe. Donald picked up one of our tables, tore off a leg and knocked the stranger out cold.

"The fellow bled only a little, but dead to the world, he was. We put him in a cart, pushed him down to the courthouse, and laid him by the flowers. He never bothered us again."

"No one saw an unconscious man in a grocery cart and stopped whoever was pushing it?" Rachel asked.

"Of course not."

It always amazed Rachel that the business people who frequented the downtown area could look right through the street people with a sort of selective blindness.

"Well, please feel free to use the apartment," she was saying when Hank's Mustang appeared at the garage entrance.

He stopped at the booth. "I have an idea," he said. "If you don't like it, we won't do it."

Chapter Thirty-seven

"You want to what?"

"Camp," Hank said.

"In a pup tent?"

"Not a pup tent, a pop-up tent. I haven't used it in ages, but it's a good one. It's bigger than a pup tent, and easy to put up and take down." A suggestion of a dimple twinkled at the side of his mouth.

Irene's eyes were moving from Hank's face to Rachel's, but in a rare moment of silence, she said nothing.

"But it's October. Almost November. Nights are getting chilly if not downright cold."

"We can stop at Sport Chalet in La Cañada and get you a sleeping bag. Down, like mine. If anything it'll be too warm."

"Too warm. Sleeping outside. In October."

"Not outside. In a tent."

"I haven't been camping since I was a kid. A *little* kid. Like seven or eight. I don't know *how* to camp."

"I have all the stuff. Lantern. Stove. All I need is you."

"And some food might be a good idea." Rachel's laugh made her realize how tense she had been lately and how long it was since she had felt the deep cleansing rush that laughter can bring.

"I have a cooler," Hank said. "We can stop at a grocery store."

"There won't be room in the car for me."

"Maybe we should take your car. It's a hatch. Probably does hold more."

She clapped her hands. "Okay. Let's do it."

"Good girl!" Irene smiled approvingly.

"But where?" Rachel asked. "We can't camp in LA. And we only have three days. Really only two and a half by the time we get out of here. I don't want to spend it all on the road."

Irene eyed Hank attentively. Apparently this was something she didn't know the answer to.

◇◇◇

Hank had a couple ideas. There was the beach at Point Magu near Ventura, but he wasn't sure you could actually camp on the beach and wasn't sure whether being there, but away from the beach, would be worthwhile. The other possibility was to take Angeles Crest Road north out of La Cañada into the mountains that overlooked the Los Angeles basin. Rachel had been working six days a week since arriving in Southern California and had never been to either place.

They still hadn't decided where to go when Hank drove Rachel's Honda Civic into the parking lot at Ralph's supermarket in La Crescenta. He filled their shopping cart with steaks, bread, cheese, and cold cuts.

"We couldn't eat that much in a week," Rachel said as he added bacon, eggs, and coffee.

"If you haven't camped lately, you obviously have forgotten how hungry fresh air makes you. And how good brewing coffee and sizzling bacon smells outdoors in the morning. Must be the extra oxygen or something."

"You have a coffee pot? Pans?"

"I told you, I've got the works."

At Sports Chalet, they decided where to spend the weekend.

Examining half a dozen sleeping bags, Rachel gazed longingly at a maroon bag on sale for ninety dollars.

"That's a helluva buy!" Hank turned the tag and read: "...to fifteen degrees. See? I said you wouldn't be cold. You won't be cold anyway, my dear," he leered.

Rachel laughed and clapped her hands like a child. "Let's go to the mountains then."

"If I remember right, the views from the road are spectacular," Hank said as he tossed the sleeping bag into the back seat. "We could run into a little snow this time of year. Are your tires in good shape?"

"New this spring," she said. "I don't do bald tires."

"Then we'll be fine."

Every inch of the Honda's back seat and hatch space was loaded. "Okay. We're off to see the wizard," he said as they got in the car.

The metropolis stretched to the horizon behind them until the road curved again and there was nothing but cliffs and scrub forest and the road snaking upward.

"I had no idea we could "get out of Dodge" so fast," Rachel said. "It's like being beamed up to a different planet."

"I used to camp up here about a hundred years ago when I was a kid," Hank said. "To tell the truth, I haven't been back since. This road is a hell of a lot better than it used to be."

They passed a sign that read *Ranger*, but when they drove into the parking area, the building looked empty. "Maybe there are some maps." Hank got out of the car and returned with a small brochure. "It doesn't say much, but it's better than nothing. The way they've cut funding and outsourced everything for the National Forests is criminal."

Rachel rolled down her window as they got back on the road, enjoying the wind in her face, ruffling her hair.

"I used to have a dog who did that," Hank laughed, and she punched his arm.

He hit the brakes. "That may be where my mom and I used to camp."

"Your mother taught you to camp?"

"Yep. I told you my dad went out to get some root beer and ice cream one Saturday night when I was six and never came back."

He turned onto a narrow lane, more trail than road, that cut through the scrub and pines. The Honda bounced hard and Hank slowed it to a crawl.

A gray cloud rose behind them. Rachel rolled her window up. "It's sure dry up here."

They reached what seemed like a natural turn-out for parking. "Yeah. This is it," Hank said.

A small weathered sign, that had once been blue but now had only a few traces of color left, read *Sugar Loaf.*

"The name may not be original," Hank said, "but I used to think this was the neatest place on earth. Let's walk up the trail a bit and see how it looks."

Chapter Thirty-eight

They wandered through a broad grassy area, then followed the path around a rock and into a canyon. Yellow-brown rock rose on both sides. A few determined shrubs clung here and there to the walls. The afternoon sky was deep blue. A few very white clouds peeked over the cliffs.

A little farther, the bottom fell away and they found themselves on a ledge. "Jesus," Rachel said peering down. They were suspended halfway between the top of the rocky canyon wall and the ground below. A few scrubby pines straggled up from the bottom.

Hank swung around a curve in the ledge. "I hope you don't have acrophobia."

"I don't think so. But I've never tried hanging right off the side of a cliff before."

"If I remember right, the perfect place to camp is just a little farther."

The ledge curled around a rock corner and a huge, spreading California oak appeared in a hollow below.

"Wow," Rachel said.

Hank swept aside a brittle shrub and she saw the trail. It was overgrown, and barely traversable, but it wound down to the hollow.

The oak tree's gnarled roots rode the top of the hard soil but there was a level place, and just beyond it, a small pit dug into the earth. Inside the pit were the whitish ashes of past fires. Two grayish birds strode along the ground pecking for seeds. A scrub jay landed and squawked at them.

Rachel sniffed the air. "This must be how the world smelled when it was young."

"Depends on what the meaning of fresh is." A grin cut across Hank's face.

Laughter percolated up inside Rachel. The muscles it stirred seemed surprised and she realized, for the second time that day, that she hadn't been laughing much recently.

Hank pointed to the flat spot. "So we camp here?"

"Are you sure? The car's jam-packed and at least a mile away. To say nothing of that ledge a million feet above the canyon."

"So we make several trips. We've got backpacks." He pointed at her cargo pants. "And you could probably carry half the entire load in those pockets."

Rachel was gazing at the huge tree. A breeze rattled its leaves. Its spreading limbs seemed to offer a sort of primal sense of security. "It's like we're the first white people to see this place."

"And we're only fifty or so miles from LA."

"You sure it's okay to camp here?"

Hank reached out and ruffled her hair. "Who's gonna know?"

It was nearly four by the time they stowed the last items in their backpacks. Rachel turned to Hank. "There's one more thing I want to take." She reached under the driver's seat and brought out the old thirty-eight.

"Why bother?" Hank said. "There's nothing more dangerous here than a deer or raccoon. I doubt many people even know about this place."

"No coyotes? Mountain lions? Snakes?"

"Well, I guess there could be. But I wouldn't make one of them mad by shooting at it."

"I'd rather have the gun with us."

Hank shrugged. "Is it legal?"

"Probably not. I'm probably not supposed to have it under the car seat."

Hank looked dubious.

"I usually never take it out of the garage. I didn't think about the gun laws when I put it in the car. We had guns at the farm. Even my mom was a good shot."

"Okay." Hank started toward the trail. "If you promise not to shoot my toes off in the middle of the night."

She checked the safety and slipped the gun into a side pocket of her cargo pants. It felt heavy. "Wait up."

They made their way across the ledge yet again. The shadows were becoming long and sharp when they arrived at the oak.

Rachel looked at her watch. "I thought it was later."

"We're in a canyon. It gets dark quicker." Hank was laying out pieces of blue and gray fabric, and plastic stakes.

Rachel surveyed the raw beauty of the area. When she turned back, Hank was popping up the tent. She pulled up the flap, unzipped the netting and peered inside. "Plenty big enough for two. I didn't know you did stuff like this. Were you a survivalist or something?"

Hank snickered. "Tents are for sissies. Survivalists don't use tents." He had begun scouring the area for bits of kindling. "Those two filets you were drooling over at the store will fit very nicely on the grill."

On a flat rock several feet from the tree, Rachel set up the Coleman stove. The sky was still blue, but dimming.

She cut up lettuce, tomatoes, and green onions into two paper bowls. "When should I put on the steaks?"

Hank didn't answer.

She was turning to look for him when someone grabbed her from behind.

Chapter Thirty-nine

Rachel spun around, eyes wild.

"Jesus, Rachel! Take it easy."

"Omigod! What were you doing grabbing me like that?"

"Being incredibly stupid. Thanks for holding off on the knee." He gazed at her a moment, then brought his mouth down on hers. "That's more what I had in mind."

"I do think I like that better." She traced his cheek with her finger. His eyes looked very dark and deep. She brushed a strand of hair from his forehead, then stood on tiptoe to kiss him again.

"Now, what were you calling me about?"

"I was asking if you had unrolled the sleeping bags," she said, taking his hand and drawing him toward the tent.

◇◇◇

"Better than I've ever imagined," Rachel said, firelight fluttering across her face. It wasn't late, but the air was cooling. A thumbnail of moon floated in the narrow gap between the cliffs like a white sail on a boat on deep blue water.

"Really?" Hank smirked. He had built a small fire while Rachel had grilled the steaks.

She chuckled. "Well that, too, but I was talking about the steaks."

"It's amazing how much everything improves with fresh air." Hank pulled a sleeping bag from the tent and wrapped it around her, then lay down with his head in her lap.

"There's something I need to tell you. I thought we'd be driving longer, and I could tell you in the car, but there wasn't time, so I guess I have to do it now."

He sat up. His face a map of worry, he stared into her face. "Okay."

At first the words wouldn't come out. Then they spilled out in a rush: "I've been arrested. For something I didn't do. I swear it."

"Oh." Hank lay down again, balancing his head on her thigh.

"It was awful. Worse than horrible. I could lose the garage, Hank. I even bought a bottle of vodka. Vodka, of all things. What was I thinking? Thank God I didn't drink it. I had to put the garage up to get bail, but I got a loan from a bank vice president who owed a favor to a gangster, who's a friend of my dad's."

Hank sat up again, a worried look darkening his features. "What did you do?"

"I got a loan from a bank president who owed—"

"I got that part," Hank cut in. "What did you do to get arrested? Or what did they say you did?"

"The people at Jefferson Medical Center said I stole a bottle of prescription medication. Something called OxyContin."

He pulled her close and wrapped the sleeping bag around both of them. "How did it happen?"

He shuddered a little as she spun out the story. "You watched an operation? A real one? While they cut someone open?"

"It wasn't as gory as you think. Hardly any blood."

"Still, why would you want to do that?" he asked.

"I was invited. I thought it might be neat to do something most people haven't done."

"They haven't done it for a very good reason."

"And I wanted the use of the scrubs, so I could get into that ward on the fourth floor."

"You seem a little obsessed with that ward." He caught her look and added, "I'm not criticizing or anything. I'm just pointing it out."

"I keep thinking it has something to do with those kids—the ones I found in that van. Two weird things at Jefferson: that ward and those kids. Doesn't seem a huge stretch to imagine they may be related."

She didn't tell him about the medical record she stole, or that someone had broken into her apartment and taken those papers. She had told him enough for one day. The rest could wait.

As the sky darkened more, a few stars appeared, trailing the moon.

◇◇◇

Rachel woke to something poking her from outside the tent. Hank was still asleep, snoring lightly. She frowned. Whatever it was poked again. Rather than dress, she wrapped herself in her sleeping bag and unzipped the tent's netting. Pushing through the flap, she looked up and gasped.

Two eyes looked back at her.

A mule deer lowered its head and, still peering at her, backed up a step.

The sky was just beginning a gray glow along the canyon edges. Shrubs and rocks were black silhouettes.

She put her head back through the tent flap and whispered, "Hank! A deer."

He rolled over.

She turned back to the deer, which had now come a step closer. She went to the backpack they had left leaning against a rock, unzipped it and took out an apple. It was a big Gala apple.

The deer watched, flicking first one ear, then the other, as she carved the apple into eight pieces and held out a slice on the flat palm of her hand, the way she had fed her mother's horses as a child.

The deer shifted its weight from one foot to another, then raised its head, picking up the scent of fresh-cut apple. It moved forward, stopped, moved forward again. When it was close enough, it stretched its neck and gently took the apple slice.

They continued in that tableau until the deer had swallowed the last bit of apple. Then it turned, and with only one backward glance, disappeared behind a rock.

"I should have brought a camera." Hank was at the door of the tent. "You look like a little kid."

She sighed. "I've been in the city too long."

"So where's breakfast?"

She picked up an apple and threw it at him.

Hank wrestled her to the ground until they were both laughing. He kissed her on the nose.

"Who are you and what have you done with Hank?" she giggled. "Hank is Mr. Grumpy in the morning. At least until he gets his coffee."

Hank rolled to his feet. "Three eggs over easy." He ducked and ran back to the tent.

◇◇◇

After breakfast, they hiked the narrowing canyon to a barely discernable trail that led upward, through pines that were soon joined, then passed, by tall firs.

Their reward was a view that gave new meaning to the word vast.

"This has to be the very top of the world," Rachel said, her voice hushed. "We must be able to see all the way to Kansas."

"On a really clear day, Mexico, maybe, but not Kansas. We're looking south."

"You are so literal." Rachel tickled his ribs until he staggered and fell, pulling her down to him. "Did you know about this place or did we find it by accident?"

"I sorta knew. I hoped I remembered it right. Last time I was here I was about ten." He tried to sit up.

She pushed him back down.

"Rachel…."

She rolled on top of him and kissed him, hard, then rolled off, put her hands behind her head and gazed at the cloudless, silvery blue sky. A solitary bird was spiraling upward. She turned on her side and traced her fingers down Hank's arm. "You still want to set a date?"

But they were soon too busy to talk.

◇◇◇

It was mid afternoon when they made their way back down to the campsite. Rachel reached it a few yards ahead of Hank.

At first, everything looked fine.

Chapter Forty

The shot came from above. It passed Rachel's ear, and chips rocketed away from where it plunged itself into a rock. A fragment grazed her cheek.

Her mind struggled to catch up with events. "What the hell?" The words were more a genuine question than a scream.

"Rachel! For God's sake, get down!" In two long leaps Hank covered the space between them.

She had already dropped into a crouch.

"Get behind a rock!" he ordered in a low voice.

She began to crawl, then stopped. "But where? I don't know where the shot came from. Maybe it's just a lousy hunter." Her mind spun to a halt as she heard another shot and more rock chips sprayed into the air.

"He's up over there." Rachel jabbed a finger toward the path that led to the car, and scrambled away from the rocks into the open.

Hank lunged after her. "What the hell are you doing?"

She began inching her way toward the tent. "My gun."

"No!" Hank's face was pale and alarmed. "Don't be an idiot. You can't have a gun fight with some berserk maniac."

"I can try. It's better than being a sitting duck, for God's sake."

Was the tent's netting zipper stuck or was it just her clumsiness?

"You're a clear target, Rachel. Get behind something!"

She was still fumbling with the zipper when another shot thumped into the dry ground. Flakes of clay-like dirt were sliced away from where it plowed into a hole a few feet from her leg. Another crack, another bullet zinged into the arid soil, this one near her elbow. The shooter was either a bad shot or was too far away for much accuracy.

It all seemed to happen at once: Hank's yell, his body landing across her shoulders, flattening her to the ground, and the sound of the gun firing again.

She wasn't sure what had happened until the blood began to pool on the ground near her chin.

◇◇◇

"You okay?" The question was a reflex. No way he was okay.

Hank seemed to try to answer. Then his weight on her back went leaden.

Another shot exploded but failed to strike either of them.

Rachel clawed at the jammed zipper and it finally gave way. With all the strength she could muster, with Hank's weight draining her effort, she pulled herself into the tent.

She had rolled out from under him, had grasped his shoulders and was hauling the rest of him into the tent when the next bullet hit with a thump.

His body shuddered with the impact and he groaned.

Blood was oozing from somewhere near his belt. Grabbing her backpack from where it lay in a corner, she slipped her hand inside to where she had put the thirty-eight the night before.

She had to crawl over Hank to get to the ripped net at the tent door.

You were wrong, Hank. I am going to have a gun fight with a berserk maniac. I have no choice.

◇◇◇

Drawing open the tent flap just enough to accommodate the gun barrel, Rachel aimed at a spot along the trail. Even if she could spot the gunman, she knew her accuracy with the thirty-eight this far away would be poor at best. If she shot now, the bullet would go wild.

Wouldn't it be worth something to warn the madman off? To prove she wasn't defenseless?

No.

He had watched her, knew where she was. He thought all he had to do now was keep firing at the tent and the chances of hitting her or Hank inside weren't bad. He was half right.

She squinted and scanned the brush around the path but couldn't find their attacker.

"Come on, you son of a bitch," she whispered.

Then she did see him. Almost indistinguishable from a shrub but moving sideways. That must be where the trail turned. Camouflage cap and shirt, melting into the landscape. A rifle pointed down his right leg toward the ground.

Gripping her gun with both hands, Rachel planted her feet apart, and pushed the muzzle through the tent flap.

She thought she saw him take aim, and it required all the control she had not to pull the thirty-eight's trigger.

A bullet tore a hole in the corner of the tent. Rachel glanced behind her. This shot had exited without hitting anything.

"You bastard!" she hissed.

Struggling to control the rush of sheer anger, she tried to think.

She moved a little farther back and to the side of the tent flap. Gaze riveted on the place where the small trail left the main path and headed into the canyon, she took a couple of deep breaths.

Her eyes began to hurt from straining to see someone who almost matched the landscape. Had she lost him?

Then he moved into the open. Rifle raised, aiming toward her. And terrifyingly close. Only a little above and nearly halfway along the short trail that would bring him to the canyon bottom. How had she missed him at the turnoff?

But he was in the open. Within range. And she had a clear shot.

She squeezed off two shots and saw him run to the left, off the trail.

He was harder to see now, crouching behind a shrub.

Rising, he stumbled farther off the trail, turned and brought the rifle into position again.

She fired.

He flopped backward.

She sank to her knees. "Thank God."

Then the tears began.

Chapter Forty-one

The moment of relief didn't last.

From behind her came the sound of a low moan. The awareness that Hank was injured, maybe way beyond serious, roared back into her consciousness.

He still lay prone, head to the side, in the position he had landed, one leg and one arm bent. She knelt by his side. Blood was pooling on the tent floor beneath him. Should she try to turn him over? What if the bullet had rattled around inside him and struck his spine? Would turning him, moving him at all do more damage?

If she did nothing, he might bleed to death.

The eye she could see flickered open, seemed to stare at her without recognition, then closed again. His face was frighteningly colorless.

"Hank." She gently touched his arm, then said his name louder.

He took a short, hard breath, but didn't respond.

One bullet apparently had thumped through the fleshy part of his upper arm. The blood there was already congealing.

The other injury was a different matter. There seemed to be an awful lot of blood. The bullet had entered his back below his ribs. The bleeding there didn't seem too bad. The puddle of blood must be coming from where the slug had exited.

Rachel tried to remember the first aid course she had taken years ago. Above all she needed something sterile and absorbent.

She grabbed her handbag, dumped out the contents, scooped up a purple tampon container, then picked up the shirt she had worn the day before and twisted it into a rope.

Turning Hank on his side as gently as she could, she slipped the end of the shirt under him. Stripping away the paper, she removed the tampon, pressed it into the wound, and held it there with her knee while she tied the shirt tightly across it.

That was better than nothing, but it was nowhere near enough.

She couldn't carry him. Couldn't even drag him very far. And he was bleeding internally.

She had to get help.

Praying he was carrying his cell phone, hadn't left it somewhere or lost it, she reached into Hank's pocket. The phone was there.

Rachel drew it out and pressed the *on* button. The little screen lit up. The battery was charged. But there was no sign of a signal.

She went to the torn netting at the door of the tent and, peered out, scanning the landscape between the tent and where the shooter had left the trail. Was the bastard out of commission? Or had he faked being hit, and was now sneaking closer?

Finally, she made him out, still lying where he had fallen.

She picked up her gun from where she had dropped it and, phone in one hand, thirty-eight in the other, stepped through the ripped netting.

Still no cell phone signal.

She walked a hundred feet into the canyon, and as far as she could in every other direction.

To no avail.

Running fingers through her hair, she grasped some strands in her fist as if that might help her think better. Maybe it did.

She would have to go to the top of the canyon. There would be a signal there.

How long would it take? The two of them had spent hours, but they had taken several side trails, and had stopped first for a snack, then for lunch.

She went back to Hank. Called his name. Touched his cheek.

He didn't rouse.

His cheek seemed cool.

He's in shock. I should have covered him immediately.

She seized a sleeping bag, pushed one edge under him, and draped the other over him.

Taking a deep breath, knowing he probably couldn't hear her, she told him, "I'm going to get help."

It was a long way to the top. No way could she run it flat out. Breaking into a jog, she mostly watched the path. The ground was uneven, and there were stones, tree branches, pine cones, and roots that could cause a stumble.

For the first time, it occurred to her that if she broke a leg, they might both die here in this place that had seemed such a paradise.

Don't think. Just keep moving.

She kept a steady pace, slowing every so often to check the phone for a signal. No luck. Each time she glanced up, the top of the canyon didn't seem much closer.

A large bird flapped up from the ground nearby, startling her. She almost turned an ankle. She was thirsty. She should have brought water.

Was the man she shot dead or only unconscious? He must have been insane. What reason could he have had for shooting at them? She should have tried to find his body before leaving. Made sure he was dead. If he was still alive, could she have killed him in cold blood? Maybe not, but she could have taken his rifle. And maybe even put a bullet through his knee.

What if he came to and went after Hank while she was gone?

Too late to think about that. Just keep moving.

Her thighs began to ache. Or had they been aching all along and she had just noticed? The ache became a piercing, unrelenting pain.

A breeze gave her a chill and she realized she was damp with sweat.

The sky seemed to be darkening. Was there a storm coming?

Lungs growing more raw with each breath, she slowed a little, but kept going.

A squirrel sat up in the path ahead and stared at her as if it couldn't believe its eyes, then scrambled up a tree.

She slowed again to check the phone. Nothing. Who should she call once she got a signal? Nine-one-one? What could they do in a situation like this?

At last, she reached the steepest part of the trail, close to the top. Agonizingly slowly, she picked her way up over the rocks.

When she finally strode along the canyon rim, it didn't look as wondrous as it had when she'd first reached it with Hank. It looked remote. The end of the world, not the top of it. A wind was whipping up, bending the trees.

Rachel fell more than sat. Breathing heavily, she took the phone from her pocket.

No signal.

She wanted to scream at God that it wasn't fair.

Was there something wrong with the phone? It had worked when she had called Irene from the car. Did the trees block the signal?

Staggering to her feet, she walked, watching the cell phone screen.

A signal flickered. *Yes!*

But before she could dial, it was gone again.

A few more steps and it showed again. Strong.

Hurriedly, she dialed nine-one-one.

A voice answered, but cut in and out.

"I'm calling on a cell phone. I'm up in the Angeles....In the Angeles....Yes, the mountains north....I don't know exactly where...a man here is injured. Badly injured....Gun shot. Someone shot him....He's losing blood. He needs medical help...now...as fast as possible."

Suddenly overcome with panic, she had to fight not to break down.

Explaining as best she could where Hank was, the turnout, the path to him about a mile long, some of it across a narrow ledge, the place they had camped, Rachel's voice began to tear at her throat, which already was stretched tight with fear. How could anyone find them? Hank would die.

"Hold for a moment please," the operator said.

Rachel tried to calm herself by taking deep breaths. It seemed like a lot of time passed. Had she been cut off? She was afraid to stay on what might be a dead line, and afraid to redial.

Finally, the phone crackled as the operator came back on line. "There is a search and rescue team headquartered not far from you. I have contacted them, but I can't patch you through." The connection faded, then came back. "Are you there?"

"Yes." Rachel turned her back to the wind and yelled into the phone.

"The rescue team is sending a helicopter. They don't want to haul an injured person on a litter for a long distance. You did say it was a mile or so to the road?"

"Yes. I think it's about a mile."

"Go back to the tent," the operator told her. She was to tear it down and take the big piece of fabric to the most open place she could find and anchor it with rocks. The rescue team would look for that.

"But time is very tight. They can't operate a chopper in a canyon after dark. The sun drops early and quickly in a canyon. If there isn't enough light, they say they'll have to go back and come in from the road."

Rachel headed back to the camp as fast as she could. It didn't help knowing she would be out of communication from here on.

◇◇◇

Hank had not regained consciousness. She probed under his jaw for a pulse. It was thin but seemed steady.

She checked the safety on her gun, unsnapped the deep pocket on the leg of her cargo pants, nosed the thirty-eight into it and fastened the flap.

With the one sharp knife Hank had packed with the supplies, she made a ragged slice through the floor of the tent end to end around Hank. Using that as a makeshift litter, she dragged him as gently as she could out into the open.

Looking up the path toward the place where the shooter had fallen, she couldn't pick out the camouflage-clad body on the ground from the landscape. Was it because the light had shifted?

Please God, don't let him wake up and come after us, now.

Should she go over there? Make sure he was still there and disabled if not dead? But there was so little time.

The tent came down easily even though she did everything wrong at least once.

She gathered the nylon, carried it about fifty yards along the canyon floor, and laid it out as best she could at the widest, most open and flat space she could find.

What if they couldn't find her? What if her directions were wrong?

Don't even go there.

She could find only one rock light enough to carry, but heavy enough to hold down the remains of the tent.

What if?

Don't think....

Chapter Forty-two

Rachel had driven tent pegs through two corners and was setting a third in the fabric of the collapsed tent when she heard the heavy buzz and steady thump of a helicopter. She had seen a lot of them on the helipad above the garage, but none as beautiful as this one.

Standing in the flattened tent, she waved both arms over her head.

"Here!" she yelled, knowing they couldn't hear her but yelling anyway. "Here!"

The thumps slowed. The chopper seemed to come to a halt almost directly above her.

"We see you!" The voice from the bullhorn came loud and weird, as if from some strange deity.

Then there was just the loud pulse of the chopper blades biting through the air. It descended a little, the wind from the blades bending the surrounding shrubs and making it hard for her to stay upright. Rachel staggered two steps, then leaned into the wind.

Would they land? Where? Was she in the way?

She was waiting for instructions from the bullhorn when she saw something begin to descend on a cable from the body of the helicopter. It became a person wearing a red jacket crossed by the broad straps of a harness. The helmet, too, was red, the field pants, olive green.

When the person, a wiry, small blond, reached the ground, she took charge immediately.

Another person began the descent. A man, followed by equipment of some sort.

Rachel called, "There's something else I should tell you."

Both rescue people gave her stern looks, clearly not wanting to hear something new at this stage.

Nor did she want to say it. But it had to be said.

"I'm pretty sure I hit the guy who shot my friend." She pointed up the trail. "He went down, fell, over there. I haven't been watching all the time, but I haven't seen any sign of him since."

The man nodded silently, without expression, and trotted in that direction.

Rachel followed the woman to where Hank lay, watched the hands moving over him, then caught her eye and asked a silent question.

The woman raised her eyebrows, then, "I've seen worse." She looked hard at Rachel, whose head had begun a slow spin, and ordered, "Sit down."

The man returned, shaking his head. "Dead. The sheriffs will want to secure the site and remove him themselves."

A second man in red jacket and helmet dropped down on the helicopter's cable. Working with amazing speed, the three put together a litter of heavy blue fabric and orange lacing. When Hank was secured to it with thick black straps and pink-and-blue bungee cords, they carried him toward where the chopper was still hovering.

Rachel followed, lurching almost drunkenly, knowing she was barely coherent.

Hank still hadn't moved. Was he okay? Well, not okay, but alive?

Don't go there.

A contraption was descending from the helicopter. The red-jacketed trio worked in unison securing Hank's litter to it. Rachel wasn't sure how they did it. The cable went up and down. She lost track of the number of times. She was scooping up the scattered contents of her purse when the woman called, beckoning her.

Rachel did as she was told. Prodded and harnessed, she was drawn upward, twisting slightly, like some crazy ride at Magic Mountain, the weight in the pocket of her cargo pants slinging awkwardly against her leg.

◇◇◇

They landed so quickly, Rachel wondered if she had somehow dozed off. "Where are we?"

"Pasadena Memorial General."

She tried to follow Hank as they transferred his litter to a gurney and pushed the gurney into an elevator. But the doors closed before Rachel and the woman from the rescue team got there. When they opened again on an empty car, the woman steered her into it, then out at a lower floor, down a bright yellow hall with white woodwork, to the door of what appeared to be a medical examination room.

"No," Rachel said. "I'm fine. I just need to find my friend."

Two men in police uniforms appeared at the end of the hall. Rachel froze. Cops. Of course, there would be cops. She had killed someone. For the first time her brain registered the possibility that she could wind up in jail for a very long time.

"Someone should take a look at you." The woman nudged Rachel into the room and closed the door.

A knock on the examination room door was accompanied by the woman's voice saying firmly, "Sorry officers, you'll have to wait out there."

Another knock. A male voice. "Hello, ma'am? Please come out to the waiting room when you are finished."

Rachel swallowed hard, then called, "All right."

The woman from the rescue team knocked lightly, then stuck her head in. "They'll want you to disrobe. There's a cover-up." She gestured to a folded, flowered piece of cloth on the examination table. For the first time, Rachel realized the woman's hair wasn't blond, it was gray.

A few minutes after she had removed her clothes and donned the flowered cape, another knock was followed by the entrance of a woman in street clothes. She handed Rachel a form attached to a clipboard and told her, "Fill this out, please, and stop at the office on your way out."

Using the pen chained to the clipboard, Rachel laboriously filled out the form. She listed her insurance, although this was sure to come under the deductible. She was adding a note about that when a person in an unbuttoned white coat entered the room.

He looked like a twelve-year-old playing doctor, but seemed efficient. Rachel answered his questions, let him poke and prod and shine a light in her eyes. He pressed a prescription into her hand, and told her she could go home.

She gazed dully at the prescription. "What's this for?"

"A sedative. In case you have trouble sleeping. Most people do after a traumatic experience."

"I need to find out about another patient," she began. "A man who was just brought in…." But the doctor was already gone.

She left the examination room on unsteady legs. Unsure whether she was angry, frightened, or both, or just tired, very, very tired, she wandered down two hallways repeating to herself how much she hated hospitals and how she kept finding herself roaming the halls of one.

Where was the damn waiting room?

What would she tell the cops when she found it?

Finally, she spotted a door marked *Exit* and pushed through it, half expecting to set off an alarm. Maybe she could get herself arrested twice tonight.

Stepping out into a parking lot, she followed the pavement around to the front door. She glanced around the lobby. There were eight or ten people in street clothes, but no cops. Where were they?

Well, that was their problem. She wasn't about to hunt for them.

She found the information desk and asked about Hank.

The woman there was at least a hundred pounds overweight, but her face was pretty and her manner pleasant. "I'll see what I can find out." She dialed a phone, spoke into it, disconnected, dialed again, spoke quietly and listened for what seemed like a long time before she turned back to Rachel.

"He's in surgery. They don't know how long it will take. Then he'll be in critical care. I wouldn't wait, ma'am. It might be all night, and then they may say no visitors."

"Okay," Rachel murmured. "Thanks." She turned to leave, then turned back and held out the clipboard. "I was just in the emergency room. They said I should stop by some office...."

The woman nodded and pointed toward a window to her left.

Rachel made her way to the window, but there was no one in the office behind it. Just as well. They would want her insurance information and money. Mostly the money. Well, they would have to bill her for it. She slid the clipboard into the space below the glass and left it there.

She sat down on one of the big brown imitation leather sofas that passed for places to sit but were so uncomfortable no one wanted to sit there long. Twenty minutes dragged by. A little girl was hanging onto her mother's knee and blowing a pink gum bubble.

Where were those cops? Had they gotten a call more important than waiting for her? Was she supposed to hunt for them? Surely they didn't expect that.

She had to figure out a way to get home. If this was Pasadena, it wasn't all that far. She could take a cab, but she'd have to find a phone book to call one. For some reason, that seemed like the task that would push her over the edge. She was barely sure she could stand up.

Remembering the cell phone, she drew it from her pocket and dialed Goldie. No answer. She left a message, then dialed Marty. He didn't answer either. She checked her watch. Almost six-thirty. He'd be down at the poker club. Rachel could have him paged there, but she didn't know the number. She'd have to find a phone book, and if she did that, she might as well call a cab.

She dialed the garage. Irene couldn't come pick her up, but she could send a cab, and at least Rachel could find out if everything was all right at home.

"Dear girl! I didn't expect to hear from you. Of course, everything is fine here. You know there's never much happens on a Saturday. A few folks who would rather work than stay home, but mostly it's just been keeping people who don't belong in, out. Good thing I know all the regulars." She paused. "However, there is a gentleman standing right here asking about you."

"My dad?" Rachel thought she couldn't be that lucky.

"No. Your friend from the hospital." Rachel could hear Irene handing the phone to someone.

Gabe?

Gordon. "You poor thing," he said when she had told him where she was and admitted she was stranded. "No, no," he added, when she asked him to send a cab for her. "I'll pick you up myself."

She waited for him in front of the hospital. She knew he drove a white Lexus and when it appeared she waved, which took about the last of her rapidly fading energy.

He gave her a worried look when she slid into the passenger seat. "Are you okay, Rachel?"

"The doctor back there seemed to think I probably wouldn't croak in the next twenty-four hours."

He smiled sideways at her as he steered the Lexus out of the parking lot. "That's good news. You want to get a drink? Dinner? Anything?"

"Thanks, Gordon, but I really just want to go home."

"Looks like you've had a nasty time of it. What happened?"

"I was camping with a friend, up in the Angeles. Someone started shooting at us. Hank was hit. We got out of there by way of a rescue team and helicopter. So I wound up at the hospital with my car still up in the mountains."

Gordon's eyebrows rose and nearly met in an angle over his nose. "You want me to take you up to your car?"

She shook her head. "Thanks, but I'm too worn out to drive it back. I'll get it later. I just want to lie down and look at the ceiling over my bed for a while."

"Is your friend okay? I mean—"

"He's in surgery. I guess they don't know yet." She hadn't thought she had any tears left, but suddenly they were burning, filling her eyes.

Gordon reached into the back seat and handed her a box of tissues. "Who was the shooter? Some moron hunting out of season after a beer too many?"

"Something like that," she said, not wanting to explain, just wanting to get home.

The Lexus swung onto the Glendale Freeway. Rachel stared at the road, willing herself calm.

When they arrived at the garage, he pulled the Lexus next to the glass booth.

"Dear girl, you look terrible. Simply frightful," Irene said. "You just go upstairs and rest, you hear me? I'll take care of things here."

"I think I'll just drive her up to the top floor," Gordon said.

"Good." Irene beamed.

When they got to the top, he parked where only a few days before Rachel had smashed the vodka bottle against the wall. She hoped he didn't get glass in his tire for his thoughtfulness.

"Oh, shit!" she said when she realized the balled-up paper in her hand was the prescription the doctor at the hospital had handed her. "I wonder if I really need this."

Gordon cast her a concerned glance. "What is it?"

Rachel sighed. "A prescription. For sleep I guess. I probably won't need it."

Gordon took the paper from her, smoothed it out. "In case you do, I've got some in the trunk."

Rachel had all but forgotten what he did for a living. Remembering that made her remember something else. She looked at the car ceiling. "Gordon, I know you heard about my being arrested for—"

. He reached over and squeezed her hand. "Yes, I heard. And I never believed a word of it. It's ridiculous."

She looked at his kind face and the tears started again.

He reached around her and gently brought her head to his chest. "There, there. Just cry it out. It'll be okay." He patted her shoulder. "My mother used to say, 'It'll all come out in the wash.'"

Chapter Forty-three

Gordon gave her some pills, but Rachel put them unopened in the medicine cabinet in the bathroom. Like many recovering addicts, she viewed all medications with suspicion.

She slept fitfully and woke early. Clancy was lying on her pillow peering into her face. He sat up and yawned, as if now that she was awake he could go to sleep. She was rubbing his head when everything came back in a rush of awful images. Hank.

She had to wake up enough to be able to call the hospital.

Waiting impatiently for the Mr. Coffee to finish gurgling, she noticed a box sitting on the floor next to her front door. Irene must have brought it up to the apartment.

The toaster popped the English muffin up too soon. Rachel shoved it down again. Her stomach growled. How long since she'd eaten? Breakfast yesterday? A thousand years ago. She dropped the jar of plum jam as she was taking it out of the refrigerator. The glass shattered across the floor of the small kitchen.

The jam was sticky. Rachel was just scraping up the last of it when she heard someone knocking on one of the garage doors.

She tried to ignore it, but it went on steadily. Then her phone rang.

She answered, hoping it would be Hank.

"Los Angeles Deputy Sheriffs," came a voice. "We're on the sidewalk in front of a parking garage. We'd like to speak with you."

She threw on jeans and a yellow tee shirt and went down to the door dreading the worst.

They were as unlike each other as any two men could be. One was built like a bear and looked like he could bring down a mountain lion with his bare hands. The other was thin and pale. He wore small, black-rimmed eyeglasses. A clipboard was clutched in a knobby hand.

Rachel smoothed back her hair, which was still tumbled from bed.

"Sorry about the early hour," the big man said. "But we need to talk with you about what happened yesterday." The stubble on his chin gave him a slightly disheveled look, which might have been deliberate.

"Up in the Angeles," the thin one said, and added, "We expected you to come to the hospital waiting room."

Rachel sighed. "I did. You weren't there. I waited quite a while."

"We most certainly were there," the big man said.

Rachel frowned. "But I was there. In plain sight, on one of those uncomfortable brown things."

"Brown things?"

"Sofas."

"Ah.... That's the lobby."

"Yes."

"We meant the emergency waiting room," the bear said. "Okay. That explains it." He paused, then started again. "You live here? In a parking garage?"

"There's an apartment upstairs."

"Mind if we come in?"

"Can I see some ID?" She didn't doubt they were cops, but buying a minute or two to clear her head seemed wise.

They flipped open identical leather cases. The blond's name was Jack Nease, the bear was Tom Walchel.

"Okay." Feeling weary already, with her day only an hour old, Rachel led them to the elevator. When it reached the top floor, she showed them to her living room and perched herself across from them on a kitchen bar stool.

The big man sank so deep into the sofa the frame creaked.

The blond remained standing. "Now it's your turn. Mind showing us some I.D.?"

"You found me, but you don't know who I am?"

"We'd still like to see some I.D.," the bear said.

Rachel sighed, then stood and started for the bedroom door. The blond moved with her. She gave him a puzzled look. "Excuse me? This is my bedroom."

"I'm afraid we can't let you go in there alone," he said, moving to block the door.

"My own bedroom?"

"Sorry."

She shrugged. "Okay, fine. If you don't mind the mess, come along."

She took her wallet from her purse, opened it to show her driver's license, and handed it to him.

"Okay," he said, glancing at it, and escorted her back to the living room. Still standing, he drew something from his pocket and held it up. "Tape recorder. Mind?"

Oh crap, Rachel thought. What would happen if she said she minded? There was something scary about having her every word recorded.

"Should I call a lawyer?"

"Up to you. We're not taking you in. Not right now anyway. We just have some questions."

She thought about that. If they weren't taking her in for questioning, it must mean they hadn't connected her to the OxyContin arrest. "Okay, go ahead," she said, her voice shaking a little. She reminded herself that if things went badly, she could stop and insist on an attorney.

In a low tone deputy Nease told the recorder the time, date, and Rachel's name, then set the machine on the coffee table in front of the sofa. "Please state your name."

"Rachel Chavez." Already she could feel her pulse quickening. You haven't done anything wrong, she told herself.

"You killed a man," Nease said.

"He was trying to kill us. I was scared to death he would do it."

Half an hour later, they were still asking questions. "Who fired first?" the big man asked for the third time.

"I've told you," Rachel said, exasperated, "he did. I didn't even see him until he had fired several times."

"Why were you at that particular place at that particular time?" Nease asked.

Rachel looked at Walcher, whose eyes were thoughtfully examining her face. "My friend and I were camping."

"In what?" the big man asked, and for the first time she noticed a dimple to the right of his mouth. Somehow it made him less scary.

"In a tent."

"Was this in a campground?" The sofa creaked as the big man leaned forward.

"No. You must already know that, you must already know a lot of what I'm telling you." Rachel wondered if camping outside a campground would be added to the list of laws she had broken lately.

"We've got preliminary reports. We'd like to hear it in your words."

"Like I said, we had hiked up to the top of the canyon and when we got back to the camp, someone started shooting at us."

"Shooting *at* you, or just a stray bullet? A hunter, maybe?" the thin man wanted to know.

"I am absolutely certain he was shooting at us and that he was trying to kill us."

The blond chewed on the end of his pen. "Both of you?"

Her shoulders sagged. "I don't know."

The sofa creaked as the big man leaned forward. "Did you get a good look at the shooter?"

"I told you. I didn't even see him until he was shooting. I know he wasn't wearing an orange cap, or anything orange. In fact, I'm pretty sure he was wearing camouflage clothes and cap. He was like part of the landscape. I could hardly see him at all. I think that was on purpose."

"That might mean he was stupid, but it doesn't mean he wasn't out there to kill deer, not people." Walcher scratched the stubble on his chin. "You have any idea the number of shots he fired?"

"I wasn't counting. But he kept it up even after he hit Hank. He was aiming at us, trying to kill us."

"You're sure you didn't know him from somewhere?"

"I didn't get that good a look at him, but I don't know a lot of people who shoot at other people."

"And you don't think it's possible he was a hunter, maybe a stupid one, or maybe one who just went bonkers?" Nease asked. "Maybe you were in his favorite site or something, and it just set him off, and he went postal."

After a moment Rachel said, "I guess that's possible. All I know for sure is he was definitely, deliberately, trying to kill either me or Hank or both of us." She said the last words slowly as if to emphasize them.

Nease raised his eyes from the clipboard to stare at her from the other angle. "If that's the case, what prevented him from accomplishing his objective?"

Her pulse had slowed a little. Now it sped again and heat rose into her cheeks. "I shot him."

In self-defense. You should have added that it was self-defense.

But Walcher was already asking, "With what?"

"An old thirty-eight."

"And you killed him," the bear said. "With a thirty-eight. At that distance."

"I guess I did. He fell over. And one of the people from the helicopter took a look at him and said he was dead."

The blond was quick to ask, "Where is this weapon now?"

"Still up where we camped, I suppose." Rachel bit her tongue. *Oh shit, Why did I say that?*

I forgot.

No, you didn't. You just don't want them to take the gun away from you. Good thing you're not hooked up to a lie detector. You'd flunk with flying colors.

"We recovered the shooter's rifle. There was no sign of the gun you describe as yours."

"I don't know what to tell you," Rachel said, knowing where the questioning would go next.

And it did. "How did this handgun get to the camp site?" Nease asked.

"You mean from here?"

He nodded.

She knew some of the rules. "Locked in the storage compartment in the back of my car." How could anyone find out now that it wasn't true?

"And that gun is properly registered?" Walcher mouthed the words as if they were rehearsed.

That they could find out, probably already had. She looked down at her hands. "I'm afraid I don't really know. It was my father's. We owned a farm upstate. That's where he taught me to shoot. For years, that was the only place it was used. And then only for target practice. I thought it might be a good idea to have a gun on a camping trip. Just in case. For self-defense. Against a mountain lion or a bear or something. At the time, I wasn't thinking of a human threat."

"Did your father transfer ownership to you, or register the gun as loaned to you?"

"To tell the truth, I don't know. I never asked."

The two deputies nodded in unison, as if they knew that all along.

Chapter Forty-four

Nease advised the recorder that he was turning it off and Walcher handed her a business card. "If you think of anything else, anything at all, give us a call."

When they had departed Rachel wondered if she had given the right answers, passed or flunked. How much had they known before questioning her? Did they know something they weren't saying? Had they talked to Hank? She should have asked. Would he have any idea who the shooter might be? She didn't think so.

She picked up the phone and called the hospital.

Mr. Sullivan was not to be disturbed. That's all the floor nurse would say.

"Did the police talk to him?"

"I'm sorry, I don't know."

Don't know or won't say? Rachel thanked the woman, hung up and dialed Goldie's number.

"Why are you calling me at this hour?"

"I'm sorry. But I need you. Big time. Real big time."

"Gimme time to put on some clothes. I'll be right there."

◇◇◇

The first hole card fell slap on the table in front of Marty. He lifted a corner. Jack of diamonds. A good start. There were nine players, which made for a nice pot. The second card landed in front of him. Another jack. Spades.

Marty scratched his head and tried to look worried, which wasn't hard. His hair was a little mussed and his five o'clock shadow hadn't been achieved by the setting on his razor. His beard had passed the point of cool macho several hours ago and was headed for seedy.

He'd lost quite a lot in the past week and needed to make it up. He wanted to do something special for Rachel. She was having a hard time of it lately. How could anyone think she would steal drugs from a hospital? She wouldn't let him help her with the expenses from that, she wouldn't accept the perfectly nice Toyota he'd bought for her. In his book, that was taking independence a step too far. But she had always been that way.

Now, though, she was getting married. He could give her a nice wedding. A honeymoon to Europe or the Caribbean or anywhere she wanted to go. She couldn't turn that down.

Marty had folded the last few hands, but now his luck was going to change.

◇◇◇

"This damn place looks more like Baghdad after a botched raid than a camp site," Goldie announced. She and Rachel had come to pick up the Civic and whatever gear and supplies they could round up.

The area was strewn with crime scene tape wrapped around shrubs and even rocks.

Goldie looked at Rachel over low-slung sunglasses. "How the hell do you get yourself into stuff like this? I just turn my head for ten minutes and someone is boiling oil and you are turning up the heat and helping 'em get it ready for you. You need yourself a keeper."

"No kidding."

From where they stood they could see the brown blotches in the scrub grass along the trail where the man she shot had fallen. Speckles of blood had even spurted onto the leaves of plants six or eight feet away from the crushed grass.

A jay sat on a flat rock watching the two women with great interest.

"You look kind of peaked," Goldie said.

"It doesn't feel good to have killed someone, even if that someone was trying to kill you." Rachel shoved her hands in her pockets and looked at the ground. "And I'm wondering how long it'll be before they find out about my two arrests, and that I'm out on bail on the OxyContin thing."

The jay hopped to the ground and strutted toward them. He opened his beak in a silent question which probably had to do with food.

"Maybe they will, maybe they won't," Goldie said.

"You're kidding. Why wouldn't they?"

"Well, first off, you don't have a conviction. Just the arrests. The first one was up north. Right?"

"Yes."

"And the OxyContin, that was LAPD. And the guys with jurisdiction up here, they would be county sheriffs. So what we got is stuff that happened in two cities and one county. These guys don't spend a lot of time talking to each other. They're more like in competition with each other. Like remember after nine-eleven there was all that flap about the CIA not talking to the FBI and the FBI not even talkin' to themselves?"

"You mean they might never connect the dots?"

"Three jurisdictions, no convictions? It's possible."

"How do you know all this?"

"My brother was a cop, remember?"

Rachel managed a small smile that quickly ebbed away. "I sure hope you're right." She pointed past the tape at clusters of little flags bearing numbers. "What's all that? Looks like some weird little golf course."

"Probably it's where they found stuff," Goldie said. "I guess they wouldn't take it kindly if we removed anything."

Rachel wondered if she should tell Goldie the cops had not found the thirty-eight here at the scene because it was at home, in her apartment, in her underwear drawer. She decided not to. Why involve her friend in something she might someday be asked about? Under oath.

They turned back up the path and she asked instead, "What could I have done that someone would come after me with a rifle?"

"Could be you should just plain stop poking around in other people's business," Goldie sniffed. "You notice nobody's huntin' me down with a gun." A few steps later, she asked, "Are we sure this guy was after you and not Hank?"

Rachel shrugged. "I just figured it was me. I'm not sure of anything. Why would anyone want to kill Hank? As soon as I can, I'll ask him if he has any ideas. I'm sure the cops will, too."

She stopped, put her hands on her hips and looked at the sky. "You think the guy shooting at us might have something to do with what's going on at Jefferson?"

"Anything is possible," Goldie said. "Come on, you can't take root there."

Rachel began walking again. "The cops seemed to think it might have been some nut-case hunter who just lost it and started shooting people. Like maybe we were in his favorite campsite or something."

"There are plenty of loony tunes out there. Probably more than one is a hunter." Goldie turned to look at her friend. "Did those deputies ask you anything about whether you might have done something that pissed off the Mexican Mafia?"

"Mexican Mafia! Where'd you get that idea?"

"You think that guy, that El whatever his name was, that friend of your dad's who got you that loan, you think he runs a nursery school or grows petunias for a living? He sounds like he's got Mexican Mafia written all over him."

"Mexican Mafia sounds so…really bad. I agree El Jefe probably operates on a less than legal basis—I've told Pop the same thing. The guy's probably a crook, a gangster, maybe, of some sort, but just an ordinary one."

"Now that sure does make sense. An ordinary gangster, not a Mexicano Mafioso. Where is your head, girl?"

"Why would El Jefe get the vice president of a big bank to loan me twenty-five thousand dollars and then send someone to kill me?"

Goldie thought about that. "Maybe the loan was honor. He owed your dad. Sending a killer after you, that was maybe money, or something he owed someone else. Those people think different than we do."

"There's also the matter of those poor kids I found in that van. What happened to them? They couldn't have just disappeared into thin air."

Goldie kicked a stone out of the trail. "You better forget about those kids. Your plate is full enough right now. You have downright made a pig of yourself with trouble."

Chapter Forty-five

The architecture was different, sort of Moorish modern, but once you were inside Pasadena's Memorial General Hospital, there wasn't a nickel's worth of difference between it and Jefferson Medical Center.

To Rachel, both hospitals seemed like foreign countries where she didn't speak the language or know the rules. Everything seemed larger than life, with a spotless lack of character. And people who worked there spoke in acronyms that must have been designed to keep ordinary folks at sea.

Whoever was in charge of reciting information about patients had told her that morning that Hank's condition was stable. He could now have family visitors, but he was still sedated and visits should be brief.

She waited in line at the reception desk. The woman behind it had pale freckles and braids the color of sand wound atop her head. Rachel had seen braids like that at a German meat market in Montrose. Sure enough, the woman had a German accent.

"He is allowed only visits from family."

Rachel didn't miss a beat. "I'm his wife."

"I.D.?"

Oh, for God's sake. Rachel produced her driver's license. "I kept my own name. I hope you don't think I carry my wedding license with me."

"Room six-fourteen."

The room was cold. Not just the temperature, but the colors—gray and white. Everything but the mattresses seemed made of steel.

One bed was empty. The other had been raised part way. Face almost as pale as the sheets, Hank lay against a small, flat pillow, chin up, slender oxygen tubes at his nose. A drip tube led from a pack that hung from a pole to his arm. A bank of digital instruments stood next to the bed.

"Hank?"

He didn't move. That frightened Rachel until she saw his chest move with his breaths.

"Hank?" she said again, softly, and took his hand. It was warmer than hers. Still she pulled the white blanket up closer around his shoulders. He was wearing one of those awful hospital gowns and she made a mental note to go up to his house and get him some pajamas. Then she realized she didn't have a key and the hospital probably had locked up whatever he'd had in his pockets when he was admitted.

His head rolled a bit and a faint sigh escaped his lips.

She straightened his pillow. "Hank, it's me, Rachel."

His eyes opened, clear blue as glass in blood-shot white. "Rachel?" His voice was high, so faint and feeble she was barely sure she'd heard it.

"How are you feeling?"

His eyebrows raised slowly, giving him a puzzled look.

"Hank, do you know anyone who might have wanted to shoot you? You instead of me?"

Very slowly, his head moved from left to right.

Was that involuntary or did it mean "no"?

His eyes closed again.

◇◇◇

The first hole card was a three of hearts. Marty's hands were getting sweaty. Almost every dime he had was on the table. He had only slept about six hours a night for three nights. Or was it four? He couldn't remember exactly.

He knew one thing though, he had to get that money back.

◇◇◇

"I just lost an argument with myself." Goldie's voice on the phone. "Where've you been?"

"You mean tonight?"

"I've been trying you every twenty minutes. My phone is gonna run down."

"I took Hank a pair of pajamas. They had him in one of those awful hospital gowns. It's impossible to find a parking place at the Galleria. I had to follow a woman to her car and wait for her to leave so I could get her slot."

"Thanks for the traffic report. How's Hank doing?"

"As well as can be expected. At least that's what they say. He was barely awake when I was there this afternoon and it was after visiting hours tonight by the time I got the pajamas to the hospital. The woman at the reception desk said she would send them up to his room. Why were you calling every twenty minutes?"

"I wasn't going to tell you. I was just going to forget about it. But I changed my mind."

"About what?"

"I just found out something I think you want to hear. Notice I said *want* to hear, not *should* hear."

"You're talking in riddles."

"Maybe. This is gonna sound crazy, but I don't want to say it over the phone. I don't even know why I don't want to say it over the phone, except my gut says maybe I shouldn't. You being shot at and all."

"Do you mean to sound that mysterious?"

"Meet me at the bench in half an hour. I'm bringin' one of the kids with me."

◇◇◇

Rachel put three cans of cola in a Trader Joe's bag and went down to the bench. A light breeze was blowing mist into pale haloes around the streetlights.

Two figures pushed through the entrance door to the Inter-Urban Water headquarters across the street. A car passed, kicking up droplets of water. The two waited, then crossed the street.

"This is Inez," Goldie said.

The girl put out a hand. "Pleased to meet you, Missus." She looked Asian, but a bit bigger boned. Her eyes were those of a street urchin, wanting to please but ready to run.

"Pleased to meet you, too." Rachel handed out the cola.

"*Gracias,*" Inez said, and waited to pop the cap on her can until Goldie and Rachel popped theirs.

"This little charmer is an Indian," Goldie said. "A Native American, if you want to be politically correct. A real one."

"Really. How nice. What tribe?"

"The feds don't recognize her tribe," Goldie said. "Her people were more or less kicked off their land by the forest service or park service or some federal agency like that. She was only seven. Her pa was dead. Her mother got a job in San Marino as a maid and raised her there. Inez came to work for us as soon as she was old enough, which was about three months ago."

The girl was nodding, endorsing Goldie's words.

"The social workers call her learning disabled. No way. She's just shy. She's quick to catch on. She knows three languages, which is a whole lot better than me."

"Or me," Rachel said.

"Tonight she happened to mention something I decided you would want to hear." Goldie turned to Inez. "Tell Rachel what you told me."

The girl dropped her gaze to her feet. "Mama, she has, how you say, *amigo.*"

"Boyfriend," Goldie said.

"Luis has a boy like I am Mama's girl."

"Luis has a son," Rachel said. "Yes, I understand."

"This boy...Ésteven," Inez went on, "he has amigo, José."

Beginning to feel she might lose the thread of the story, Rachel nodded encouragingly.

"José is the principal player in this tale," Goldie said. "It'll take a little patience but you'll see why I brought her over."

Inez looked up at Goldie. "You say it. *No bueno, mi inglés.*"

"No. I want Rachel to hear it from you."

The girl fixed her eyes on Rachel and took a deep breath. "José, *Méxicano. Muy fino.*"

"He's a nice guy. Inez here is dating him," Goldie added.

"José, he come *aquí* go hospital."

"Hospital?" Rachel asked. "Do you know when that was?"

The girl stared at her for a moment. "*Uno año.*"

"About a year ago," Goldie translated.

"*Un hombre* in *México* say to José do he want be *Americano?* José say *sí.* So they make the deal. José go hospital. They...."

Inez looked at Goldie. "Cut?"

Goldie nodded.

"They cut him." Inez slowly finished her sentence.

Rachel frowned and stared, intent now on the girl. "Hospital? What do you mean, cut him?"

"Some kind of surgery, apparently," Goldie said.

A deep frown swept across Rachel's face. "Where did they cut him?"

Inez looked down and brushed an index finger across her stomach.

"Did he want to do this?" Rachel asked.

Inez shrugged. "He want be *Americano.*"

"Then what?" Rachel asked.

"After they cut, they send José to a *casa* where he meet *compadres.* Now José *Americano.*"

Goldie looked at Inez. "Tell her the name of the hospital where Jose went."

"I not say it good."

"Yes, you do," Goldie said. "Tell her."

"Hef-er-sun."

Chapter Forty-six

"Good girl," Goldie told Inez. "You said the whole thing very well. I told you, you could."

Inez was nodding, looking shyly pleased.

"Now you go on back to the crew, sugar. Rachel here and I need to talk."

Inez crossed the street, then turned to wave at the two women.

"Jesus Christ." The words burst from Rachel. "Maybe you were right when you said there might be some kind of ghoulish thing going on at that hospital. Something experimental. And illegal."

Goldie looked up and down the street as if she expected some-one might be lurking. "I don't know about ghoulish, but it seems pretty clear there's something weird going on. And somehow they're able to trade American citizenship for the right to do it."

"Whatever it is, I think it happened to that Mexican kid I took to the emergency room. That's where he disappeared to. I'd stake my garage on it."

"I figured you would say that."

Rachel stood up. "I'm going up there. Now."

"Good idea. Wake everyone up. Why not get yourself arrested for trespassing? Might as well add that to your rap sheet."

Rachel sat back down. "You're right. I'll wait till morning." She turned to look at Goldie. "Wait a minute…." She paused, considering the unthinkable. "No. It can't be as bad as I think. That would be grotesque, almost like vampires."

Goldie's eyes widened until the whites showed all the way around the dark irises. "Of course not…. Nah. Vampires do the neck, not the gut."

Rachel was nodding slowly and steadily, as if in time to something in her head. Finally, "No, it all fits," she said quietly, more to herself than to Goldie. "I just have to prove it."

"Prove what?"

"I think I know what Dan Morris was shipping by chopper four or five times a week."

◇◇◇

Rachel's alarm clock got her up at 4:30. She wanted to be fully awake and alert when she got to the hospital. And she wanted to get there a little after 6:30. The night shift should be getting ready to go home, and the day shift wouldn't have arrived yet.

She sat on the sofa in the dark, in the oversize tee shirt she wore for a night gown, listening to the chug of the coffee pot. Clancy stood in her lap, put his paws on her shoulder, and purred in her ear as she thought about what she wanted to do, and how she would do it.

"Is it worth the risk?" she asked the cat.

He only watched the ceiling intently as if he could see something that wasn't there.

The choice, she decided, had already been made for her by whoever had planted that bottle of OxyContin in her jacket, then had her arrested; by whoever had tried to kill or at least disable her; by the person who shot Hank.

She had been fairly sure the shooter in the Angeles was after her, not Hank. But it had been a fuzzy gray sureness. Now she was certain. A white-outlined-in-black certainty.

Something seriously shady, and probably criminal, was going on at Jefferson Medical Center. And she had gotten way too close.

Rachel drank her first cup of coffee as the light outside the window grew a little brighter. Hoping they provided the energy their wrappers claimed, she ate two trail bars. Then she put on sweats, changed tees and went out to jog for twenty minutes on city sidewalks that were blessedly empty at this hour. Only two cars and an SUV passed her.

Jogging helped. So did the shower she took after. She dried her hair and toweled off.

Is this how suicide bombers feel on the morning of their big day?

Dressed in jeans, she took another half cup of coffee, but it tasted of the pot, so she poured it down the drain.

She petted Clancy, who was certain he had done something to earn this attention, then told him goodbye and went down to open the garage. It was early, but she couldn't take the chance of not getting back soon enough to do it later. With any luck, the local criminals would sleep late.

Yellow rays of sun were just beginning to make their way between the high-rises. A few more cars roamed the street, but the air still smelled sweet.

What would she do once she had proof?

Go to the police? Yes. She would have to. They'd think it was trumped up because of her arrest for the OxyContin. She would insist someone accompany her back to the hospital and up to that ward. Maybe she should start by telling her attorney. Something should be done very soon. Maybe today.

What would she do if she was caught in that ward?

I'll have to wing it.

Would whoever caught her try to kill her?

In a hospital there must be dozens of interesting ways to do that.

Chapter Forty-seven

Rachel entered the hospital through the side door and took the stairs up four flights. A male nurse passed her going down. She smiled at him and nodded. He followed suit. If she got caught at this stage, the hospital would claim she was intent on stealing drugs.

But she went on climbing.

At the entry to the ward, the door made a metal-on-metal shriek when she pushed through it.

If there's a staff person nearby, I'm dead.

But no sound of footsteps came from the adjacent hall.

She inched her head around the corner of the wall. No one was in sight.

One of the rooms must serve as a nurse's station. Which? Hard to know. And there was no point spending any more time in the hall than necessary. Rachel swung around the corner and entered the first room on her left.

Three beds. Three boys. Smallish. Early teens, probably. Two sleeping, one yawning.

"Hello," Rachel said.

The yawner closed his mouth and gave her a puzzled stare. *"Hola?"*

Trying to look friendly and non-threatening, Rachel asked, "Do you speak English?"

He sat up, shook his head. Which meant he must have understood the question.

"Por favor." Please. "English. *Inglés.*" That rounded out about a quarter of Rachel's Spanish vocabulary.

The boy shook his head again.

"He speaks *inglés?*" She pointed at one of the sleeping boys.

"No."

Rachel looked over at the occupant of the third bed, who was beginning to stir.

"No."

The frustration must have shown on her face.

The boy who had just awakened got out of bed. Barefoot, hospital gown flapping about his narrow flanks, he took Rachel by the elbow. *"Inglés. Sí."* He took her arm and walked her into the hall, down two rooms and toward a door on the right. Rachel was suddenly terrified that he might be leading her to a nursing station.

But the room was like the other: three beds, three boys.

Her escort led her to the bed next to the window, where he shook the shoulder of the boy asleep there. "Miguel," he commanded. *"La señorita, de necesidad, inglés."*

The eyes of the boy in the bed slowly focused and he sat up. He looked a little older than the others. *"Está bien."* He turned to Rachel. "Yes, Miss. I help you?"

"Thank you," Rachel breathed. "Yes, please. First, are there nurses or doctors near here?"

"Now?"

"Yes, now."

Miguel started to get out of bed. "I find for you?"

"No!" Rachel said quickly. "I do not want to meet a nurse or a doctor."

"Ah." He seemed to recognize furtiveness and relate to it. "Someone here all night, then she go and another come."

"Is she here now?"

The boy looked at a clock on the wall near his bed and shook his head. "I think no."

"How long.... " Rachel hesitated.

"One hour, *más o menos.*"

Rachel nodded, trying to be sure she understood. "When did that hour begin?"

He stared at her frowning, and she decided the question had outstripped his English. She would have to assume it was roughly the hour that overlapped the two shifts.

"I am looking for a boy who was brought—who came here," she tried to keep the verbs simple, "about a month ago. He was unconscious." With her hands and cheek, she mimed sleeping. "Small. Smaller than you or that other boy." She touched the top of her head, then brought the flat of her hand down below her shoulder.

"*Sí.* I understand," Miguel said. "But is no boy like that."

The other two boys in the room were awake now and listening intently. He turned to them and spoke in rapid Spanish. When he finished, one boy shrugged. The other nodded slowly, then let out a short rush of Spanish syllables. "*Inconcienti?*"

"*Sí,*" Miguel said.

There was a long pause, then, "*Soledad,*" came the reply.

"*Ah, sí. Quizá. Es posible.*" Miguel turned to Rachel. "No boy like you speak of is here."

Rachel, who had been sure the exchange was the news she sought, frowned. "No? I thought…."

"*Esta niña.*" Miguel said. "Is a girl."

Chapter Forty-eight

"No," Rachel said. "Thank you for trying, but no. This was a boy."

"How you know? You see?" Miguel stood up and tugged his hospital gown an inch or two above his knees.

"Good heavens, no. Of course not." Beginning to wonder herself what made her so sure, she frowned, thinking back. "I'm not sure." Was it just the hair?

"Boy or girl, why you want this person?"

"I own a parking garage down the street. I found two kids locked in a van. I brought them to the emergency room here. They told me one was dead. When I came back the next day to see how the other was doing, they said there was no one like that here. But I know better. I brought him here."

"Aaah…." The sound was collective, from all three. It was hard to know how much they had understood. They began jabbering quickly in their own language.

Rachel glanced at her watch and knew she had little time left, if any.

"Come." Miguel drew her to the door of the room and gently pushed her against the wall. "You stay." He and his cohorts padded out into the hall.

Rachel tried to quiet her nerves. The last time she'd been in this ward she was arrested when she left. What would happen this time?

Miguel reappeared, put his hand to her forearm, and drew her through the doorway. "Is okay now."

Did he mean he understood, or that there was no staff around? Rachel desperately hoped it was at least the latter.

He half pulled, half pushed her down the corridor. Three rooms down on the left she could see the heads of the other two boys poke out to peer down the hall. One motioned for them to hurry.

There were three beds in the room, but only one in use.

Miguel pointed to the child in it. "Soledad."

The child frowned, sat up, peered shyly at Rachel. "Who you? You want me? *Porqué?*"

Rachel moved toward the bed. Yes. The face seemed faintly familiar. This might be one of the kids she had taken to the emergency room. The hair was a little longer but still boyish. "You are a girl?"

The child's nod was so tentative Rachel suspected that if she preferred a male, Soledad would do her best to be a boy.

"How old are you?"

"*Once.*" She pronounced it *own-say.*

"*Diez y uno,*" Miguel said. "Ten and one."

"Eleven?"

"*Sí.*" This from both Miguel and Soledad.

"Why are you here?" Rachel asked her. "Here in the hospital?"

The girl looked puzzled. "I wake. I here."

Thank God the child spoke some English. "You just woke up and you were here?"

Soledad nodded.

"How long have you been here?"

The girl held up three fingers. "*Tres semanas.*"

"Three week," Miguel agreed. "*Más o menos.*" More or less.

Three weeks, plus or minus. Time-wise, that fit.

"Maria?" Soledad asked.

"Who is Maria?"

"*Quién,*" Miguel inserted.

"Mi amiga." Soledad said and added something in rapid Spanish to Miguel.

Oh, no. The other kid. The one who died. Rachel dodged the question. "Do you remember being locked in a van? A truck?"

Soledad's brows drew together.

"Van." Rachel looked at Miguel, whose expression was blank.

"Car? Automobile?"

They all exclaimed, *"Coche."*

A faint dinging came from somewhere in the bowels of the hospital. Rachel's eyes darted nervously to her watch. "I have to go. I'll come back. Will you talk with me again?"

The four in hospital gowns nodded solemnly, but she wasn't sure how much they understood.

◇◇◇

"Meet me for lunch," Rachel said into the phone.

"I don't get up till then. I have breakfast at one," came Goldie's groggy voice.

"Okay, one."

"What time is it?"

"Eight o'clock. I waited as long as I could."

"Eight o'clock? I just got to bed. Why are you doing this to me?"

"You aren't going to believe what I found out this morning."

There was a long pause on Goldie's end, then, "I don't think I want to know."

"Please. You know I wouldn't ask if it wasn't important."

"Okay, okay. Where?"

"Philippe's."

"Oh, well. Twist my arm."

"Come on. How long has it been since you had a good French dip."

"I ain't never had a French dip, honey. That's for you white girls."

"Goldie!"

"That's what you get when you don't let me sleep. Okay!" she added quickly. "I'll be there. Two o'clock, right?"

"One," Rachel said, then, "Wait. Can you pick me up?"

"Something wrong with your car?"

"No. It was due for a tune-up, oil change, all that stuff. Johnny Mack says he has time now, so I want to get it out of the way."

As soon as Rachel hung up, she dialed the main number at Jefferson hospital. "Can you page Dr. Johnson? Emma Johnson."

How much did Emma know about all this? Could something like that be going on right under her nose without her knowing it? Very unlikely. Possible? A small maybe, but still a maybe. Jefferson was big, old and sprawling. The people who knew every inch of it were probably few.

"Dr. Emma Johnson. Paging Dr. Emma Johnson." Rachel could hear the hollow tones of the PA system. She ran her mind over what she would say when the doctor came to the phone. She would invite her to lunch, and once seated across a table, she would ask some very direct questions.

The receptionist came back on the line. "Sorry. Dr. Johnson isn't here. I've been told she is out of the country."

"When will she be back?" Rachel asked, but the line had gone dead.

◇◇◇

Marty stared at the second card that fell face up on the green felt tabletop in front of him. He squeezed his eyes tightly shut, then opened them wide. Both cards were clubs. The nine and ten.

His hair was shaggy, his eyes felt like two burned holes in his face. He had been up for how many hours? He looked at his watch. Thirty? The effect was worse than jet lag.

He tried to do the math, figure the odds. This was important. Real important. Rachel had called. Things were going from bad to worse for her. Now some stupid hunter had shot Hank.

Someone called from across the table, "Hey, Marty. Let's go."

"Hang on, hang on." Marty lifted the corner of the first hole card, then the other. The queen and jack of clubs.

He moved a stack of chips into the pot.

Chapter Forty-nine

There was a distinct bounce to his step as he moved through the parking lot. The silver 4Runner gleamed under the lights. The lot was sparsely littered with cars. An old man with a cane was hobbling along on the sidewalk. Marty thought his gait looked a little like Charlie Chaplin's.

He took a deep breath. The air tasted so good he wished he could liquefy it and drink it, get drunk on it. It was just after three a.m., but he wasn't tired.

His wallet no longer fit in his back pants pocket. It barely fit in his jacket pocket. For that matter, he could hardly fold it. The wallet was probably ruined, the jacket pocket might be ruined, too. But he didn't care. He could buy others. He could buy a thousand others.

Marty always took his winnings in hundred-dollar bills. For luck. To prime the luck-pump for the next game.

Wait till he told Rachel. He would call her as soon as he got home. Wake her up.

He punched a button on his key ring, the 4Runner's lights flashed, and he heard the click as the locks opened.

He was reaching for the door handle when a wooden hook grabbed his shoulder and twisted him around. Marty looked into the face of someone who was definitely not Charlie Chaplin.

A fist ground into his face and he slumped to the ground. Sharp pebbles bit into his cheek.

Something slammed into the back of his head, and the world faded to black.

◇◇◇

Goldie crossed her arms and looked over her eyeglasses at Rachel. They were standing in line at Philippe's. "I guess it would be asking too much for you to tell me what the hell I'm doing here."

Rachel rubbed the toe of her sneaker on the sawdust-covered floor and glanced around. "Wait till we get a table."

Goldie reached the counter and ordered a beef sandwich and potato salad. "What do you want?" she asked Rachel.

"Turkey, coleslaw, and lemonade."

They took their trays of paper-plated sandwiches and found a table at the back.

"Okay, what's up?"

"They were girls in the van. Both of them. One is up in that ward."

"No shit?"

Keeping her voice low, Rachel started a rapid blow-by-blow of her visit to the ward in the east wing of the hospital's fourth floor.

"You're talking with your mouth full," Goldie observed.

"I don't want my lunch to get cold. Since when do you stand on ceremony?"

"I don't. It's just harder to understand what you're saying."

Rachel put her sandwich down and sipped her lemonade. "What do you think they're doing up there with those Mexican kids?"

"Nothing good."

"I've got more than a sneaking suspicion. I'm just about certain."

Goldie took a bite of potato salad. "Like what?"

"Think about what Inez said. Her boyfriend was 'cut.' They're stealing body parts."

"Gak!" Goldie put her sandwich down. "Arms and legs? I swear. You must want my lunch telling me stuff like that."

"No, I mean organs. It's pretty obvious that's what Inez was saying."

"I thought she was talking about experimental operations. Some kind of research."

Rachel shook her head. "Think money. There's not enough money in developing new surgical procedures. But there's probably a lot of money in something like black-market human organs."

"Jesus, Mary, and Joseph. You think they're killing those kids?"

"No. At least not most of them."

"How else can they steal their gizzards?"

"Well, I read or saw somewhere recently that if they take out half your liver, it grows back. And if they transplant the part they took into someone else, that part grows back whole, too."

Goldie made a face. "I don't know about you, but I think that's a little creepy."

"And these kids are poor, young Mexican kids."

Goldie's face knotted into a frown. "You think they're kidnapping them in Mexico and bringing them up here to steal their livers?"

"Maybe half a liver. Or a kidney. Or who knows what else."

"How much can you get for a kidney or half a liver?"

"No idea." Rachel set down her lemonade.

"Well, if there's a lot of money in it, no wonder they didn't like you nosing around."

"If it really is a lot, and it just might be, I can even see how they might send somebody to take me out—because I got too close. I watched that surgery and then I saw that ward, both on the same morning."

"And the thug they sent got Hank instead," Goldie said. "Which means you're livin' a risky life right now. Real risky."

"Mind if I join you?"

They both looked up, startled, to see Gabe standing there with a tray.

Rachel brought her napkin to her mouth, tried to think of an excuse to say no, but couldn't. "Sure." She gave Goldie a look that said, "Why this, why now?"

"You got me, kid," Goldie said.

When Rachel had introduced them, and moved her tray to make room for Gabe's, Goldie stood up. "I'm going to get some lemonade. You make it sound good slurping it through that straw."

"Good sandwich," Gabe said when he had taken a few bites.

Rachel was wondering how much he had heard. "I guess that's why this place has been around more than a hundred years."

"You must know all the funky restaurants."

Goldie returned with a cup and straw. "Yessir, she does. What she doesn't know is how to stay out of trouble."

Rachel tried to think of something innocuous they could talk about until Gabe finished his meal.

Goldie solved that by asking, "You're a pharmacist, right? One of those guys who just fills prescriptions all day."

"Well, not exactly "just." At Jefferson, we work with various medical teams. I work with the pain program. There are so many medications these days, no doc could keep up with them all. We give advice to MDs, DOs, even to dentists, as well as to patients. And yes, of course we count out pills and fill prescriptions."

"You must have to take a course in reading bad handwriting," Goldie said.

Gabe chuckled. "Well, yes. That is a problem."

"I guess prescription drugs are pretty expensive these days," Rachel said.

Gabe nodded, chewing.

"I mean, that OxyContin they accused me of stealing, you said that was worth maybe a thousand bucks."

"Drug prices are getting worse by the day," Gabe agreed.

"Is OxyContin the most expensive one in your pharmacy?"

"Oh, no." Gabe shook his head. "Not even close."

Rachel wished he would finish his sandwich and leave. She was wondering about something else now and wanted to talk to Goldie. If she shut up, maybe he would chew faster. But that might seem rude. "What high-priced drugs do you sell the most of?"

Gabe thought about that. "Jefferson has a big transplant program. So for our pharmacy it might be immunosuppressants."

That was a more interesting answer than she expected. Rachel forced herself not to shoot a look at Goldie.

"Immunosuppressants are expensive?" Goldie was asking in a voice that sounded half bored.

"You better believe it." Gabe finished his sandwich and stood up. "Sorry to eat and run, but I gotta get back."

"Oh, no problem," Rachel said.

"Nice meeting you," he said to Goldie, and to Rachel, "Good to see you again." And he was gone.

"Jesus H. Christ," Goldie said. "Immunosuppressants. Isn't that what they give to people who get someone else's kidney, or whatever?"

"You got it. To keep the body's immune system from rejecting foreign tissue."

Goldie narrowed her eyes. "You think he heard anything?"

"Didn't seem like it."

Goldie stacked their paper plates and cups. "That doctor friend of yours, you think she might be in on something?"

"I've been wondering about that, but I really don't think so. If she is, she's the best actress I've ever seen. Emma has a real strong feeling for the Mexican people. It seemed hard for her to even talk about how poor they were down where her clinic was."

The two women made their way out of the diner.

"I ran out of time this morning," Rachel said. "I'm going back tomorrow."

"If you get caught, girl, it's gonna be *splat.* There won't be enough of you left to mop up with a paper towel."

A cell phone tootled. They looked at each other.

"Mine." Rachel pulled it from her handbag. "Yes?" Her face went startled, then puzzled. "You're kidding….No, that's crazy. I have no idea….Can you take it off? Yes, for God's sake, get rid of it."

"What's going on?" Goldie asked when Rachel had disconnected.

"You won't believe this."

"From your end of the conversation, you may be right."

"That was Johnny Mack."

"That's all you need. Something expensive is wrong with your car?"

"No, the car's fine. This is totally bizarre. I'd been wondering why some random goon took it into his head to shoot at Hank and me."

"I'm kinda hoping it was just some lunatic hunter gone postal," Goldie said. "Like the cops suggested."

Rachel gave her head a couple small, slow shakes. "I was, too. But apparently that was no accident, no coincidence at all."

"How would Johnny Mack know anything about that?"

"He found a tracking device under the Civic's rear fender."

Chapter Fifty

When Rachel got back to the garage, there were four voice-mail messages. Three were from places where she had applied for loans and she enjoyed deleting them. The fourth was from the attorney, Edgar Harrison. Her attorney. Her arrest. She was out on bail. It wasn't even a month ago, but it seemed like a year, almost another life.

She dialed Harrison's office.

"I have some news," he said. "I think it's good news."

"Okay," Rachel said warily. At this point it seemed to be getting more and more unlikely that there was good news anywhere.

"They're offering a plea."

"Like what?"

"They drop the charge to misdemeanor. You plead guilty and you'll just get thirty days and a year probation."

"No."

"Rachel, you should think about this. The drug was found in the jacket you were wearing. Trials can be iffy. Thirty days would be over in no time."

"And on my record for the rest of my life. No. Not just no, hell no. I didn't do it and I'm not going to say I did."

"I'm going to wait until Monday to respond. If you change your mind, give me a call."

"I won't change my mind, Mr. Harrison. I'm not going to say I did something I didn't do."

"Okay, okay. But remember, I won't call them until Monday."

Rachel disconnected, then dialed the main number of Pasadena Memorial General.

"Could you ring the room of Hank Sullivan?" she asked the receptionist. "I think it's six-fourteen."

The phone rang five times before he answered, and it sounded like the receiver had been knocked off the cradle rather than picked up.

"Hank?"

It seemed like a long time before he said, "Yeah."

"You okay?"

Another pause. "Yeah."

"You don't sound too good."

"Prob'ly the drugs." His voice sounded hoarse.

"What drugs?"

"Hospitals....They stuff you full of 'em."

"You sure you're okay?"

"Mmmm...."

"You got the pajamas I left for you?"

"Uh-huh."

"You like them? At least they're better than those stupid gowns."

"Uh-huh."

"I'm going to try to get over there this afternoon. Anything you want me to bring?"

"No. Won't be here."

"You won't be there? Why not?"

This time the pause was longer before he said, "Tests."

"Well, maybe this evening?"

She was still waiting for an answer when the line went dead.

◇◇◇

Rachel spent the rest of the day worrying. Who the hell had put a tracking device on her car? Maybe it was there when she bought the car—which was not all that long ago. But in the end, that didn't seem nearly as likely as the possibility that the device was what brought the shooter to the Angeles, and ultimately to their campsite. Which meant he was no mere hunter, berserk or otherwise.

Goldie thought Rachel should call the police about the device, but she put it off. Johnny Mack had already dumped it, but the cops would want to talk to him. He, like Rachel, had an arrest record, and she didn't want to subject him to questioning when it was unlikely anything could be learned.

Why was Hank sounding so out of it? They sure weren't kidding when they said he was sedated. Or was everyone lying to her? Was his condition worse than she thought?

◇◇◇

She had trouble finding a parking space at the hospital in Pasadena. The whole area was humming with activity. Families with hyperactive tots with runny noses and teens who looked like they would rather be elsewhere were streaming through the lobby when Rachel finally reached the main door.

The line for visitor sign-in was long and slow. When she finally got to room 614, Hank was asleep in the bed by the window, his mouth slightly open, his sandy hair looking a bit damp, his face a little flushed.

This time, the other bed was occupied as well. An elderly man in a dotted blue hospital gown was sitting upright gazing at the television high on the wall. He seemed to be all bone except for wisps of reddish gray hair that stood out at odd angles.

Nodding at Hank, he said to Rachel, "Been like that all day. Sure wish he'd quit the snoring."

Rachel moved one of the green-marbled plastic visitors' chairs close to Hank's bed, sat down, and took his hand in both of hers. He only snored a little louder.

"Hasn't he been awake at all?" she asked the old man.

"Not when I was watchin'."

Touching Hank's cheek, she softly called his name. He turned his head but slept on. The bank of instruments next to his bed showed numbers, but she wasn't sure what they meant.

She found a clean washcloth in the metal cabinet next to the bed and took it to the bathroom. There were pools of water on the floor. At least she hoped it was water. She tiptoed to the sink, dampened the cloth, went back to Hank, and gently wiped it across his face.

He felt warm. Was he running a fever? He turned his head back and forth as if trying to avoid the damp cloth, but still not waking.

Rachel folded the cloth, laid it on the cabinet, found the nurse call button, and clicked it on. Then she sat down, taking Hank's hand again.

The old man was watching a sitcom and from time to time he cackled, although Rachel thought the show was seriously unfunny.

At least half an hour went by and still no nurse came in response to the call button. Rachel checked to be sure it was still on, then went down the hall to the nurses' station. Inside the big square of countertops, five people in white were staring intently at papers or computer monitors.

She waited, cleared her throat, then tapped on the counter. "Excuse me?"

A dark man with long, straight jet-black hair and eyes that showed white all the way around the black centers looked up. "Yes?"

"The patient in room six-fourteen. Hank Sullivan. What's going on with him?"

The man behind the counter tapped several computer keys and stared at a screen. "Sullivan, yes. Gunshot."

"Is he okay?"

"Yes. His condition is stable."

"Are you sure? He doesn't wake up."

"Gunshot damage like this, you can't expect too much yet," the man said, still looking at the screen, that and the counter-level fluorescent lights giving his face a bluish cast. "But he is stable, really, ma'am."

"He seems feverish. Is there an infection?" Rachel asked.

The man scribbled something on a pad of paper. "I'll have someone check."

"The call button has been on for more than half an hour."

"We're extremely busy tonight. This wing is full up first time all year. Accident on the freeway."

"You won't forget to check him? Room 614."

"I promise."

Rachel made her way back to Hank's bed. Still no sign of consciousness. She sat, took his hand, and put her forehead down on the blanket next to it until a voice on the PA system announced the end of visiting hours.

Wanting to scream, wanting to be hysterical, she instead stood, then bent and kissed his forehead.

"Sure wish he'd quit snoring," the old man said as she left.

Chapter Fifty-one

When her alarm clock went off at 4:30 Rachel tried to remember why she had set it so early. Then the reason came to her and she hauled herself out of bed to begin the exact same routine she had followed the day before. Except this time, she opened the box that had been delivered while she was up in the Angeles with Hank. The box Irene had put in the apartment. Inside was the hospital scrub suit she'd ordered, and she was glad to see it looked very similar to most of those worn at Jefferson.

As soon as she had finished her coffee, done her jog along the sleepy city streets, showered and changed, and eaten some trail mix, she slipped the flat, folded scrubs under her shirt.

Having stuffed as much of the folded green fabric as she could into the side of her jeans, where her arm could keep it from falling to the sidewalk, she made her way to the hospital.

Entering this time by the lobby door, because only from there was she sure she could find a ladies' room, she waved boldly at the night-shift security officer, betting that there was no way he could remember the face of every single Jefferson employee.

He nodded and gave a small wave back.

Inside a stall in the restroom near the main lobby, Rachel shucked her jeans, shook out the scrubs, and donned the pants and top. She rolled up her jeans, shirt and jacket and shoved them down into the trash bin below the paper towel dispenser.

She took the elevator to the fourth floor and headed immediately for Miguel's room, arriving a little earlier than she had the day before. This time all three boys in the room were asleep.

She went to Miguel's bed and touched his shoulder.

He jolted awake, eyes startled, and sat up in bed frowning at her. *"Que paso?"* he asked sharply.

Didn't he recognize her?

The boy in the next bed either hadn't been asleep or was a light sleeper. He rolled over, sat up, and shot a sentence of low staccato Spanish at Miguel.

Miguel went on frowning and Rachel realized it was the scrubs that kept him from recognizing her.

"Remember me?" she asked. "From yesterday. I told you I would come back."

"Sí?" Miguel sounded unsure.

Rachel pinched some of the pale green material at her shoulder. "I'm wearing this so people will think I work here."

"Disfraz?" Miguel asked.

Not understanding the word, but recognizing the first syllable as sounding the same as that of "disguise" or "deceive," Rachel ventured a tentative, "Yes."

"Comprendo." The boy's face relaxed.

"I thought maybe you would go with me to Soledad's room." The limited English of both Soledad and Miguel would double Rachel's chances of being understood.

He nodded, got out of bed, and padded barefoot across the room. At the door, he stopped and touched an index finger to his lips, then motioned for Rachel to wait. The other boys, both awake now, sat on the edges of their beds, apparently unwilling to be left out.

Miguel inched his head past the door. Trying to do something without being seen clearly was not new to him. He looked both ways, then signaled her to follow him. She heard the bare feet of the other boys traipsing behind her.

Soledad's big dark eyes were open and watching the door of her room. Had she heard them or had she somehow known

Rachel would come back at this time on this day? The girl frowned and peered at her visitor suspiciously.

Miguel said, *"Disfrazo."*

The girl opened her mouth in a silent "ah," and her face lost its tenseness.

All four youngsters watched Rachel expectantly and she wondered why these kids were so interested. They had no real reason to be fascinated by her own comings and goings. Maybe it was unusual for an adult to pay attention to them. Or maybe they were bored. Hanging out in a hospital couldn't be much fun.

Soledad pulled her sheet and blanket chastely around her, as she had the day before.

The girl's unwavering eyes met hers as Rachel asked, "Why are you here?"

Soledad gave an exaggerated shrug.

Rachel looked at the three boys, who had clustered around the bed. "Why are you here? Any of you. Why are you here in this hospital?" She pointed at each of them, then jabbed her index finger at the floor.

"Porque aquí," Miguel said.

"*Doctor* say eat," the girl said. "*Señora Doctor furiosa.* No girl. More fat. More old. *Muchacho.* Boy."

Miguel took Soledad's hand and encircled her wrist with his thumb and forefinger. *"Muy pequeña.* Too little."

Rachel nodded. "Yes, she looks too young, too small, to even be away from home."

"*No es verdad* if home *es mal,* bad," Miguel said.

Rachel tilted her head, examining Soledad's face again. "I guess that's true."

Miguel pointed at Soledad and rubbed his belly. "*Éste muchacha,* she eat and eat and eat."

Puzzlement deepening, Rachel glanced at each of the boys. All were barely a notch or so above skinny. "Is that why you're here? All of you? To eat? To fatten you up?" The latter suddenly struck her as macabre.

"No mas que." Miguel pantomimed, moving a finger in diagonals across his abdomen. "Knife. *Hacerce operar.*"

The boys were all nodding.

Rachel's eyes narrowed. She had promised herself not to lead them into saying anything, and she hadn't. "You are all here for surgery? For operations?"

"They are here to eat, gain weight, save themselves, and in the process, save someone else."

The voice came from behind Rachel. How could she have been so stupid as to turn her back to the door?

"And now I must ask you to come with me."

Chapter Fifty-two

Rachel turned, not sure whether to be relieved or aghast. "Emma?"

"I'm afraid so." Emma turned to the boys and spoke in stern Spanish. "Get back to your own room."

They pushed past Rachel, then past Emma, and fled the room.

"Soledad," Emma said, "breakfast is coming. Chorizo and eggs and a tortilla. You must eat it all."

Soledad's solemn eyes were very large. She nodded.

"Now, come with me," Emma said to Rachel.

And Rachel, like the boys, obeyed.

The nursing staff station was in the center room across the hall. Emma led the way through that into a small windowless space that might once have been a wheelchair-accessible bathroom. It was now furnished with a small desk, a table, and two chairs.

She closed the door behind Rachel, turned the latch, then slowly and deliberately moved to the front of the desk and leaned against it. She was wearing a white lab coat, short navy skirt, black stockings, and flat black shoes. A turquoise and green scarf had been tucked into the neck of the lab coat. "What are you doing here, Rachel?"

Back against the door, Rachel wondered how long it would take to twist the lock and make a run for it. Ignoring Emma's question, she said evenly, "I thought you were out of town, out of the country as a matter of fact."

Emma's face remained expressionless. "I was. I'm back."

"Did you bring more kids from Mexico so you could lock them up and steal their organs? Kind of like keeping a chicken alive until you want to eat it? That way you don't even need a refrigerator."

"Dear God!" Emma drew back as if she'd been struck. "How can you say such things?"

Their words hung between them like icicles in frozen air.

A muscle in Emma's jaw twitched. She raised her chin and turned her full blue gaze on Rachel. "I asked you what you are doing here."

"I came to find the child I brought to the emergency room. The one who went missing at this hospital."

"As I understand it, you are out on bail after having stolen some drugs from this hospital."

"I didn't take that bottle of OxyContin, Emma. I think you, of all people, know that."

Two vertical lines appeared over Emma's nose.

"You want to tell me what's going on here?" Rachel asked.

Emma lowered her chin and stared first into the middle distance, then at Rachel. "I don't think you really want to know. But I will tell you this: What we do here does far more good than harm."

"I'd like to believe that, Emma. I really would. But what are all these kids doing here? Why is there this secret, very busy ward with a closed sign on the door? Why did someone in this hospital plant a bottle of OxyContin on me?" Rachel paused, then said slowly, "Most of all, I'd like to believe you don't intend to kill me right here in this neat little room with no windows and acoustical tile on the ceiling."

Emma's brows drew down and her eyes snapped. "Rachel! How can you—"

"Why would I think that? Because if you let me out of this tidy little room, I am going straight to the police."

"And what makes you think they would believe you?"

Rachel stared at her. "Oh...my...God." Her voice was barely audible. "So that's why."

"We couldn't very well let you go on nosing around. But now, I would like to save you some trouble—and embarrassment."

Rachel found herself nodding like a toy with a spring-mounted head. "Okay. What do I have to do to avoid trouble and embarrassment?"

"Not a thing, actually. In fact you just might even find your arrest removed from the Rampart's books."

"You could do that?"

The doctor met her look and nodded. "I might."

"What is going on here?" Rachel asked again.

"Sit." Emma pointed at the chair in the corner.

"I'd rather stand." Rachel didn't want to get that far away from the door.

"Rachel, get a grip. The last thing in the world I want to do is harm you. This is not what you think."

"Just the same, I'd rather stand."

"Have it your way." Emma went to the chair behind the desk and sat down.

Rachel took a deep breath. She felt a little safer with the desk between them.

Emma leaned forward, propped an elbow on the desk and her chin on her hand. Somehow that pose made her seem less threatening and Rachel allowed herself to relax a little.

"This is the truth: The children in this ward are going to be better off because they were brought here."

"Better off? With an organ missing? A kidney or half a liver? Or what else do you relieve them of? A cornea or two? Jefferson Medical Center gives the term chop shop a whole new meaning."

Emma stared at her for a long moment, then said quietly, "Rachel, you don't understand the kinds of places these kids come from."

"Well, at least they aren't missing body parts. Not until they get here. How much do you sell them for?"

"I am not going to dignify that with an answer."

"I hope it's a lot," Rachel said. "I would rather think you don't risk their lives on the cheap."

"I, personally, don't get a dime, not one thin dime, if that's what you mean."

"Then why the hell do you do it?"

"If I answer that honestly, will you listen?"

"I don't seem to have a lot of choice."

Chapter Fifty-three

"I think you mentioned you've never been to Mexico," Emma said.

"No, I haven't."

"Do you know much about Mexico?"

"No."

"I thought maybe since your name is Chavez...."

"I wish I knew more about the Chavez end of things, but I don't."

"Okay, for the moment, you'll have to take my word for it," Emma said. "Where these kids come from there is more poverty—abject poverty—than you can probably imagine."

"Are they from the area where your clinic was?"

"Some. All are from places where the men feel helpless and that makes them angry. The women feel betrayed, so they, also, are angry, and when they are not angry, they are depressed. At least a quarter of the boys will not reach thirty. Their lives are likely to be cut short by a knife in a bar room brawl. The girls live in a fantasy world until they are old enough to bear children. Then they become betrayed women. I don't take girls, by the way."

"Why not?"

"Because things are not exactly rosy here in the land of milk and honey either. A lot of kids take some hard knocks here. Chicanas, Mexican girls can easily fall into prostitution or worse, become sex slaves."

"How thoughtful of you to refuse to take them."

"I don't take boys under the age of seventeen, either."

"A couple of the boys out there don't look much more than thirteen or fourteen."

"They're small for their age. You can imagine the nutrition. Or maybe you can't. I don't do surgery on anyone underage or seriously underweight."

"You fatten them up for the kill."

"I feed them, they gain weight. They become more healthy. Is that bad?"

"Maybe. Especially if you then remove some of that weight and sell it."

"Rachel, we do not, repeat, *do not,* sell anything."

"That's hard to believe."

"Why?"

"Because when criminal, corrupt, unethical things are done, it's almost always for money. Why else do it?"

"I am proud of what I do," Emma said. "You simply don't realize the desperation, the terrible need for transplantable kidneys. The Global Organ Sharing Network has more than a hundred thousand on its waiting list and that list grows by at least ten percent per year. And far too many of them die waiting."

"What about that little sticker on my driver's license?"

"Those stickers provide only about eighty-five hundred trans-plantable kidneys per year. Don't take my word for it, look it up. Less than ten percent of those needed. That's common public knowledge. Don't you know anything about this?"

"I didn't know it was that bad. I've heard about people offer-ing kidneys on eBay. I've read that there's a regular organ market in India, that China sells the organs of executed criminals. But this is Los Angeles. Using poor Mexican kids...."

"I swear to you, Rachel, those kids are better off. And for the people who receive an organ or tissue from them, it's the differ-ence between life and death. This is not a crime, it's a win-win situation."

"Really." Rachel eyed her for a moment. "Exactly how does it work? Who pays for it—the running of this whole ward, all of it?"

"The transplant team, mostly. It comes out of our budget."

"The transplant team is part of Jefferson Medical Center?"

"Yes."

"And everyone at Jefferson knows what's going on here?"

"Of course not."

"Everyone must know. The kitchen sends up trays, the O-R receives these kids for surgery and sends them back, the janitors have to clean the place." Rachel hesitated a moment before adding, "The pharmacy has to provide pills."

"Of course a lot of people know these rooms exist. But this is a big hospital. The kitchen sends up trays, they don't ask where the patients came from or why they're here. The cleaning staff mops floors, they don't know anything about the patients in these rooms. We kind of imply that it's a charity ward for young Latinos, and people have no reason to believe otherwise."

"Even the O-R staff? They don't question anything?"

"They know Jefferson has a big transplant program. They look after surgical patients, they don't ask exactly how it was decided that someone should have a particular procedure. They assume the admitting doctors, the surgeons, are responsible for that."

Rachel was remembering how Gabe had described the pharmacy's big volume in sales of immunosuppressant drugs using the same words: Jefferson has a big transplant program. "What about the hospital administration?" she asked.

"Of course, a few of them know. They have to. A few very near the top. The ones who sign the papers, the checks. You think hospitals aren't capable of a little Enron-style bookkeeping? They tell us fairly frequently that Jefferson is not an altruistic organization, it's a business enterprise."

"Some others must guess what's going on."

"A few probably do, but they look the other way."

"Why?"

"Probably partly because they know we are doing so much good and so little harm. In other cases, okay, it may be because their pay envelopes are pretty fat."

"And you're not worried about law suits?"

"Filed by whom? Certainly not one of the kids. They know they're better off. They also know they are in this country illegally. The last thing they want to get involved in is a law suit. The transplant recipients don't know anything about the donors, and even if they did, they are desperate. They are very literally dying. They want to live.

"Last but certainly not least, our medical practices here are on the cutting edge, among the best anywhere."

Rachel shook her head. "What's the money angle? How can you pay higher staff salaries, pay the people who smuggle these kids across the border? If there's no big profit, where does all that money come from?"

"The revenue from roughly three thousand additional transplant procedures per year."

"How much is that?"

"I don't know exactly."

"Roughly."

Emma thought for a moment. "It could be as much as thirty million."

Rachel stared at her. "A year."

"Yes."

"You're telling me you don't sell the organs, you transplant them into other patients right here at Jefferson?"

Emma nodded emphatically. "I am unequivocally telling you we do not sell organs. Period. We do, however, keep quite a few transplant surgeons busy."

"But the shelf-life, so to speak, of say, a kidney, can't be very long. How do you work that fast?"

"For one thing, we can do tissue matches with our own transplant patient waiting list before the donor's surgery. And, secondly, we trade."

"Trade?"

"The closer the tissue match, the better chance the graft will survive. We send kidneys, for example, all over the country, and receive others from all over. Our patients have some of the best odds for survival anywhere. That's because we trade some of the organs we remove. If they don't provide our own patients the very best match, we trade for organs that do."

"How can you transport organs that quickly?" Rachel's eyes widened as she realized the answer. "Omigod. They leave and arrive by helicopter."

"Yes."

"And what about the kids who happen to lose a kidney, or whatever, in your self-styled philanthropy?"

"First, I assure you that we are absolutely state-of-the-art here. Organ excision by laparoscopic surgery may not be risk free, but it is quite low risk."

Emma bit her lower lip and determined eyes drilled into Rachel's. "You may have heard that kidney donors are neglected at some transplant centers. There was a TV special about that a year or so ago. That does not happen here.

"Our donors get the best of everything, food, treatment, medical care. I, personally, see to that. Even with ordinary care, the odds of the remaining kidney ever failing are small. Most kidney donors live long and normal lives. And, I repeat, the kids in this ward come from unimaginable destitution. They are much more likely to die in that environment than from having only one kidney here."

"How do they get here? Are they kidnapped?"

Emma picked up a ballpoint pen from the desk and rolled it between index finger and thumb. "Not one comes here by force or coercion. Every single one volunteers. They are carefully chosen for their age and general health."

"And they enter the country legally?

"Of course not, Rachel. Don't be naïve. You've heard the guessed-at statistics. Hundreds of thousands, maybe a million undocumented foreigners crossing the Mexican border every year. A tiny percentage are boys brought to us here before they enter new and better lives. A coyote is hired to have them smuggled into this country. As I understand it, the coyote hires a *brincador* who brings them through a tunnel under the Arizona/Mexico border. I don't much care for all the middlemen, but that is how it's done."

"That van in my garage was hardly testimony to how well the kids are treated on the way here," Rachel said.

Emma turned her head sharply as if she'd been slapped. Her cheeks reddened. "That was inexcusable. The man responsible will never do another job for us."

"He should be in jail."

"If I could figure out how to make that happen, I would. But thousands of farm workers, restaurant workers, hotel workers, have come to this country through that same tunnel, in the same way. And in their case, it's because American corporations want illegal workers who can't protect themselves from exploitation. That's far worse that what we do."

"Are you saying you're not exploiting these kids?"

The doctor shook her head. "Instead of spending years running from the authorities, and ruining their backs crouching over strawberry plants in order to be paid a pittance, our boys are brought here where we feed them, care for them, and do every possible test to be sure they can be donors with minimum, absolute minimum risk."

"You say they volunteer. What do they volunteer for? To come to California? I'll bet they don't volunteer to donate a body part."

"As a matter of fact, they volunteer to do exactly that."

Rachel gave Emma a doubtful stare. "I would bet they don't understand."

"I assure you, they do. I insist that it be explained. They volunteer because they want to better their lives. They want to become American citizens."

"And just how do you manage that?"

"Once they're well enough, and strong, we send them to what could be described as halfway houses in east LA, where they learn

English. We give them some money. Not a huge amount, but enough to tide them over until the people at the halfway house help them find jobs. A couple of our kids have even taken the GED and started community college."

"How do they get around the citizenship questions?"

"Where do you think birth certificates are generated?"

Chapter Fifty-four

Rachel's mouth dropped open.

"That's right," Emma said. "Birth certificates usually originate in hospitals. On forms signed by doctors and notarized. Copies are sent to the state. But of course the system isn't perfect. And a small stack of the forms went missing a while back. It was assumed they were somehow thrown out by mistake."

"How can you get away with that?" Rachel asked. "Aren't there cross-checks?"

Emma shrugged. "You would think so, but it's really remarkably simple. And a notary's stamp isn't all that hard to come by."

"You said you don't take girls, but there's one out there. Alone in a room. Soledad."

"As I said. The kids who are here want to come here. Some have a friend or relative who did it. Others hear about it from someone who knew people who came here. Some want to come here so badly they lie about their age and even their sex. Soledad originally arrived here with another girl. Both had their hair shorn, hoping to pass for boys. Naïve, yes. They have good intelligence, but little or no education. Both the girls were way under age. They may have been sold to the coyote by their parents."

"Sold? By their own parents?"

"A parent may want a better life for a child, as well as for themselves and the children who remain. But please remember that I refused to take the girls." Emma's eyes flashed. "I didn't want the coyote to think he could get away with that. I should have realized what would happen. As you obviously know, both girls came back to the hospital through the E-R. Maria was dead. Soledad was in serious condition."

"So you are keeping Soledad? For your, shall we say, purposes?"

"To tell the truth," Emma said, "I don't know. And this won't be the only time girls will be smuggled in here. So I have to think of something."

Rachel was shaking her head. "No matter how you spin it, pretty it up, Jefferson Medical Center is stealing kidneys. And that ward out there is a black-market organ ward."

There was a long pause before Emma said, "I wouldn't call it that."

"If everything is so clean and nice, why did someone try to kill me last weekend?"

"What?" Emma sounded shocked, but Rachel wasn't sure the doctor's look was not just carefully studied surprise.

"Exactly," Rachel said. "Whoever it was, missed me and hit my friend."

"My God," Emma said. "Believe me, there's no connection to Jefferson, to the transplant team here. I guess I can see how you could think there might be, but that event has to be a coincidence. We *save* lives here. We don't *take* them."

"I'm not convinced, Emma."

"Well, forgive me for this, but if you tell the police your suspicion, they won't believe you. We've seen to that. I'm sorry, Rachel, but we had to. What we're doing here is too important."

◇◇◇

Rachel walked back to the garage trying to order her thoughts. This must be what it would be like on another planet, where enemies were friends and some friends could not be trusted.

Eventually, Emma had come to some decision and allowed her to leave, had escorted her out of the hospital. They stopped at the ladies' room on the first floor and while Rachel dug her clothing out of the waste paper bin, Emma watched, head slowly shaking. "You really are very clever."

At the garage, she barely stopped at her cubicle to check phone messages before walking up the ramp to her Civic and heading for Pasadena. She had to see Hank.

Making her way through the hospital lobby, she took the stairs to the sixth floor. The door to 614 was open.

Both beds were made up with fresh linens. Both were empty.

Now what?

Rachel hurried down the hall to the nurses' station.

"Where is the patient from room six-fourteen?" she asked the man behind the counter.

"Bed A or B?"

The look he gave her seemed wary and a tide of panic rose inside Rachel. "I don't know," she faltered. "The bed by the window."

He went to a computer, tapped a few keys and squinted at the monitor. "Sullivan?"

"Yes."

"He's been transferred to an isolation unit."

"Isolation? Why?"

"You are a relative?"

"Yes," she lied.

"Apparently there's an infection. This is just a precaution until the antibiotic takes effect."

"Can I see him?"

"No ma'am. No visitors allowed in isolation."

"How long will he be in isolation?"

"If the antibiotic is successful, it could be only a few days."

◇◇◇

Back at the garage, Rachel called Goldie's number and left a message. Marty's line rang six times. Rachel hung up. His voice mail was likely full. He probably hadn't been home in a while. She knew what that meant. She looked up the number of his favorite poker club, punched it into her phone and asked for him. Everyone there knew him. "This is his daughter," she added, suspecting they protected men from fuming wives.

"I don't think he's here, but I'll check. Hang on."

The line went empty for what seemed like a long time.

"Nope, not here. I asked around. They say he hasn't been in since his big win."

Rachel thanked him and hung up. Big win? A new big win or the old big win? They usually didn't come in pairs. But no way could Marty stay away from a poker table very long, and he was not only loyal to One-Eyed Jack's, he never switched clubs after a sizeable win. Supposed to be bad luck or something.

Rachel chewed on her pencil. Something didn't feel right.

If there was worrying to be done, she'd have to do it later. Right now, her head felt like it was going to explode. She had to find someone to help her reconcile all this bizarre information.

Looking up, she saw Irene pushing her cart up the garage ramp. The woman was carrying an umbrella, although there was no sign of rain. That and the high-collared prim blouse she wore today made her silhouette look like a plump Mary Poppins. She parked the cart in the space Rachel always saved for her and, umbrella still in hand, came to the booth.

"Dear girl! It is such a lovely day and here you are looking so glum."

Wondering if she could trust Irene with her quandary, Rachel gave a small shrug and decided no, probably not. Not right now, anyway. Irene might be on first name terms with just about everyone over the age of six in Los Angeles County, but she loved nothing more than a nice morsel of gossip. Rachel needed to think things through. And helping with that was probably not Irene's strong suit.

As it turned out, she was wrong.

"It isn't your friend, is it, luv? He hasn't taken a turn for the worse, has he?"

"No." Rachel shook her head. "At least I don't think so."

Today, Irene's hair was in gray pin curls. The woman's mouth made a broad smile below apple-red, round cheeks. "No, of course not. I knew that."

"How do you know that?"

"Oh, from time to time, I take me a look into the unseen present as well as the past and future. Things will be not quite as expected, but he will be in fine fettle in no time. You'll see."

Rachel knew Irene wanted her to ask for details, but she never quite believed the woman when she was playing the mystic, so instead, she pulled out the handbag Peter had given her. "I need to pay you for the weekend. I'm sorry. I should have done it before. Can I give you a check?"

"Of course, dear girl. But just this once. I don't care to have the tax man poking about in my business."

Writing out the check, Rachel realized she didn't know Irene's last name.

"Never mind. It's very long and hard to spell. Just write it to Irene. And thank you kindly. But I dare say, you do still look peaked. Tell Irene what is troubling you."

"Oh, it's just that I have to decide what to do about something. And I haven't quite got it sorted out in my head yet."

"You don't want to talk about it?"

"Not right now, no."

"You have to decide something on your own say-so and you don't know what that say-so is."

"That probably describes it."

"Then you would be well advised, dear girl. Very well advised, indeed, to consider the words of Dr. Reinhold Niebuhr."

"Who?"

"Never mind, luv. The man's name is not important. It's the little prayer he wrote for a service at a church in Massachusetts that has helped so many folks make the choices they have to make. It was a Congregational church. Nineteen forty-three."

"All right." Rachel waited for some bland little homily that had caught Irene's attention.

"Give us the grace to accept with serenity the things that cannot be changed, courage to change the things which should be changed, and the wisdom to distinguish the one from the other."

◇◇◇

Rachel went through the motions of the day's work, stopping a couple times to wonder how Irene had managed to come up with virtually the same lines so many alcoholics kept in their wallets or posted on the doors of their refrigerators. Was the woman really clairvoyant? How did she know the name of the person who authored it and where and when? Or did she make up that part?

Whatever, Rachel gained a smidgen of serenity from it, enough to get through the day with reasonably sensible thinking. What did she have to accept? That Hank had been horribly injured, for one thing. That now he had an infection dangerous enough to land him in isolation.

Was there anything in her power to change? By mid afternoon, when she saw Emma come through the street door, she knew at least one answer to those questions.

She motioned to the doctor, walked over to where Emma waited, leaned against the wall, and crossed her arms. "I have a proposal."

Faint alarm seemed to register in Emma's eyes. "Yes?"

"I will not go to the police about this," Rachel began. "At least not right now. But I have a price."

"And that is…?"

"Soledad."

Chapter Fifty-five

"What are you saying, Rachel?"

"You said yourself you don't know what to do with her. You said her parents probably had sold her. And I have very little doubt that whoever locked her in that van in my garage left her there to die. Your system, if we can call it that, is set up for boys. Apparently Soledad has no one to take care of her and nowhere to go. And she's only eleven years old. In the long run, you don't have many choices. You can send her back to the people who sold her and try not to know when they sell her again."

"There is the Department of Social Services," Emma said.

"Oh, sure. I'll bet people are lining up to provide a foster home, let alone adopt, an eleven-year-old Mexican girl who barely speaks English and is in this country illegally. Do you know how Social Services even deals with a case like hers?"

Emma gave Rachel a long look as if sizing up her intent. Finally the doctor said, "Frankly, no, I don't. I've been thinking I should try to find out, but I'm afraid of tipping my hand."

Rachel raised her chin and stared hard at Emma. "So here's another option. I want to ask her if she would like to come live with me."

◇◇◇

The autumn sun made their shadows very long as the two women threaded their way along the sidewalk among pedestrians newly freed from offices and anxious to get to their cars and go home.

"You're sure you've thought about this enough?" Emma asked. "The job you'd be taking on is not a small one. Soledad is nearing puberty. What do you know about teenage girls?"

"Not a lot," Rachel had answered. "Except I was one. A long time ago."

"Shouldn't you wait another few days?"

"Not really. Look, I don't want to take her right away. Not until you say she's strong enough. Not until she says she says she's ready. But everything in my life is so frigging uncertain right now that one more uncertainty will drive me straight over the edge."

"Given your emotional state, you think you're up to the task?"

"I'm probably a better option than the county or the coyote or someone who deals in sex slavery which, as you mentioned, may be right around the corner for someone like Soledad."

Emma stopped on the corner and looked into Rachel's face. "Forgive me, but I have to ask. What if you're convicted for drug theft?"

Rachel drew in a long breath and was silent a moment. "I told you, Emma. I didn't do it."

"As a matter of fact, I know you didn't. But I didn't say what if you're guilty, I said what if you're convicted."

Rachel ran her gaze along the tops of the buildings across the street, lined in red by the lowering sun. "I have a father, friends. If worse comes to worst, I can make arrangements." She hoped that was true. "It's better than the people who sold her or left her to die."

They walked the rest of the way to the hospital in silence, went in the side door and took the elevator to the fourth floor. Pushing the button inside the car, Rachel asked, "Is that ward the reason for the weird floor numbering?"

"I don't think so," Emma said. "I think they originally used European floor numbering for some obscure reason, and never changed it."

The elevator stopped at the ground floor and three people in whites entered. One looked at Emma and said, "I thought you had left."

The doctor shrugged. "Forgot something."

Rachel wondered if these and all the other Jefferson staff members knew about the special ward. Despite Emma's explanations, it seemed like a lot of people to trust with a secret. Maybe it was a case of hiding in plain sight.

The answer was obvious when they all got off on the same floor. Emma was clearly well versed in the charade. The doctor turned left instead of right, and with Rachel following, walked around another ward until the others veered off, then headed back in the right direction.

"Surely a few other people besides me have stumbled across that ward," Rachel said.

"Not many, actually. Most people are in a hurry and they know the building rambles. They see the *Closed* sign and turn back. Almost everyone knows we used that area at one time as a celebrity ward, long ago, actually, but celebrity gossip hangs on. Employees know the celebrities were moved to the top floor, the old wing was closed and slated for revamp. All that is reported in the employee newsletter. Supervisors were asked to announce at staff meetings that the old ward was unsafe due to earthquake damage. Now we mention from time to time that we're using it as a charity ward for young Latinos.

"People are busy. They don't remember exactly what they've been told, or when."

"Smoke and mirrors."

"Whatever." Emma shrugged. "It works for the politicians. Why not us? Only four employees have gotten too curious. They no longer work here."

"Did they have a bottle of some controlled substance planted on them?"

Emma didn't answer. She swung open the door that bore the *Closed* sign and moved quickly down the hall.

Soledad was laughing at a television show on a Spanish language station. She jumped, startled, eyeing Emma and Rachel worriedly as they entered her room.

"It's okay, Soledad," Emma said in English and followed it with Spanish that sounded calm and sedate compared to the Mexican boys' rapid-fire sentences.

When Emma paused, Soledad began shaking her head. "No." Then she began chattering quickly in Spanish.

Rachel asked Emma, "What did you say to her?"

"I said I can't keep her here much longer, that she is too young for the organ donor program and that in another week or so, when she has gained a little more weight, she can go home."

"What was she saying no to?" Rachel asked.

"She doesn't want to go home. Not exactly surprising. She says her father left the family long ago. Her mother died last year. She says the people who handed her over to the coyote were kind to her, but they aren't her family. She worked for them. She did laundry and took care of their children. The people gave her food and clothes and let her sleep on the floor of a shed with a goat and a donkey."

"Good God. That passes for kindness?"

"Actually, where Soledad comes from, it does."

"And it was out of kindness that they sold her?"

"I would guess that they couldn't afford to feed her anymore," Emma said. "And they probably thought Soledad was going to live the good life in America, so why shouldn't they take a little money to ease their own lives in exchange."

"She speaks a little English. Let me ask if she wants to come with me. Maybe let me say it and you translate."

"Go ahead."

"Soledad," Rachel began, "I own a parking garage, a place for cars. I have an apartment there." She waited for Emma to translate, then went on. "The living space not very big and there is no yard to play in. I don't know of any kids your age in the area. I don't even know where the school is." Rachel waited again.

Soledad, watching her very carefully, seemed to be studying every nuance of word and expression.

"That said, would you like to come stay with me for a while?"

Soledad was nodding slightly as if she understood the words but wasn't sure it was a question she was supposed to answer. She moved her eyes from Rachel to Emma and back, then nodded vigorously. "*Sí*. Yes. For me." She grinned broadly, showing a splash of white teeth in a face that promised to be very pretty one day.

Rachel put her arms out and Soledad threw herself into them.

Chapter Fifty-six

"Are you out of your ever lovin' mind?" Goldie said when Rachel told her about Soledad. "You have flat out taken leave of your senses."

They were sitting on the front steps of the InterUrban headquarters across the street from the garage. The night was chilly. Both wore bulky sweaters.

"Maybe," Rachel said, thoughtfully. "But somehow it seems like a good idea."

Goldie threw up her hands. "The road to the hot place is paved with ideas like that. Teenage girls want hundred-dollar aerobics shoes, ninety-dollar jeans, fifty-dollar blouses that are eight sizes too small. They do drugs, they get their body parts punctured. They get pregnant."

"I thought you liked kids," Rachel said.

"I come from a big family. Eight of us. I'm the oldest. I love kids. Right up to about age six. After that any adult should have the right to strangle one."

"They aren't all that way."

"No, but you aren't likely to be getting one of the point-oh-five percent that isn't."

"Soledad has nothing and nobody. She needs an anchor."

"Yeah, well, people who get caught in anchor lines get drowned. As in dead."

"You trying to talk me out of this?"

"You could call it that," Goldie said.

"Maybe *I* need a purpose."

"What you need is to take off those rose-colored glasses. They have made you blind and warped your mind. Have you talked to Hank about this? He just might have some little bitty notion about it."

"I tried to. I tried to see him twice. The first time he was still under heavy sedation. The second time, he was in isolation."

"Isolation for what?"

"Some kind of infection."

Goldie swung to face Rachel. "Hank is in an isolation unit and you didn't tell me?"

Two cars went by, their headlights making holes in the dark.

"I guess I don't want to face whatever that might mean," Rachel said.

"Tell me it isn't flesh-eating bacteria or anything like that."

"They just said infection. I don't know what to think."

"Wound like that, smack dab in the middle of all those inner parts. Can't be good." Goldie's gaze shifted to the sky. A few stars were barely visible above the omnipresent glow of city lights. "So you gotta make this earthshaking decision about this kid right away?"

"Not immediately. Like I told you, I thought I could keep her with me for a week or so and then the two of us could decide whether to make it permanent."

"Like taking a dog back to the pound if it pees on the carpet?"

"Jesus," Rachel said. "There's no way to win with you."

"It's just that I've seen some pretty awful stuff."

"Like what?"

"Like you don't even want to know."

"What about the kids who work for you? You're crazy about them."

"That's different."

"How?"

"I don't know, but it is. For one thing, I'm not responsible for them. If they do something bad, it isn't my fault."

"You helped raise your brothers and sisters. Weren't you responsible for them?"

"I sure was."

"Your brother was a police officer."

"Yep. Shot dead in uniform."

"I know. I'm sorry," Rachel said. "What about the others?"

"I got two brothers sitting in prison, even as we speak."

"I didn't know that."

"I got two sisters who are doing fine. One's a teacher."

"Three brothers, two sisters, including you, that's seven. You said there were eight of you."

"My sister Flo. She had a kid when she was only fourteen. Hannah. When Hannah was fifteen Flo caught her shootin' up. My sister tried everything. She even moved to Bakersfield. But that kid never saw sixteen. She got hold of some angel dust and stepped off the roof of a twelve-story building."

"Christ." Rachel pulled her sweater around her as a gust of wind come around the corner of the InterUrban headquarters building. "You're sure doing a good job of trying to talk me out of this."

Goldie turned up the collar of her sweater. "You're right. That's exactly what I'm trying to do. But I don't expect it'll work. And you know perfectly well that if you are hell bent to do it, I'll help you every way I can."

The next morning Rachel called the hospital and had Emma paged. When the doctor came to the phone, Rachel told her, "I want to spend the afternoon with Soledad away from the hospital."

Chapter Fifty-seven

Soledad's eyes were huge and glowing when Rachel arrived to pick her up. The child's pointed little chin and broad high cheekbones spoke of an elegant sort of beauty in the making. She giggled and shrugged when Rachel asked her where she would like to go.

"I guess you don't know about many places around here, do you?" Rachel asked.

"No, *señorita.*"

"Rachel. My name is Rachel."

"Su nombre? Ra-shel?"

"Yes." Rachel nodded appreciatively, then pointed at the girl's pants, which were too short by at least a couple inches above her bony ankles. "First we'll get you a few more clothes."

By the time they were on the freeway headed for Santa Monica, Rachel realized that the language barrier was far less a problem than she had anticipated. Soledad knew quite a bit of English but was afraid she would "say it bad."

"No matter what, sweetie, your English is a lot better than my Spanish. Maybe you can teach me a little Spanish and vice versa." It took a while to explain the last two words of that sentence.

She turned off the freeway and headed for her favorite thrift shop. Rachel bought most of her own clothes there and had seen kids' clothes on the racks.

Soledad's mouth made an astonished O when she realized she could choose some clothes for herself. She headed straight for the girls' jeans and selected a pair of Calvin Klein.

When she tried them on, Soledad posed, thumbs in pockets, in front of the dressing room mirror, then rolled her hips.

"Hey," Rachel laughed. "You're only eleven."

Soledad grinned. "Almos' too-elve."

Rachel suggested she find two more pair of jeans, and this time Soledad had to settle for L.L. Bean. For shoes she picked a pair of Reebok high-tops identical to Rachel's. They added a denim shirt and four tees. The whole bill was forty-one dollars.

Soledad took Rachel's hand as they walked back to the car. When they passed Baskin Robbins, Rachel pointed at the ice cream cone and Soledad nodded vigorously. "*Sí.* Oop. *Yes!*"

The girl's simple responses to small pleasures were so contagious that Rachel found herself in a better frame of mind than she'd been in since the first hours in the Angeles. She wished she could tell Hank about the girl. He would love Soledad.

With two double-dip white chocolate cones in hand, they found the Civic and Soledad held both cones while Rachel eased the car into the street.

"You want to go to the beach?" she asked Soledad.

"Beesh?"

"Sea? Water?" Rachel realized Soledad probably hadn't been more than a few miles from where she was born until she was brought to Los Angeles. And the coyote probably had not taken the scenic route.

"*Agua?*"

"*Sí,*" Rachel said. And they both laughed. "Maybe more *agua* than you have ever seen."

And apparently it was. "*No es lago,*" Soledad said after her jaw dropped and her eyes fixed on the horizon beyond Venice Beach. "Is not lake."

"You got that right. That's the Pacific Ocean."

"Ah. *Océano.*"

"Yes. Say it again."

Soledad repeated the word.

"*Oh-say-a-no,*" Rachel said.

"*Sí,*" Soledad shouted and ran toward the water.

"Be careful," Rachel called. But the girl ran straight into the water, making huge splashes almost as tall as she was.

Suddenly frightened, Rachel dashed after her. "Wait! It may be too deep."

As Rachel reached the water's edge, Soledad giggled and splashed water at her.

Finally, with Soledad sopping wet from head to toe, and Rachel far from dry, they headed back to the car.

It was late enough in the year that the beach was all but abandoned. They passed only a couple holding hands. Both men. Rachel decided to leave that subject for another day. The other person on the beach was a very tall man with what appeared to be a huge live snake curled about his shoulders. This made Soledad's eyes bulge and she raised a finger to point.

"There's no end of nutty people in the world," Rachel said after he had passed. She circled her finger around her temple. "You'll have to get used to that if you stay in Los Angeles."

They drove east next to westbound rush-hour traffic that had completely bogged down.

"Why *alto?*" Soledad asked. "Why they stop?"

Rachel shook her head. "Just more craziness."

"*Loco,*" Soledad said. Rachel repeated it and they laughed most of the way back to Los Angeles.

When they pulled into the garage, Irene was standing in the doorway of the glass booth talking to two men. Both men turned, stared, and waved. Gabe and Gordon.

She parked, and with arms filled with their purchases, she and Soledad walked back to the cubicle. "Hi, you guys." Rachel was still flushed from laughing. They had to wait while a string of cars whizzed by, their drivers anxious to get home for the weekend.

"Well, look at you, dear girl, if you aren't a sight for the sore of heart," Irene said.

"Thank you. And I'd like you to meet my…little cousin, Soledad."

"Allo." The girl bobbed her head looking half embarrassed, half gleeful, then raised her chin and declared, "We chop."

"Chop?" Gordon gave a perplexed glance at Rachel.

"Shop," Gabe said. "She means shop."

"Yes," Rachel said. "We did a bit of shopping."

"The pair of you look a bit damp, as well," Irene said.

"We went by Venice Beach on the way home."

Irene smiled at Soledad. "Ah, and I'll bet you liked that, young lady. It must be a grand thing to visit your cousin."

Soledad nodded uncertainly.

"She doesn't speak a lot of English," Rachel said. "But we're working on it."

"Have you been to LA before?" Gabe asked Soledad, then asked the same question in Spanish.

"No," Soledad said solemnly.

Gabe looked at Rachel. "Actually, I was looking for you to see if you'd like to go to the Day of the Dead celebration tomorrow. Your cousin might like to come, too."

"Day of the Dead?" Rachel had heard of it but knew little about it except that it was some kind of event for Mexicans to honor their dead.

"*Las Dias del Muertos.*" Irene said the words to Soledad so smoothly that Rachel wondered if the old woman was fluent in Spanish.

Soledad's face split in a grin. "*Sí.*" She looked at Rachel. "Yes?"

"There's a big festival right downtown here," Gabe said.

"Is it during the day?" Rachel wanted to do something nice for Soledad, but would going somewhere with Gabe upset Hank? She didn't want to do anything that might. Especially now. Even if he never found out.

"Noon on, from what I've read," Gordon said.

"Afternoon is what I had in mind," Gabe said. "It's a great family do. Music, dancing, costumes, if it's like the festivals in New Mexico. And great food, too."

"If you like tacos and quesadillas," Gordon put in.

"Authentic, not ersatz," Gabe added. "No teriyaki tacos."

Soledad was clapping her hands.

Irene wagged her head up and down. "You should go, dear girl. Take the day off. We never know how many days we will have. Enjoy this one."

Soledad skipped in a little circle. "Yes. Yes. Yes?"

Rachel was thinking that the last time she took a day off it hadn't turned out too well. Plus, what would Hank think? She was pretty sure she knew what Goldie's advice would be.

But Soledad's eyes were so excited, so hopeful.

Those eyes won. "Okay," Rachel agreed. "But just for the afternoon. I have a lot of things that need doing."

When the others had left, Soledad asked, "The woman, she is *bruja?*"

"Bruha? What is bruha?"

"I think…you say witch."

"Good heavens. Irene is no witch. Why do you think that?"

Soledad picked words carefully from her limited lexicon. "*La vista doble*…see…*mañana.*"

"See tomorrow? You mean see the future?" When Soledad nodded, Rachel said, "Well, Irene does consider herself to be a fortune teller, but I don't know how much there is to that." Then Rachel yielded to a sudden whim and asked Soledad, "Would you like to spend the night here?"

The girl glanced about the garage.

"I don't mean in the parking lot, silly. In my apartment." Rachel pointed upward. "*Mi casa.*" Even she knew those words.

"*Aquí?*" Soledad asked. "*Su casa?* Your house, it is here? This place?"

"Yes," Rachel said. "*Sí.*" And Soledad repeated the same words in reverse.

"Okay, we'll go upstairs and call Dr. Johnson."

Soledad skipped beside her up the ramp.

"Glad I caught you, Emma," Rachel said into the phone as Soledad explored the apartment. "She's fine. We had a wonderful time. That's why I'm calling. I want to keep her for a few days.... We bought some clothes. Yes, I think it will work out."

The evening for Rachel was like a trip back to her own childhood—a little like a pajama party, before all the storms in her life had broken loose.

They had bought everything Soledad needed except pajamas, so Rachel loaned her an old tee shirt. It hung down below the girl's knees and for some reason they both thought that was funny.

She called the hospital, but Hank was still in isolation and there was no new information.

Chapter Fifty-eight

Rachel and Soledad were on the sidewalk in front of the garage by 1:30. Rachel wasn't sure exactly why, but she didn't want Gabe coming up to the apartment.

The day was balmy and clear. In her new jeans and a purple shirt, Soledad sat primly on the bench where Rachel often sat with Goldie.

Gabe pulled his car into the garage entrance, parked in his usual place, and ambled back down the ramp. He was wearing a shirt with thin red stripes, open at the collar. Rachel realized she had seen him only once before without his pharmacist's jacket.

When he reached the sidewalk he removed the toothpick he was chewing and twirled it in short, thick fingers. "Hello, little lady. And big lady, too." He nodded to each. "I called a taxi," he said to Rachel. "With all the festivities, parking is likely to be impossible."

He was putting the toothpick back between his teeth when a taxi rounded the corner and stopped, its tires scraping the curb a little. They climbed into the back seat with Soledad between them. Gabe leaned forward and told the driver, "Anywhere near César Chavez and Olvera."

Rachel noticed that his pronunciation was more Spanish than English. Soledad was watching him intently.

"Ah, *el muerto*." The driver eased the cab into traffic.

"Have you been to a Day of the Dead celebration before?" Gabe asked.

Rachel shook her head, no, but Soledad said, "I, yes."

"I haven't been to any here," Gabe said as the driver took a sharp corner, drawing a honk from another car. "I assume they're something like those in New Mexico, although our Hispanic customs may be a little different."

"I barely know what it is," Rachel said. "I gather it's something like a cross between Halloween and Memorial Day."

"Yes and no," Gabe said.

"*Los muertos…*go to…*familias,*" Soledad pronounced carefully.

Rachel pulled a frown. "The dead visit their families?"

"That's basically it," Gabe said.

"Maybe it's me, but that doesn't sound like much fun. The Day of the Living Dead? Like your dead relatives?"

"Sort of," Gabe said. "Except it's a couple days. Technically, the spirits arrive on October thirty-first and leave on November second, although lately it's the closest weekend to those dates."

"This close enough?" the driver asked, pulling the cab to the curb.

"Fine." Gabe paid the man, shaking his head at Rachel's protest that she should pay half.

The sidewalk was milling with people. Decked out for Day of the Dead, Olvera Street was an assault on the senses—the smells, the sounds, but above all the colors. Wild, untamed oranges and reds. Flowers, from big Hawaiian-lei-like necklaces, to unabashedly gaudy plastic petals, to pot upon pot of brilliant marigolds. The whole area was seething with a proud flamboyant garishness.

"Wow." Rachel could barely absorb it all. "Sorta takes your breath away, doesn't it."

Skeletons were everywhere. Some huge, on stilts, some tiny and ornamental. There were dolls in lavish evening dress with skulls for heads, marionettes, puppets, and dozens and dozens of skeleton costumes bouncing along the walk, some above feet shod in black sneakers, others with patent leather shoes. Even some of the food laid out for purchase was brilliantly colored bread crowned with what was made to look like bones.

Soledad ran to a table of bright little skulls in colors of lime, scarlet, gold, and turquoise. She grinned up at Gabe, who chuckled and handed her a five-dollar bill. She handed it to the woman behind the table. "*Tres.*"

The woman put three shiny skulls in a bag and gave the girl a fistful of change. Soledad popped a skull into her mouth and held the bag out to Gabe and Rachel.

Rachel took one tentatively. "What an in-your-face way to deal with death. Eating skeletons, of all things."

"That," Gabe said, "is exactly the point."

"It does take a little getting used to."

Many people in the crowd sported skull masks, some ghoulish, some silly, with lace doilies, no two alike.

Gabe, Rachel, and Soledad strolled past shops and stalls. A marionette merchant was working the strings, making a doll—a dark-eyed female in a blue ruffled dress—bow and sway. Soledad fell in love with it. She looked at the price tag, and shook her head sadly.

"How much is it?" Rachel asked.

Soledad showed her the tag. Seventy-nine dollars.

Gabe spoke to the merchant in quick staccato Spanish. The merchant threw up his hands, shook his head, and walked away. But by the time Gabe had turned to walk away, the merchant was back. Soledad watched the two men, her head bobbing each time Gabe spoke.

Rachel was both fascinated and a little embarrassed.

Gabe took out his wallet and handed the man some bills. The merchant handed him the marionette.

Soledad jumped up and down and clapped. Rachel wasn't sure whether it was praise for his performance or thanks for the doll. "What did you have to pay?" she asked. "I don't have that much cash with me now, but I'll pay you back."

"No way," he said, watching Soledad working the doll's strings. "I haven't had this much fun in a long time."

"Is it fair to ask them to take less?"

Gabe laughed and dug another toothpick out of a little plastic vial he kept in his pocket. "Don't ever travel in Mexico or the street merchants will think one of two things: that you're a dumb, rich American; or that they've died and gone to heaven. They'll probably think both. Bargaining is expected. And respected."

They walked around a clay donkey hitched to a cart made of slats of every color Crayola had ever put in a box. The donkey wore a serape and a necklace of bows.

They reached a small square and Rachel gazed at a sign that read, *Bienvenidos A La Placita Olvera.* "This place almost feels like a foreign country."

"In a way, it sort of is," Gabe said. "But don't let it fool you. This is a total set-up for the *tourista.*"

"I don't think I care. It would be impossible to be sad here."

Gabe pointed to a relatively small white building on the opposite side of the street. Two bells hung in a short tower on one side, a palm tree framed the other side. They crossed and went inside, where a grotto made of rocks was fronted by a mass of brilliant flowers and a long red leather kneeling bench. Flames flickered on dozens of candles, some in brightly decorated tall glasses, some small in plain glass.

"Is there someone you'd like to light a candle for?" Gabe asked.

Soledad didn't wait. She opened her hand, which was still clutching the change from the five-dollar bill Gabe had given her. Extracting three singles, she pushed them through the slot on top of a small metal tube, picked up three small votive candles from along the side wall of rock, and handed one to each of the adults. Then she picked up a lighted candle, lit the one she had kept for herself, set it down at the edge of the flickering flames, knelt on the bench, and closed her eyes.

As Rachel and Gabe followed suit, it gave Rachel a pleasant, but almost eerie, feeling. She wondered what her Jewish mother, dead several years now, would think of having a Catholic candle lit to her memory at a Mexican Day of the Dead celebration.

On the street again, they passed a display of shocking-pink guitars. Rachel eyed them doubtfully. "People don't really buy those, do they?"

"Maybe someone from Texas," Gabe guffawed. "I'm sorry. I hope you weren't born in Texas."

"Nope. California native," Rachel said.

"Well, through the centuries, Texas has tried more than once to take over New Mexico, so we natives of that state occasionally think unkind thoughts of Texans."

They passed a shop with leather goods literally spilling out the door. Patch leather suitcases, Mexican huaraches, tooled belts and handbags. Rachel wanted to take a look.

Soledad tapped Rachel's arm and gestured toward a table piled high with round loaves of bread.

"Hungry?" Rachel asked.

The girl gave a small, solemn nod.

"Can you wait a minute? I need to find someplace quiet to make a phone call."

"Tell you what," Gabe said. "The little lady and I will buy some bread and maybe find some burritos and meet you back at the fountain in, say, twenty minutes. That should give you time to peek in the leather shop, too. I saw the amorous glances you were casting over there."

"Okay," Rachel said, and watched them wend their way through the crowd, Soledad hanging onto Gabe's hand. "Don't let her go," she called after Gabe. "She could get lost."

They looked back and waved. She wasn't sure they had heard.

The three of them had passed a big, double-deck, blue fountain twice. Was it in the plaza? She couldn't remember for sure, but the whole area wasn't that large.

The sound of slightly off-pitch mariachi music came from one direction, a sad sort of ballad came from another. She pulled her cell phone from her handbag and looked around. Was there any place quiet enough to make a call?

She followed a narrow walk between two buildings and found herself in what appeared to be an alley. This might do.

She dialed the hospital and asked if Hank was able to have visitors yet.

"Mr. Sullivan has been discharged."

Rachel felt like her breath had been knocked from her. "Discharged?"

"That is correct."

"When?"

"Let's see….It looks like right before noon."

Rachel clicked off the phone.

How could he have left the hospital? His car was in her parking garage, not anywhere near the hospital in Pasadena. It was a godsend that he was well enough to leave the hospital, but why hadn't he called? Had he not got all the messages she'd left? Why hadn't he called her to come pick him up? She had been home all morning. Surely he wouldn't take a taxi. Who else would have picked him up?

She clicked the phone on again and dialed his home, but got only his voice mail. She had his cell, so she couldn't very well reach him on that.

She was putting the phone back in her handbag, when a hand dug hard into her shoulder.

Chapter Fifty-nine

Rachel tried to turn around, but the hand was pushing her across the alley toward a narrow space between two utilitarian-looking brick buildings that might once have been factories.

She staggered and nearly fell, then brought her arm up. Wrenching her shoulder away from the hand, she spun around.

Two eyes stared at her through the sockets of a skull mask.

The air was like dry ice in her throat. Her heart seemed to halt, then erupted in a violent pulsing that thudded in her ears.

He was stocky and well muscled. She was hopelessly outmatched.

But she couldn't just give up.

She rammed the side of her fist up into the throat just below the mask. He gave a gagging sound. His grip loosened. She dodged.

Run. But where to? He was blocking the way back to the plaza and Olvera Street. She took off in the opposite direction. In two beats, she heard his feet pounding after her.

A mugger? A rapist? Or—?

The buildings on either side looked like old industrial structures. Probably empty. She had to keep going. No time to try doors.

She ran a block down the alley. Looking back wasn't necessary. She could hear the feet, and they were gaining on her.

If she could just get to a street. Somewhere, anywhere with people. How could Olvera Street be teeming with noise and laughter and here it was bare of anything living? Except her and the man behind her.

Rachel darted into an open space between buildings.

Mistake! It was too cramped for all-out running. Then she got a good look at what was ahead: a dead end.

Gasping for air, she stopped, tried to clear her head. Her brain was fiercely demanding flight but couldn't tell her how to get away.

Then she saw a break in the wall ahead. A door? She raced toward it. Yes, a door. She grabbed the knob. It wouldn't turn. Locked. Of course. No one with any sense would leave a door like this unlocked.

Was this it, then?

She slumped against the door and desperately twisted the knob again.

It still refused to turn.

But under her weight the door swung inward.

Rachel careened over the sill into darkness. There were only two windows, both high up. Large boxes were strewn across the floor, some obviously empty. A warehouse of some sort?

She slammed the door shut, but it bounced back toward her. She tried to slam it again before seeing that the bolt was extended just enough to hit the frame and prevent it from closing. She struggled to slide the old bolt, but nothing budged. Two syncopated thumps pounded at the door from outside.

The skeleton-head had arrived.

She threw her weight against the door. She already knew he was built for trouble. Years ago, she had taken a few lessons in self-defense but had forgotten most of it. She might stall him a bit, but there was no way to keep him out indefinitely.

With wild eyes, she explored the walls for another exit or something she could use as a weapon. Finding neither, she waited for the next assault on the door, then yanked it inward, toward her.

Grunting, he stumbled over the sill as she had. But his momentum was too great. He fell.

Rachel kicked him, tried to land another blow on his throat, but missed.

He lunged, catching her by the hair.

She grabbed a wad of soft flesh on the inside of his upper arm, dug her nails in and twisted.

He yelped, let go of her hair, then raised his fist and came at her again, roaring like a wild beast, terrible eyes staring through the skeleton sockets.

She brought up her knee, but the angle was bad. His roar barely hiccuped, growing instead even louder.

He reached for her neck, but the mask was now askew and must have been blocking his vision.

She seized his wrist and pulled it toward her. His first two fingers clawed at her. She grasped them, bent them back, hard, and heard the cracking of two knuckles.

"Bitch!" he howled. The first sound she had of his voice other than the grunts and roars.

"What do you want from me?" she screamed.

"Nada," he snarled.

As his wrist bent, she caught sight of a tattoo on his forearm, the letters EME above an eagle with a snake.

"Who the hell are you?"

"Ha!" he grunted, reaching behind him with his other hand. "You never hear of Mexican Mafia?"

"Yes."

He whipped his fist forward and she saw the muzzle of a gun.

"You never will again."

The gun bucked. She wasn't sure whether she saw the flash of light at his fist level first, or heard the explosive pop first.

Then the second shot came, and with it a roaring pain as her body folded up like a carpenter's ruler and sank to the concrete floor.

Chapter Sixty

When Rachel came to, she was in a crumpled position in a dark, cramped space. And something seemed to be jolting it from below. Her left arm was numb. Something was wet. Very wet. Her shirt.

Then she remembered the jarring staccato of the gunshots, the sparks of light, the rising pain.

How badly was she hurt? There seemed to be a lot of blood. Her jaw was sticky with it. And her hair.

She tried to turn over to see if she could see anything, some clue to where she was. Pain blazed through her arm and shoulder and her breath rasped like sandpaper in her throat.

Something thumped under her again.

Understanding began like a tiny pinpoint of light and grew.

She was in the trunk of a car.

Mr. Skeleton-head was taking her somewhere. Somewhere he could either leave her to die or finish killing her at his leisure.

And there was nothing she could do about it.

A pale glow near her forehead slowly penetrated her consciousness. Rachel raised her chin and stared at it. She wasn't sure whether she was having trouble focusing her eyes, or whether there was just nothing to focus on.

The car ran over something and she bounced off the trunk lid. A groan rose in her throat.

Something long and heavy slid into her side.

The driver turned a corner, sluing Rachel's head against something hard. Here the street was smooth and she could hear the wheels skimming across the pavement beneath her.

Awareness of the source of the pale glow came all at once: a taillight. She ran her fingers over the space where the light was coming from. It was not large, but maybe....

She groped in the darkness behind her for the object that had slid into her. One end was angled to a small recessed cup, the other end was pointed. A tire iron. Grasping it, she scooted herself deeper into the trunk, and thrust the pointed end of the iron into the glow of light. A sharp pain stabbed through her chest, stopping her breath.

When the pain ebbed, she saw that the metal bar had missed its target.

Screwing her eyes shut, she willed herself to ram the bar again.

This time something buckled as it hit.

Slowly, agonizingly, Rachel forced herself to turn as far as she could onto her side and raised herself on her elbow. She tasted blood and realized her clenched teeth had bitten into her lower lip.

It hurts too much. I can't.

But she managed the turn, and rammed the bar again. And again. From this angle her aim was better. At last the whole taillight assembly gave way, and the next blow brought the sound of heavy plastic cracking, then breaking away.

Did the driver hear it?

Apparently not. The car didn't slow.

Now she could see daylight. The lens of the taillight must have fallen out into the street. If she could just get her hand out through the hole where it had been. She hated to give up that little bit of light, but could think of no other way, no other chance.

She eased her fingers toward the daylight.

Something bit into her wrist. She put her hand out into the open air, hoping against hope that there was a car behind this one, that someone, somewhere, would see her hand.

Minutes that seemed like hours passed. Rachel was wondering if she had passed out again when she heard the sound she wanted to hear more than any other—the *whoop-whoop-whoop* of a siren.

Not sure whether the police car was close enough to see, not even sure it *was* a police car, Rachel waved her hand wildly.

The wheels beneath her leaped into drag-race acceleration.

An electronically amplified voice rose over the sound of the engine: "Pull over and stop. Now."

Mr. Skeleton-head did not slow. The car barreled on, picking up even more speed.

The electronic voice issued more orders. The car she was in didn't change direction or pace.

Two claps, like lightning strikes, were followed by a loud hissing sound right beneath her head. The car began to rattle and sway, and something slapped rhythmically at the pavement as the driver finally braked.

The stop was sudden and Rachel was thrown to the back of the trunk, her bloodied hand ripped back inside, her entire body throbbing with wave after wave of pain.

Barely able to breathe, she heard the driver's door open and the sound of feet running fast and hard. More than two feet.

Chapter Sixty-one

Soledad had let go of Gabe's hand and run toward the plaza to bring Rachel a burrito she had chosen herself. Gabe called after her, but she was too excited to stop.

She was at the far end of the plaza trying to look into the face of every passerby who might be Rachel when she heard the noise. Soledad knew immediately what the sound was. She had heard more than a few shots fired back home in Mexico, and seen the blood that followed. Knives were more common, but there was always someone in town with a gun.

Face full of wariness, she tried to see where the sound might have come from. It was close enough to hear, but not nearby. A couple of kids followed by three adults came running toward her. "Gunshots," someone yelled. The word echoed, gaining momentum, up and down Olvera Street.

Swept up in the crowd running away from the sound of the shots, she tried to look for Rachel and for Gabe, but she was too short to see anything but chests and armpits. She tried to stop and wait, stop and think, but the crowd would have none of that and kept pushing her along. She could do nothing to hang onto the burrito or the marionette and the thrashing bodies swept both away.

Soledad stumbled and fell against a heavy-set woman.

"*Perdón,*" the girl said, but the woman only scowled and kept moving.

The mass of people finally began to thin out and head in different directions. She leaned against the side of a building and tried to examine the tide of humanity as it passed. She stood there for a long time.

If only she had come here in a car, she could maybe find that. She began walking along César Chavez trying to retrace the path of the taxi they had arrived in.

She kept going, hoping to see something familiar. When she came to the freeway, she recognized that and followed the street past it, then turned left at the first stoplight. But nothing else looked familiar. If only she had paid more attention.

"Are you lost?" A car slowed, a window rolled down.

Soledad shook her head uncertainly. *Policía.* The face looked kind, but she didn't like police. Maybe they were different here, but at home they could be rough and mean and one stayed out of their way.

Then her mind shook loose the perfect solution. There were a few scattered pedestrians. Soledad chose an old black woman hobbling along the sidewalk with a walking stick.

"*Hospital?*" she said. "*Por favor. Dónde esta hospital?*"

The woman frowned at her, but it was a thoughtful frown, not a forbidding one.

Soledad remembered the English words and pronunciation. "Where-is-hospital?"

"Are you ill, child?"

The girl shook her head vigorously, then said slowly. "I want hospital." English words came better to her when she wasn't nervous.

"Well, the closest one is Jefferson."

Soledad nodded her head as vigorously as she had shaken it.

"Two stop lights." The woman pointed behind her. "You understand stop light?" She pointed at the one on the corner where they stood.

"Yes."

The woman held up two fingers. "Two stop lights. Then go that way." She pointed north. "Keep walking. You will come to it."

"*Gracias.* Thank you," the girl said and began running. She did not actually want to go to the hospital, but she knew if she could find Jefferson, she could find Rachel's garage from there.

◇◇◇

Rachel had no idea how much time had passed when she opened her eyes again.

She blinked and glanced around the small, plain room trying to remember where she was and why. It looked like a hospital room. Her bed was narrow and railings had been raised on both sides. A couple of rectangular steel instruments, looking a little like robots in some space movie, stood just out of reach. There was a window, but she was too far from it to see much outside.

The walls once were yellow, but the paint was dull with age. The light from a ceiling fixture wasn't bright and only succeeded in making things uglier. She lay there half conscious for a long time.

When her brain finally rid itself of sleep, a rush of dread went through her. Was this part of Jefferson's secret black-market-organ wing?

Someone was sitting quietly on a chair in the shadows next to a closed door. He crossed his legs and folded his arms over his chest. The look on his face was one of patience. It bore the knowledge that he had been there for a long time, and would be there a good deal longer. Dan Morris.

She tilted her head toward him and now realized there was a tube at her nose and various other tubes elsewhere.

"What are you doing here?" Her voice was thin and hoarse. She tried to clear her throat but the effort made her chest hurt. "Why am I here?"

He nodded at her, raised a cell phone to his ear, pushed a button with his thumb and said something into it she couldn't hear. Then he moved to the side of her bed and put his hands on the steel crib railing. The bright white of his shirt made his face seem even darker than it was.

"Welcome back," he said, his eyes soft and dark. "We were hoping you would decide to stay with us."

A woman in white pants and tunic pushed through the door to the room, moved immediately to the bed and put her fingers on Rachel's pulse, her eyes on her own watch. The fingers were cold.

Morris went back to his post at the door while the nurse took Rachel's blood pressure, then took her temperature with an electronic gadget that pinged.

"Well, now," the nurse said cheerily, "this looks very good." She jotted something on a clipboard and left.

Not to me it doesn't.

The nurse had barely disappeared when the door swung open again and Emma, in a loose green dress and open white coat, strode to the bed.

"Why am I here?" Rachel asked as the doctor lowered the bed rail and went through the exact same process the nurse had.

"So we can monitor your progress. You were in critical care for a few hours. This is excellent improvement."

"What happened?" Rachel asked, her voice still husky but becoming stronger. "How did I get here?"

"You were shot, Rachel. One of your lungs is collapsed, but it will re-inflate and you'll be good as new."

"Why was I shot?"

Emma's eyes went blank. "I have no idea."

"I think you do know, Emma. I think this whole thing, this whole cycle of strange happenings is tied together. And I think the link is this wing of this floor of this hospital."

The three sentences exhausted Rachel. She looked at the ceiling, then back at Emma. "This thing have a contraption so I can sit up a little further?"

"Of course." Emma pushed a button on the side of the bed and the head of the bed slowly began to rise.

"What do you know about something called *La Eme*?" Rachel tried to say it, then spelled it.

Emma's brow wrinkled. "I don't think I've ever heard the term."

"How about the Mexican Mafia?"

"Of course I've heard of them, but I can't say I know much about them."

"Well, that's how the guy who shot me identified himself. He was no mugger, he didn't even try to take my purse. He didn't try to rape me. I asked him what he wanted from me and he said *nada*. Then he shot me. Seems that all he wanted was me dead."

"Maybe."

"That's my problem," Rachel said. "I can't think of anyone in the whole world who would want me dead, especially bad enough to pay to see it happen. Except you."

Emma drew back, looking shocked. "Me?"

"I threaten your little operation here, don't I?"

"Rachel, I have never in my life wanted to see anyone dead. And certainly not you."

Rachel looked over at Dan Morris, who appeared to be napping in his chair by the door.

"Why is he here?"

"To guard you."

"Why do I need a guard?"

Emma sighed, raised the bed's railing, snapped it into place and leaned her elbow on it. "Someone shot you. They may try again."

"Does your little operation here have anything to do with the Mexican Mafia?" Rachel gulped a breath.

"I'm told they are the only ones we can rely on to hire the coyotes. In Mexico, it isn't regarded as criminal activity. The coyotes and *brincadores* are service providers."

"Like UPS or FedEx."

"Something like that."

"Why does someone who calls himself Mexican Mafia want me dead?"

"I want to know that myself," Emma said.

"Why am I in this ward?"

"You were brought in by ambulance. Jefferson was the nearest emergency room. Apparently a couple of police found you in the trunk of a car they had chased down."

Rachel felt a chill as the fog in her head lifted a little and she began to remember.

"The driver got away," Emma said. "I heard it was a choice of getting you to the hospital in time, or catching him. They opted for you. I happened to learn about your admission to critical care and when you stabilized, I had you brought here."

"Something about all this doesn't pass the shudder test. I want to trust you, Emma, but I don't."

The doctor rubbed her temple and Rachel noticed how tired she looked. "Obviously someone tried to kill you. You say it was Mexican Mafia. Maybe it was. Whatever, you're probably safer in this ward than somewhere more open to the public."

Chapter Sixty-two

Soledad had slept the first night on the bench in front of Rachel's garage. It was cold, but she had been colder. The next morning, she woke to someone gently shaking her shoulder. She leapt up from the bench, but it was only Irene.

Soledad told her as best she could what had happened.

Irene's face went from worried to stricken. "That's a terrible, frightening tale, dear child. Something dreadful must have happened. Rachel would never have left you alone. Never on this earth would she do that. Has anyone reported her missing?"

The girl gave an eloquent shrug.

"I will do so immediately. I will talk to the Gray Panthers. They may know something. And I will call her friend Goldie. Her young man is in the hospital, but I should call him, too. Here, take the key. Run up to the apartment. Clean yourself up and I'll see what I can do. I'll let you know the minute I find out anything."

Soledad took the key. But she had no intention of waiting to hear news of Rachel from Irene.

She changed clothes, carefully folded the worn ones and put them neatly in the laundry basket in Rachel's bathroom. Then she went down the stairs and out the side door where Irene wasn't likely to see her.

Minutes later, she was at the hospital.

The lobby seemed vast. Soledad had never seen such a huge room, except maybe the church in her village. The problem was, she had no idea where to go from there. She had never seen any part of the hospital except the area where her own room had been. She and Rachel had left the hospital by a side door. She tried to walk as though she knew where she was going and hoped none of the adults would stop her.

Turning left, she passed the cashier and a shop with furry toys. Then, through a glass door, she saw Gabe. Thrilled at her luck, she pulled open the door and ran to the counter.

He looked up, then rounded the counter, hands out. "Thank God, little one. Thank God." He squatted down and put his hands on her shoulders. "Where have you been? Where is Rachel? I have tried to call the garage, but the woman who answered was as worried as I was."

Soledad shot a stream of Spanish at him like a verbal fire hose and he had to think for a moment. Then he said he had tried to get into the garage the night before and hadn't seen her on the bench.

His Spanish was okay, but his accent was different, so she had to listen carefully. He told her he had called the police, but they hadn't sounded like they planned to do much real hunting for Rachel anytime soon. He took a card out of his pocket, scrawled something on the back, and handed it to her. "That's my *teléfonos, aquí y mi casa.* Here and at home. You know how to use a phone?"

She nodded.

"Call me as soon as you find out anything about Rachel, or if you need something." He walked her to the door and waved as she left the hospital.

But Soledad didn't want to leave. She wanted to see her friends in the hospital. She went back into the lobby and this time turned to the right. That led her to a bank of elevators. She didn't understand elevators. But there was a door just beyond the elevators. Soledad opened it and was pleased to find something she did understand: stairs.

She ran up the steps, stopping on each floor to open the door, but nothing looked right or smelled right, so she kept climbing.

When she reached the top, she realized she would have to leave the staircase and look around a little. The hall where her room had been had to be somewhere in the building.

After prowling what seemed like miles of corridors and becoming thoroughly confused, she found the place she was looking for just a floor above where she had begun her search. She hugged the wall where the main hall began. She wasn't sure why she didn't want to be seen here; after all, this was where she belonged. But somehow it seemed better to be invisible.

It was early. The breakfast trolleys had not arrived yet, but they would be coming soon. Soledad ran to the first room and shook the boy in the bed closest to the door. "Luis!"

He turned over and sat up when he saw who it was. *"Su amiga está aquí,"* he blurted out immediately and added that everyone was worrying about Soledad.

"Ra-shel *aquí?*" She ran to the door of the room, then back to the bed. *"Dónde, dónde?"* she wanted to know. Where?

He went to the door with her and pointed down the hall. *"Cuarto tercero."*

Soledad thanked him and sped down the hall.

Rachel was almost masked from the door by a dull green curtain gathered at the wall by the bed.

Soledad rushed in, eyes flashing with worry. She touched Rachel's cheek and began chattering.

Rachel opened her eyes, shook her head slowly, and put a finger over Soledad's lips. "English...if you can."

Soledad's eyebrows drew into a straight line and she touched the clear plastic tube that passed below Rachel's nose.

"Oxygen," Rachel said, knowing the girl wouldn't understand. She took a couple breaths to try to demonstrate, but that made her cough. "No, no. I'm all right," she said as the girl's expression became even more worried.

By the time they had told the briefest outlines of their tales, they could hear breakfast trays rattling in the hall.

"Can you get out of here okay?" Rachel pointed toward the door.

"Yes."

Rachel motioned the girl closer and whispered into her ear.

Soledad drew back, looked into Rachel's eyes, and nodded slowly. When she turned, she noticed for the first time the man in the chair by the door. She threw an alarmed look at Rachel, who responded, "Not to worry. He's okay."

"Have you been there all night?" Rachel asked him when Soledad had gone.

Dan Morris said that he was.

"You know about what's going on here?" Rachel thought he must indeed know everything and wondered why she still felt comfortable with him. Maybe it was because his face seemed so honest. But she well knew how deceptive looks could be.

"I guess I do," Morris said, trying to smooth his tie and shirt and not having much success.

"Those packages you were sending from my helicopter pad were stolen organs, weren't they?"

The man frowned and pinched the bridge of his nose. "Well, not exactly stolen."

"What would you call it? Not exactly borrowed, were they?"

"You just don't know how bad it gets, do you?"

"How bad what gets?"

They were interrupted by the arrival of breakfast. The pretty girl who brought it was fair-complected, annoyingly cheerful, and looked barely sixteen. She left a tray for each of them.

Rachel pushed the button to raise the head of her bed and drew the tray table toward her. Balancing his tray on his lap, Morris said, "Desperation. How bad the desperation gets."

"I know a little about desperation."

He gave her a long look. "People handle it different ways."

"Like having me arrested?"

He heaved a sigh. "Okay. I know you can't see it any other way. If I were in your shoes, I'd see it that way, too."

"Does a kid like that one with the trays know about all this?"

"Of course not." Morris picked at his pancakes. They finished their breakfasts in silence.

Rachel clicked on the television and was dozing through a Sunday news show when Soledad burst through the door carrying a shopping bag. She presented it to Rachel, who propped it under her arm.

When Soledad left with instructions for Irene to look after the girl, written on a piece of paper Morris provided, Rachel asked him to draw the curtain around her bed so she could sleep.

◇◇◇

Soledad was watching television in Rachel's apartment. She had started with a Spanish channel, but flipped to English. Maybe that would help her learn the new words faster. Having the command of a television was still an amazing thing to her. There was only one TV in her village. That was in the cantina and it didn't work very well.

When the commercial came on with a man in a white coat, she remembered Gabe. She had forgotten to call him. Taking Rachel's phone from the kitchen, Soledad carefully punched in the numbers written on the card he had given her that morning.

Chapter Sixty-three

She was awakened by cool fingers on her wrist. Emma. "Don't you ever get a day off?" Rachel mumbled.

"Tomorrow, maybe. One of the on-calls is sick, so I took the late shift tonight." The doctor thrust a thermometer into Rachel's mouth.

"It's night?" Rachel asked as soon as the device pinged.

"About eight. They said you ate a good lunch, so we didn't wake you for dinner. If you're hungry I could probably have something sent up."

"No, I'm fine."

Emma finished taking Rachel's blood pressure. "Actually, you are. I didn't expect you to make so much progress so fast." Emma tapped the mattress. "I don't want you lying flat, but we could put the bed down a little."

"It's fine, thanks."

The doctor started to step back through the curtain that surrounded the bed.

"Wait," Rachel said. "I do want something."

"Yes?"

"But it's not food. I want you to fix a birth certificate for Soledad."

Emma gave her a long look before answering. "All right."

"I'd like to take it with me when I leave here. Is that possible?"

"Probably." Emma turned to go. "You want a book or a magazine or anything?"

"Not right now," Rachel said, then, "Is that guy still out there?"

"Dan? No, they decided to let him get some sleep."

"Is anyone out there?"

"They decided it probably wasn't necessary." Emma slid the curtain back partway and disappeared before it occurred to Rachel to wonder who "they" was and why they thought she was now safe.

She lay awake watching the play of lights on the on the curtain from somewhere on the street beyond her window.

The door to the room opened. She rolled startled eyes toward the figure that halted in the shadows at the curtain opening.

"Rachel?"

She knew the voice.

"Can I come in?" Gabe.

"It depends." Rachel pulled the sheet up, then reached for the light on the table beside her bed and clicked it on. The glow it threw was pale, leaving Gabe still in the shadows.

"On what?"

"On how much you had to do with this whole mess someone has made of me."

Gabe moved forward, out of the shadows, but stopped several feet short of the bed. "Jesus. How can you think such a thing?"

"Hey, from my point of view, it isn't hard. For one thing, you took me to Olvera Street where some thug abducted me."

"Jesus," he said again. "I don't know any more about why or how that happened than you do."

She frowned, wanting to believe him, but not quite ready to. "What about that OxyContin? Who planted it on me?"

Gabe shrugged. "I wish I knew. This whole damn thing is pretty horrifying. Even from my point of view. I'm going to look for another job. This place is beginning to smell as bad as Denmark."

"Pretty rotten, all right." She waited for him to say more. When he didn't, she asked, trying not to sound suspicious, "So how did you know I was here?"

"Soledad called me. She probably told you we got separated when the gunshots stampeded the crowd. We reconnected at the pharmacy. She knew I was worried."

Rachel studied his face for a moment. Finally, "Okay. Maybe I'm stupid, but I believe you."

"Ask Soledad."

"I don't mean about that. You going to look for another job in LA?"

"Nope. I never much liked it here, and now I'm liking it even less."

"You going back to Albuquerque?"

"Maybe," he sighed. "Probably. I don't want to lose touch with my daughter."

They were interrupted by a nurse. This one, wearing thick glasses and no lipstick, marched toward the bed.

"I guess I'll be going."

"Thanks for coming by, Gabe. I don't mean to be disagreeable."

"If I were in your shoes, I'd be downright surly," he said, and left.

The nurse was taking Rachel's pulse. The name tag on her white pocket read *Anne Christian*.

She proceeded to retake her blood pressure as well. "Ah, very good," she said, as if Rachel had deliberately produced the desired results. Taking the steel pitcher from the tray table, she poured water into a paper cup and handed that to Rachel. Then she handed her another paper cup, this one tiny and fluted as if made for baking miniature muffins. Inside were two pink tablets.

"What are these for?" Rachel asked.

The nurse gave her a surprised look that said patients simply didn't ask such questions. "Doctor's orders," she chirped. "Swallow them down. Go on, now."

Nurses had given her medications earlier when she was too out of it to question anything, but Rachel didn't like swallowing anything when she didn't know what it was. *Well, that's how it happens in a hospital.*

She tipped the tablets into her mouth, and took the water.

"There, now," the nurse said. "Should I turn out the light?"

"Huh-uh."

"Sleep well," the nurse piped and departed.

Rachel opened her mouth, reached under her tongue and removed the two tablets.

Chapter Sixty-four

The room was almost totally dark when she woke again. Someone had turned out the light next to her bed.

Rachel wasn't sure exactly when or how she realized she was not alone in the room. The eerie feeling one sometimes gets that someone is watching from behind made her skin prickle.

Then she heard four slow, soft steps.

"Who's there?" she called.

With a clicking sound, the curtain slid along the ceiling track that drew it in a semicircle around her bed.

A bright light hit her eyes. Hard. Was the night nurse cruel or only an idiot?

Blinded, Rachel crossed the backs of her hands over her eyes. "What the hell are you doing?"

"Ah, Rachel…. This is such a shame."

A man's voice. It sounded familiar. But she couldn't quite place it.

The flashlight tilted, jerking the beam momentarily to the curtain. He aimed it back at her face immediately. But she had glimpsed the intruder, the somewhat narrow shoulders, neat haircut, shirt and tie. The boyish Tom-Sawyer face.

"Gordon?" Her voice broke on the first syllable.

"I am so sorry, Rachel."

This was too bizarre for words. Had he come to rape her or something?

"What are you doing here?"

"Well, it seems incompetence is rampant these days. If a job is to be done right, it seems one has to do the job oneself."

The flashlight beam shifted a little as he moved closer and Rachel had trouble believing what she was seeing: a gun.

It wasn't trained on her, just held loosely in his right hand.

"You? Wh—why?"

Gordon's eyes went hard. "Frankly I wasn't crazy about the idea. And when it became obvious it would have to be done, I really didn't think I'd have to do it myself. But hired goons are like everything else these days. You can't get a good one. They totally fucked it up. Both of them. So now I don't seem to have much choice."

"You hired the guy who shot at us up in the Angeles?" She was still trying to absorb what his words meant.

"Pretty third rate, the bastard. It was supposed to be a hunting accident."

"Who put that tracking device on my car?"

He gave her a tight smile. "I did that myself. Amazing how easy it was."

"And the guy in the skeleton head. He was yours, too?"

"Another third rate SOB."

Rachel was staring at him, trying to read his face. "What have I done to you that you want to kill me?"

Gordon gave a dry chuckle. "I kept hoping it wouldn't be necessary, but you just had to keep butting into my business."

She gave him a puzzled look. "The pharmaceutical business? I don't have anything to do with the pharmaceutical business."

"You had to keep on poking around about those kids."

"The kids?" She tried to make these pieces fit together. When he didn't offer an explanation, she asked, "Are you involved in the black-market organ business?"

"You could say that." He set the flashlight end-down on the tray table. The beam shot to the ceiling, giving the space around them a dim yellowish glow.

"Why?"

He only stared back at her.

"There can't be enough money to make it worth all this."

"That's where you're wrong, sweet lips." Gordon moved a little closer.

She could see a small contraption on the muzzle of the gun. Dear God. A silencer? He really meant to put an end to her. Forever.

Considering kicking out at the hand that held the gun, Rachel tensed her legs. Was she strong enough? No. She might dislodge the gun from his hand, but he would surely pick it up again before she could get out of the bed, much less out of the room.

"Won't it be a little messy to explain how a hospital patient got shot?"

"Not really," Gordon said. "A lot of crimes are committed in hospitals. They try to keep that quiet. Not just this hospital. Security is mostly old retired guys. Deputy Dogs. You already know that people can get in and out of Jefferson pretty easily. And in your case, the cops already know someone tried to kill you."

"A stolen kidney must be worth a lot."

"Not all that much, really. Maybe ten grand or so, max."

She gave him a long stare. "So how can it be worth…this?"

"You're doing the wrong math. I thought you were brighter than that." The boastful expression on the scrubbed choir-boy face made him look more like a cocky teenager than a middle-aged murderer.

"What math?"

"You've been talking to Emma. She thinks the problem is that there aren't enough kidneys available. She's right, but she's wrong. If it weren't for the crazy system we use, there would be many more."

"What system?"

"The way it is now, people willing to be donors have a sticker put on their driver's licenses. That's an opt-in system. A lot of people don't opt in, including kids—who might be the very best donors—and those who don't have a driver's license. Then there are those who might be a little squeamish about the idea, those who think it's bad luck to contemplate their own death. What we need is an opt-out system. Unless you have it tattooed on you somewhere that you don't want to be an organ donor, you take your last breath and the nearest doc takes whatever he or she can use."

"That sounds gross."

"If I had more time, I could make it sound prettier. Matter of fact, we've been lobbying Congress for years. But those morons in Washington aren't clever enough to push it through. So we're trying to see if anything can be accomplished state by state. Unfortunately, that's a very long process."

"What does any of that have to do with you?"

Gordon scratched his chin with his left hand. "I told you, you were doing the wrong math, Rachel. Right here, from this ward, Emma gets about a thousand extra kidneys a year."

"I thought it wasn't about the organs."

"You have any idea the annual cost of immunosuppressants and other medications for a thousand kidney transplant patients?"

"I guess I don't."

"Ballpark, maybe one hundred million." His voice put spaces between the words.

"Jesus Christ!" Rachel caught her breath and added slowly, "And you provide all of those drugs."

"Zyrco manufactures just about everything a transplant patient needs. Of course, some of the other companies have their own brands, but we're very competitive, and the transplant teams know they can rely on us."

"And how much of that money is yours?"

"Only about twenty percent is bounced back to me."

Twenty million a year? It was mind boggling.

"You said, 'we.' We who?"

"Christ, Rachel, you don't think I could do this on my own, do you? For one thing, this isn't our only operation. There are a couple more cooperative transplant teams in California and two more in Arizona and Texas."

"Your whole company is in on it?"

"Don't be silly. It really doesn't take a huge number of people. There's a little shadow operation at Zyrco that gets run through books kept at an off-shore subsidiary, and ninety-five percent of the people at headquarters are none the wiser."

"I don't see how you could keep things like smuggling kids from Mexico, hiring thugs, a huge increase in transplant medication sales—how could you keep all that secret?"

"Money is a great little persuader. And if that doesn't work, there are ways to arrange accidents. We've only had to do that once."

"And there are more of these…these organ snatching schemes?"

"This, however, is our Lexus enterprise. Which is to say the head surgeon here is something of a pain in the ass."

"Emma."

Gordon nodded. "Dr. Johnson has the conscience of a nun. She insists on having only kidneys-on-the-hoof so she can do all the pre-op tests and post-op care. It's an expensive way to go, but the organs are top quality, with such good graft survival rates that this particular supply is in high demand."

"You make it sound like a factory."

"What would you call it?"

Rachel narrowed her eyes. "No one wonders why there are so many organs available here?"

"You're forgetting the desperation," he said. "The transplant teams don't like to see their patients die. They may suspect something is a little out of the ordinary, but they're willing to look the other way. They believe they're saving lives. And they are."

"So you're talking five hundred million a year?" Rachel asked, running trembling fingers along the edge of the bed.

Gordon smiled. "Somewhere between that and a billion. Of course, that isn't all profit. And don't forget, the sales are perfectly legit, so a lot of it goes to a good cause—the research and development of life-saving medications."

"That's bullshit." A hand swept aside the curtain behind him, startling them both. Even in the dim glow that spilled from the flashlight beam still trained on the ceiling, Rachel could see Emma's eyes were blazing. "Zyrco spends at *least* three times as much on advertising as it spends on research. Far, far more if you include the sponsoring of continuing medical education courses for doctors, which amounts to hours and hours of lobbying the very people who prescribe your wares."

"That doesn't seem to stop the docs from accepting invitations to our courses, which just happen to be given aboard cruise ships."

"I don't," Emma said.

"I grant you that. You, my dear Emma, help us in other ways."

The doctor backed up a step, as if she had gotten too close to something rotten, then said in a stronger voice, "Now please explain exactly what the hell you are doing in this room."

In apparent surprise at the outburst, Gordon had taken two steps toward the head of the bed.

As he turned to face her, Emma's eyes caught on the gun in his hand. "Dear God in heaven!"

She put her arms out toward him, palms forward, as if they could stop a bullet.

"You've become a greater and greater liability, Dr. Johnson, with your picky ways and your aversion to the Mex mob's coyotes, to say nothing of your objections about what to do with Ms. Chavez here." Two sounds, more like puffs of air than shots, came from the gun.

Emma's expression contorted. She slumped to the floor, blood spurting from somewhere near the lapel of her otherwise spotless white coat.

Gordon swung back toward the bed. "I'm afraid it's your—"

He stopped short as Rachel rammed the muzzle of her old thirty-eight up under the chin of Gordon's little-boy face.

Chapter Sixty-five

She didn't shoot. She didn't have to.

Gordon's gun, silencer and all, clattered to the floor. In his stunned face, the eyes bulged.

Rachel drew a cell phone from under the covers and pressed the number seven, the code she had programmed days ago for the hospital's main number.

"I am in a room in the west wing of the fourth floor. A man here has shot Dr. Johnson.... No, he has dropped his gun and I have mine where it will make a mess of his head if I fire it...." Her voice had a slight quaver and she struggled to steady it. "Please send someone up here to help me. Someone armed.... The west wing. There's a sign that says it's closed, but it is quite full and busy.... Thank you."

Chapter Sixty-six

"I'm very sorry to disturb you."

Rachel rolled over and blinked at the face near her shoulder. Six security people had come and taken Gordon away, and then two nurses had rolled her onto a gurney and through what seemed like endless darkened hospital halls to another room. The linen of the bed they rolled her onto was cold and she had lain there unable to sleep for what seemed like a long time. But finally, she had dozed off.

Now there were eyes peering at her anxiously. Early morning light was beginning to glow at the window. When the stranger's face swam into sleep-fogged focus, she gasped, half sat, pulled the sheet to her neck, eyes searching him for anything that looked like a weapon.

Was this another attempt to silence her? Gordon had said it wasn't a one-man operation. Why hadn't she asked for a guard? How could she have been so stupid? How could the security people be so stupid? But the orderlies had whisked her off so quickly to her new room, and left her alone.

"Who are you?" she asked, staring straight into the man's face. "What are you doing in my room?"

She ran her hand along the side of the mattress. Where was her gun? Then she remembered that the security cops had taken that, too, promising to keep it for her in a safe.

Her visitor was tall but looked slight, hollow-chested, past middle age, with a too-short haircut. Pale brown eyes were somewhat enlarged behind thick-lensed eyeglasses.

A hit man didn't have to be a wrestler. One who looked like this might find it easier to get into a hospital.

"I'm sorry," he said again, looking ever more like an absent-minded professor.

"What do you want?" Rachel's eyes kept darting to his hands, but nothing resembling a weapon appeared.

"Hamilton Baker," the man answered her earlier question in a surprisingly take-charge, but not intimidating, voice. He handed her a business card that gave his name above *Attorney at Law*.

In spite of herself, it was hard to maintain her distrust. He looked so Midwest-decent. An Indiana farmer fresh from Sunday church. "What do you want?" she asked again, her tone less tense.

"A small business deal. Nothing more."

Rachel's eyes narrowed. "Like what?"

"A business deal that will provide you quite a lot of capital."

Wondering where her cell phone was, she tried to digest his statement. "In exchange for what?"

"Very little," he said, nodding. "Just your cooperation."

"What kind of cooperation?"

"That you don't talk to anyone about recent events—detectives, attorneys, the media, anyone at all, about recent events."

"Recent events," Rachel repeated, trying to figure out exactly what he was talking about.

"Specifically, the unfortunate finding of OxyContin in your jacket pocket, the tracking device that somehow got attached to your car, your acquaintance with one Gordon Cox, and most especially, anything at all about a certain group of rooms on the fourth floor in the east wing of this hospital."

Rachel's tired brain tried to assimilate all the possible meanings. "You're offering me hush money?"

He nodded, apparently pleased that he would not have to go into further detail. "You could call it that."

"From whom? Hush money from whom?"

"I am not at liberty to say."

"Maybe I can guess. Gordon Cox."

Baker looked down at large-knuckled hands that nevertheless were too well manicured to belong to an Indiana farmer. "I'm afraid Mr. Cox isn't with us any longer."

"Isn't with you? What does that mean?"

"Unfortunately, Mr. Cox tried to escape from the police station. Apparently, he grabbed an officer's weapon. He was shot by another officer. I'm told this happened in the men's toilet."

"Holy shit. Gordon is dead?"

"Correct."

"You know that he shot a doctor here in this hospital, in my room, the room I was in before they moved me here?"

"I believe that is why he was at the police station."

"And now, you're telling me I should forget that someone here at Jefferson planted OxyContin on me, virtually destroyed my good name, to say nothing of costing me a hell of a lot of money for bail? And I'm supposed to forget the whole organ scheme that was taking place here, right under everyone's noses? To say nothing about Gordon's drug company underwriting the rest of the enterprise. Plus the connection to hired thugs who tried to kill me, which he admitted a few hours ago."

"That is correct." Baker gave her a thoughtful look. "In exchange for your cooperation, that bail bond will be taken care of."

"Who planted that bottle on me?"

"LAPD already has what amounts to a confession from Dan Morris, head of Jefferson Medical Center's security department. Apparently, his adult daughter has a brain tumor. She doesn't have insurance, she isn't covered by his, and the drug needed to shrink it costs nineteen hundred dollars per dose."

"And Gordon supplied it."

"So it appears."

"In exchange, Morris ignored that ward on the fourth floor, and planted the OxyContin on me."

Baker gazed at her, neither confirming nor denying.

"What about Zyrco?"

"They know nothing about any of this. They have no idea why Cox killed Emma. Perhaps he was partaking in some of his own samples."

"They never noticed the up-tick in his immunosuppressant sales?"

Baker shrugged. "Ignorance is a beautiful thing. It almost let Ken Lay get away with something even bigger."

"What about the thug who tried to kill me, who tossed me into the trunk of his car like a sack of garbage?"

"Hard to say, unless Cox named him. And he probably did not have sufficient time."

"So he's free to come after me again?"

"But why would he do that? I'm sure he had no personal grudge against you."

Baker leaned a little closer. "You haven't asked about the amount of the monetary benefit."

"Okay, consider that I'm asking now."

"One million dollars."

"Jesus God!" She gave a hollow whistle. "You people must have one hell of a lot at risk."

"You could say that. There are federal agencies, law suits, to consider. Entire corporations at stake. I'm not trying to hide that from you. I admit it."

"That makes my silence worth a lot. Why don't you just have me killed?"

"This has been much too messy already. The less said and done now, the better."

"How do you know I won't tell everyone I know?"

"We are willing to assume that you will have sufficient interest in preserving both your financial assets and your life, that you will keep your mouth shut about this matter. And that you will not want to risk other people's life and welfare." He paused before adding, "Keep in mind that the money, of course, is tax free. Transferred to your account from an off-shore source."

"That can't be legal."

"My dear woman, a very great deal of what you, yourself, already have done is not legal."

"What if I take the money and then go to the police?"

"This is not child's play. The moment you accept the money, the moment we have your signature on the check, you will be implicated. Believe me, at the very least, the jail time would not be short."

"You don't miss a trick, do you?"

"We're not foolish. Things have been thought through."

"This offer is from Zyrco and Jefferson, right?"

"I am not at liberty to say."

"What about the other parts of Zyrco's operation? Gordon said there were other hospitals besides Jefferson."

"Even as we speak, these activities are disappearing." Baker's face was utterly blank. "I realize this is a complicated decision. Perhaps you would like a little time to think about it."

"What do I tell the cops when they come to question me?"

"I think the police will not be bothering you. At least not for a time. Maybe never."

Rachel frowned at what that statement seemed to mean. "Are the people you represent that powerful? They could keep the police from even questioning me?"

"They have considerable influence, yes."

Rachel was wondering how she could bring herself so accept so much tainted money—more than tainted, filthy. "And what if I don't agree to keep quiet? Another goon comes to silence me?"

Baker had the grace to look uncomfortable.

A nurse carrying a white envelope came through the door and stopped short. "I didn't realize you had a visitor."

"Just leaving," Baker said, then to Rachel, "I'll check back this evening."

"I don't know if you know about Dr. Johnson," the nurse began.

"Is she going to be okay?"

"They tried." The nurse was obviously struggling to keep her lower lip from quivering. "For a while we thought she might make it. But we lost her."

Rachel's eyes filled but did not spill. "Oh, God, I'm sorry to hear that."

"This was on the desk in her office. It's addressed to you." The nurse handed the envelope to her and left, pulling the door closed behind her.

Rachel tore open the envelope and drew out the paper inside. It was a birth certificate in the name of Soledad Chavez.

Chapter Sixty-seven

Goldie strode into Rachel's new room, a private one on Jefferson's top floor. "Mmm-mmm. You got more tricks in you than a triple pinochle deck."

Rachel pushed the button to raise the head of her bed. "Have you heard from Hank? Do you know where he is, how he is?"

Goldie stared at her. "How should I know? Don't you?"

"I called the hospital in Pasadena from Olvera Street, just before that guy jumped me. They said he'd been discharged. Last time I talked to Irene, she didn't know where he was. I thought he might have contacted you when he couldn't reach me."

"Shit. This does not sound good."

"I'm worried. He would have called me to pick him up when the hospital discharged him. I don't know what's going on."

"I will try to find out where he is. I'll go to Pasadena myself, if I have to."

"Thanks. I'd really appreciate it."

"So what's this I hear about you having a gun right here in this very hospital? How did that happen?"

"Soledad brought it to me. In a shopping bag."

"You had that little kid walking the streets carrying a concealed weapon?"

"Without her or the gun I wouldn't be here now, talking to you, would I?"

"Aside from the fact that you're probably guilty of child endangerment?"

Rachel rolled her eyes. "I never thought of that."

"And nobody's been here asking questions, including where that gun came from?"

"Not yet anyway," Rachel said as it dawned on her that Baker's fingerprints might well be all over the lack of official question asking. "I guess they had a little more on their minds than an old thirty-eight that I didn't even fire. At least not here."

Goldie squinted at her. "You look guilty about something."

"How much would it cost to buy your own cleaning company?"

Goldie rolled her eyes to the ceiling. "Are you crazy? You been doing crack or joy juice or something?"

"Of course not. But it's possible I may come into some money and I may want to invest it in something like a well-run cleaning company."

"Whee-ooo. I do not want to hear any more."

"There's my girl," came a voice from the doorway.

"We can talk about it later," Rachel said to Goldie as Marty made his way to the bedside.

"What's this I hear from Irene, that you've been going around attacking men with guns?" he asked, trying to sound jovial but not quite succeeding.

"Where—?" Rachel's breath nearly stopped as she got a good look at him. "What...what happened?"

The right side of his face was an awful combination of green, blue, and yellow hues. His right eye was swollen nearly closed. "Nothing exactly good," he said.

"Why? How...?"

"I won, again, Rache. I won big. Really big. And I was getting into my car, and this guy, well, I guess I was mugged." Marty looked down and muttered, "He took the car, too."

"How did....Where have you been? I've been trying to reach you. No answer. I even called the club."

"A cab driver saw me lying on the ground. I'm surprised he stopped. Goes to show there are some decent people left in the world. He offered to take me home. I couldn't even think where

I lived. So he said he'd take me to a hospital. I told him I couldn't pay him but he took me anyway. The hospital people looked me over, put in a couple stitches, did some kind of scan of my head, and said I could go home in the morning. So that's what I did. After signing my life away promising to pay the bill."

"Oh, Pop." Rachel was thinking how a load of extra dollars might help straighten this out. Including finding the cabby and thanking him. "Why didn't you call me? Why didn't you answer the phone?"

"For a while, I couldn't talk very well. And then, it was you not answering the phone."

Marty brushed her hair away from her forehead and kissed it. "Jeez, Rachel, you gave me a terrible scare."

"About time I scare you rather than the other way around."

Marty looked at the floor. "Well, there's that, too."

"So you won big and then some crook on the street stole it?"

Marty couldn't quite meet her gaze. "That and the car, too. I told you, you should've taken the SUV. At least then we'd still have it."

"But you still have your earlier winnings."

Marty hung his head. "'Fraid not, Rachel. I may as well say it straight out. I'm dead broke."

They were interrupted by a man in khakis, yellow knit Izod shirt, and golf shoes. He strolled toward the bed, both hands in his pockets. Rachel's attorney, Edgar Harrison.

"I have to admit," Harrison said, "when we first met, the last place I would have expected to find you was in a private room at Jefferson, with all expenses waived."

"You and me both," Goldie said, and Rachel introduced them.

Harrison announced, "LAPD is dropping the charges on the OxyContin."

Rachel's smile froze. Was Baker so sure what her answer would be? "You're kidding. Why?"

"Well, for one thing, it seems your fingerprints were not on the bottle found in your jacket."

Goldie glanced at Rachel. "Amen."

A nurse arrived and, ignoring them, went about the business of taking Rachel's pulse. The room fell silent until the woman smiled. "Very good." Turning, she brushed something from the table next to the bed. Goldie picked up a large envelope from the floor and handed it to Rachel.

In that moment, Rachel knew exactly what she was going to do.

The nurse glanced at everyone around the bed. "Sorry, but I'll have to ask you all to leave. Our patient needs some rest. You can come back after dinner."

"Let's you and me go to the cafeteria," Marty said to Goldie.

"Good idea. And hey, if you like greens…." She turned back to Rachel. "We'll be back in an hour or so."

"I have a date with a golf cart," the lawyer said.

"Wait." Rachel put out her hand. "Could I have a few words with you, Mr. Harrison?"

"Of course," he said, turning back toward the bed as the door whisked shut behind the others.

"Can you draw up a trust?"

"Sure. How much money are we talking about?"

Rachel thought for a moment. She might keep enough to help her dad one last time, enough to get Goldie started with her own company, if she could get that stubborn woman to agree. And enough to pay off the debt that covered her bail bond—money that Gordon's little operation had cost her. "Maybe seven hundred thousand dollars. Something like that."

Harrison's eyes widened. "All right."

"Even though I would give you the money to put in the trust, could you fix it so nobody, not even me, could take any money out of it?"

"No one except the person in whose name the trust is held. Sure."

"Like maybe when that person turned twenty-one?"

◇◇◇

Marty glanced at the paper Rachel was holding. "What have you been up to? Who is that?"

"Holy shit," Goldie said softly, looking at the birth certificate. "Now you really got your hands full."

All three were still staring at the certificate when something began bumping against the door to the room. Goldie pulled the door open. "Jesus, Mary, and Jehosephat!" She stepped aside, held the door open for a wheelchair that was having some difficulty navigating its entry.

Rachel threw a puzzled look toward the door. Her features moved from surprise to disbelief.

Hank was slapping the arm of the wheelchair. "There must be a knack to running this infernal machine." He flashed a grin at them like someone who had just won the lottery.

Rachel gaped at him. "Why are you in a wheelchair? What are you doing here? Why were you in isolation? How did you leave that hospital in Pasadena without your car?"

Marty went to the door, turned the wheelchair and guided it toward the bed.

"Tell us you drove that wheelchair down the Pasadena Freeway," Goldie chortled. "I'll bet that would back up traffic."

"I was transferred here in an ambulance as soon as they were sure the infection was under control," Hank said. "I needed more surgery and the doctor they referred me to wanted to do it here. The wheelchair is just so I don't overdo."

"How did you know where I was?" Rachel asked, still looking astonished.

"I called the garage this morning. Irene told me. She even gave me the room number. Is that all I get? Questions?"

"You look wonderful." Rachel almost shouted it. "I was so worried. You have no idea how good it is to see you." She held out her arms.

He rolled the wheelchair to the bed and she leaned over for an awkward embrace. He planted a kiss on her cheek. "What's that?" he asked, pointing at the certificate still in her hand.

Rachel dropped her glance to the paper. "I guess it's something we need to talk about."

To receive a free catalog of Poisoned Pen Press titles, please contact us in one of the following ways:

Phone: 1-800-421-3976
Facsimile: 1-480-949-1707
Email: info@poisonedpenpress.com
Website: www.poisonedpenpress.com

Poisoned Pen Press
6962 E. First Ave. Ste. 103
Scottsdale, AZ 85251